TEDDY AND THE
HORDESMEN'S MASTER

Simon M Garrett

grŵpgwyn

First published in Great Britain in 2012
grŵpgwyn "The Forge", HR2 8BU

Simon M. Garrett has asserted his moral rights
A CIP record of this book is available from the British Library

ISBN 978-0-9569246-9-8

Fouth Edition

http://www.grwpgwyn.com/books/teddy-and-the-hordesmens-master/

To my friends,
who have supported me more than they know

Contents

Preface

The years from 2005 to 2008 were quiet and long, without a hint of adventure; then, one outstanding day, a million things seemed to happen at once. Some things burst, apparently from nowhere, and left us stunned; other things that had seemed stable and true, were changed in a blink ... and then there were those things that ended, forever. Sad things that have left a hole in us, and yet somehow reminded us about the value of life.

Since that single onslaught of a day, Teddy, Gundy and the rest of us have been working to record what actually happened, and why. You are holding the results of our labour in your hand. However, if you haven't read "Teddy and the Darkgate" you won't know the details of what happened to Teddy in the late summer of 2005 — how he ended up on a mission to the Darkgate, and met the Yorebear. You might want to read that first: it's available for free.

I said it was 'quiet' between 2005 and 2008 but it wasn't, of course. Joanne and I were looking after baby Bertie, who grew to become three-year old Bertie, and his baby brother Oli was born in May of 2008, so things certainly were not 'quiet'. But there was no sign of the Yorebear, nor of the trouble he'd stirred up that had affected Teddy's friends The Dolls, The Dwarves and Ramgar.

It all began to tip over into chaos when a note was dropped onto our doormat warning us that the Yorebear was awake again. For days, we didn't know what to do, so we thought about it at length, and paced up and down discussing it among ourselves ... and did nothing. Until one day: the day described in this book.

Anyway, the things we've written here will hopefully explain that strangeness that happened near the border between Wales and West England back in 2008 and 2009. Most people excuse it in one way or another, and find some story that explains it for them, but that doesn't do it justice, which is why we've written down what really happened. Many of the questions left dangling in Teddy's first book will be answered here, and some new questions will be raised.

This book is also an account of what happened to Gundy, now that she's Alive and part of Teddy's life, in fact Teddy and I considered calling this book "Gundy and the Book of Llanguirig", but we didn't.

Oh, and Teddy says thank you to all of you who bought or read or shared or commented on the last book. He says he hopes you enjoy this one just as much.

Simon and Teddy, Nr. Aberystwyth, October 2011.

- CHAPTER 1 -

A Pale Reflection of the Past

The last thing you expect, when you're taking tea in a gazebo, is someone shooting an arrow at you.

Gundy tracked the darting shaft until its stone tip reached her stomach and pressed in, distorting her fur into a deepening, concave dip. She waited for it to rip the weave and burst into her stuffing — but it didn't, the stone was too blunt. Instead she felt an increase in pressure that winded her and forced her backwards, initially leaving her feet paws behind, yanked just above the ground; then they too started moving, stuck out in front of her as if she was on the back-breeze of a fast swing in a children's play park.

The arrow's pressure pained her and continued to drive her into the gazebo, towards its rear wall. Adults and children came into view around her, and her mind began to rewind through the mad day she had just had — flashes of violence, the smell of an old car and the stab of dark emotions — toward the early hours when she had been reading words written down hundreds of years ago. She remembered Pale, and her hope that he could save them now, all the way from the past ... near a pond ... meeting a man ... uncovering a plan ... shouting ... falling asleep.

Gundy's head hit the back wall of the gazebo and the swarm of thoughts shook into a jumble — fading Pale, and everything else, to black.

::

Standing by the Peredur fish-pond, Pale was sullen and still. He was looking at something, vaguely aware of a tightness in his breathing, surrounded by the chirrup and chatter of dawn birdsong — wren, chaffinch, blackbird, chaffinch, crow, pigeon, crow, crow —

near and far, echoing like a symphony around the spring-green valley of Llandegley. While studying his reflection in the water at his feet, he puffed out a low, slow sigh.

Around him, the breeze strengthened for a moment, agitating the pond and whipping wisps of grey, shoulder-length hair in to the air. It rippled his watery image … and died away. Pale cleared his hair from his eyes and waited. Eventually, the pond settled and he returned to studying his gently undulating likeness. He hated the lumps on his face; he hated what he had become — but he wanted to memorise himself, as precisely as possible, before he did what he was about to do. He sighed again.

The Yorebear had never been particularly pleasant, but this recent cold violence was sickening: destroying an entire family because one of them had touched The Darkgate. It was too much; he had to be stopped, and Pale knew how to do it.

He knew because he had learned to read, and reading amazed him. He could actually see the thoughts of others, written down; he'd learned the skill at the church. Not in a pew on a Sunday morning with the rest of the village; that wasn't possible. Pale had gone there late at night, when he could be alone.

The wood of the church door was thick, but it had a poor lock. Gaining nighttime access was easy for someone with Pale's skills … however, he didn't always have to break in. Sometimes, the rector's plain, studious daughter met him, and let him in with the key. She sat with him and taught him, touching him incidentally whenever the excuse presented itself. And, whether she was with him or not, Pale studied for hours, learning, investigating, understanding: turning pages by candlelight until dawn. The poor girl waited and loved him, but Pale hated himself too much to believe anything could happen; in any case, she was far too young, only nineteen. It wasn't fair to continue to spend time with her, so he determined never to see her again. He'd already found and read what he really wanted; her company was just a beguiling luxury.

It was safe to assume that the rector would have objected to him breaking into the church, to use it like a personal library — and, without a doubt, he would have been highly defensive about Pale rummaging through the crypt with his daughter — but the fact that Pale was small, light grey, lumpy and not even human would have been asking to be captured, so he was careful to leave everything as he'd found it, and always left the church while the dawn light was dim. When the rector's daughter was with him, she would look into his eyes and squeeze his arm before creeping back towards the rectory; otherwise, Pale would simply lock the door with his tools and return to his hut in the woods — on the edge of the Yorebear's camp — to sleep for a few hours before searching for some food.

If the rector might have caused trouble for Pale, it was certain that the villagers in the congregation would have responded rather more viciously. Only last Tuesday, there had been a 'witch' lynching over in Llanfihangel, so someone would surely consider Pale's appearance to be a sign of something diabolical — and yet he was a perfectly ordinary goblin, albeit with an unpleasant skin condition. So he kept himself to himself, unless the Yorebear called him.

The one redeeming feature of the Yorebear was that he could see past people's appearances to the person within. Sometimes he could see it all too clearly. It wasn't a Darkgate gift; it came from centuries of observing people's behaviour … it made Pale uncomfortable. Only the rector's daughter really talked to him, and he liked it; it made a change from the gruff mumbled words of the Yorebear's horde, or random scared villagers shouting, "What *are* you?!" or "Kill the offspring of Beelzebub!" Luckily, Pale was a good runner: better than the villagers, at least.

In this moment, standing by the pond, Pale could feel the Darkgate's pull. The Yorebear wanted him, so The Darkgate called directly to Pale — to its life inside Pale's body — for him to come home now. He was ignoring it.

He took a last look at his tired, grey eyes, reflected in the water, and determined it was time to do this, so he plunged his foot into the cold wetness, and waded in. The fine mud at the bottom oozed through his distorted, grey toes, and little brown fish swam around his legs, but they didn't hinder his progress towards the island in the middle. A minute later he was walking up out of the water, dripping onto the island.

The question was, where was the stone? The island was overgrown with weeds and brambles and small trees. As Pale rummaged through the undergrowth, he repeatedly snagged and scratched himself on needle-stiff thorns, and drew blood. He searched behind bushes and under big-leaved plants; he *needed* to find it. This was taking far too long — even though it was still very early in the day, an early-riser might see him … but he needed to do this while it was light.

A detail caught his attention: there was one small tree, with red leaves, on the whole island. His mind rummaged for a lost phrase … and he had it, remembered from a book. Until now, it had meant nothing: 'The stone under red will complete three sides.' Perhaps, the red-leaf tree meant something?

Pale started excavating with his hands in between the roots, then snapped root after root out of the ground where they impeded his progress, leaving them lying on the surface. After a while he grasped the thin trunk of the tree and levered it from side to side, and from front to back, to loosen its hold on the ground. But he hadn't dug enough, and he needed to pull up more roots. After a few more busy minutes of earth-digging and root-ripping he tried again to loosen the tree. With effort, it yielded and he pulled it over onto one side, exposing the soil under the tree's slim trunk. He dug down into it with renewed vigour, and about ten inches into the soil, his dirty, blooded hands touched the top of a flat stone. He finger-brushed the dirt from the top of the stone, tracing the square edge of its outline, and wiggled his fingers down opposite sides to grasp it.

Shaking the stone as best he could, while it was still embedded in the ground, he was surprised how much he could move it. He paused, took a breath and pulled; it came clean out of the ground. And he looked at it, cupped in his hands in front of him, then held it to his chest and closed his eyes, as if it were a lost keepsake of a broken love.

If this really did help to destroy the Yorebear, he would be alone. He would have to leave the rector's daughter, and the Hordesmen he had lived with would drift off, leaderless, and eventually he would have no one. He shrugged: he might not survive what he had to do next — absentmindedly, he scratched a bulbous facial growth to ease its itch — but loneliness made no difference: whatever the cost, this was the right thing to do.

Before leaving the island, Pale took out a book, some ink and a quill from the bag he was carrying on his shoulder, and sat on the ground. He dipped the quill in the ink and wrote: '*May 23rd, 1618 (approaching six o'clock in the morning). Remembering the red tree on the Peredur Pond island. Destroyed by the hand of Pale. Remembered forever by Pale.*' When he'd finished writing, he put everything back into his bag, along with the stone, and waded through the water towards the shore.

::

Almost twelve hours before she would be hit by an arrow in a gazebo, Gundy was calmly placing her bookmark in Pale's notebook, then setting it down on the pouffé on which she'd been sitting. She looked around the make-shift room she shared with Teddy, paced up and down a couple of times, and sighed.

These last few weeks, it had not been fair to sleep next to little Bertie in his bed; she was too restless. Instead, each night, she'd help to settle him, stroking his hair until he was asleep before leaving. Bertie didn't mind, he slept soundly. She made a point to sit with him at breakfast and ask if he'd dreamt of dinosaurs or monsters, and she'd laugh with him, or cuddle him, and smile at his beautiful face, so full of fun.

So she and Teddy had taken to sleeping together in their 'toy room' downstairs: a tiny one-and-a-half metre square, ex-cupboard with a single small curtained window. The floor was completely covered by two duvets, with the round pouffé under the window, shelves on the walls for their things, and covers to sleep under. Although the room was so small that the door had to open outward, it was theirs.

While her big, beloved Teddy slept (and occasionally snored), Gundy spent most nights reading and thinking and — once the sun was up — standing on the pouffé, looking out at the sheep in the field over the road. Yet again she had watched the sun come up, and yet again she had failed to find anything in Pale's words that could help them. Teddy, on the other hand, wasn't much of a thinker, so he slept at night and played his role during the day as a kindly, jolly source of support for Gundy and the family; meanwhile, Simon and Joanne looked after the boys. They all did what they could, and they all knew it wasn't enough.

Three weeks ago, someone posted a note through their front door, telling them that the 'Third Yorebear' was awake again. Pale's notebook seemed to be the only clue about who they were facing and how to defeat him, but no matter how much Gundy and the others studied it, there didn't seem to be any clue about how to defend themselves. Gundy's mind was too tired to think. She closed her eyes, breathed in and out, tried to calm herself.

Pale's words were old words from another time, and to begin with it had been hard for Gundy to decipher his seventeenth century way of writing. By now, however, Gundy read them as well as if they were her own words ... and she still couldn't find anything to help them in their predicament.

So she sat, on the floor, Pale's book beside her on the pouffé, tapping her leg paws together and wiggling her snout from side to side, with no idea what to do next. She looked down at her wheat-brown fur, ruffled and in need of a brush, and puffed her cheeks. The blue digits of Teddy's LED clock ticked to the next minute: *07:12, 16 Aug '08, 17°C.* Hazily, Gundy leaned back against the wall and gazed up at the light trying to burst through the curtains.

Although it had been three weeks since the warning note about the Yorebear, it had been three years since Teddy had found Pale's notebook in a rabbit skin bag under a low bush at a farm twenty-five miles away. A bag never to be claimed by Pale because he'd been blasted by the Yorebear soon after the sun had risen. And all of that was nearly four hundred years after the events in Llandegley that Gundy had just read. Time was so long, and yet Gundy was panicked that they didn't have enough of it. She knew Teddy felt it too; she saw it in his eyes at times, and indeed in the eyes of Simon and Joanne who had never asked for their family to be put in danger.

Again, Gundy huffed in frustration at her failure to find anything to help them, and this time Teddy stirred.

Teddy and Gundy had learned so much about Pale after he died; it helped ease the fact that Pale had tried to kill Teddy three times. But it still didn't explain how Teddy had put the Yorebear to sleep just after Pale's death and, more importantly, why the Yorebear was awake again. Three things were certain though: (i) the Yorebear was old; (ii) if he had lasted this long then he wasn't easily defeated, and (iii) Pale's book didn't contain a section entitled, 'Why Yorebears Wake Up, and How to Put Them to Sleep Again'. There was a rather obvious section that had excited them when they first read it, a section that Gundy was about to read, but they soon realised it was almost certainly of no value today.

Teddy yawned wiggled his feet under the covers, brushed his snout with his paw, and slowly sat up, yawning. When fully upright, he opened his paws to Gundy, his eyes soft with affection. She padded the few steps towards him, and they shared a long, first embrace of the day.

"Mornin', my lovely," yawned Teddy.

"Morning," said Gundy, her stuffing glowing in the middle, and she stroked his furry face.

"Der book again?" asked Teddy, knowing there was some reason Gundy was already wide awake.

She nodded.

"D'you want to read sum more?" Teddy asked.

She nodded again. "Just another five minutes?"

"Okie-dokie, I'll look after Bertie if he wakes up den; good luck my lovely."

He hugged her again, pushed their door open, and wandered off to see if Bertie was awake.

Her mind returned to the problem of the Yorebear. Simon had suggested returning to Llandegley, to walk to the Yorebear's Darkgate so Teddy could attempt to regain the power he'd received the last time he touched it. But Teddy was scared it would fill him so full that he'd kill someone again, maybe someone he loved. And what if the Yorebear and Hordesmen simply rode of the wood and killed them all? Simon had considered buying some infrared binoculars, to check the wood from afar for the body heat of its murderous inhabitants, but Gundy wasn't sure. Maybe they didn't have any body heat ...

So Teddy and Gundy and Simon and Joanne had done nothing, not because they were afraid of doing the wrong thing, but because they had no idea what to do at all. As for the Dolls, they and Rufus had heard no news from their sources. All seemed quiet and normal, except Ramgar the ram had gone unusually quiet, and there had been no word from the Dwarves for over a week. But that sort of thing had happened before and they'd always been a reason for it. No one had any idea what to do, but time was marching on, and they all felt they had to do *something* soon before the Yorebear had the chance to harm them. Gundy continued reading where she left off.

::

Pale stomped through the trees by the main track, looking around continually. There was one person who might listen to Pale before they killed him: Robertson, the village leader. It was still early enough to avoid attention and Robertson's cottage was nearby.

Hiding behind a witch-hazel bush, Pale checked for movement. He peered through branches and young leaves, left and right. Just sounds of the morning. He had almost hoped to see someone, because it was time to act — he left the security of the bush and bolted towards the house.

Thirty seconds later, he was knocking on the back door of Robertson's home, panting. The sound of stirring within; feet on stairs; a clattering; a low grumbling; the grumpy stomping of feet on floorboards, marching closer, and the door was flung open by a man who was very annoyed to have been woken up so early.

"What the hell do you wa—" Robertson stopped talking when he saw the short, grey, bobble-covered, skinny goblin standing at his back door. "What *are* you?" he asked.

"I'm Pale and I'm here to help you save the village from the Yorebear. You probably won't believe me, and you may kill me, which I don't want but, before you do, there's a stone in my bag and you can use it to destroy the Yorebear if you listen to what I have to say."

"Huh?"

"Hm. Can I come in? People try to tie me up and burn me you know."

"Oh. I suppose so. Yes. I'm going to get my axe first though."

"Of course."

Robertson called up to his wife that she shouldn't come down because he had some 'private village business' that needed his attention, then he beckoned Pale to come in and close the door, and stood in front of him holding his axe vertically between his legs.

"Go on. Tell me more."

"Do you know what this is?" asked Pale, holding up the stone cube.

"It's a stone," said Robertson, dryly.

"Yes, but do you know what it can *do*?"

"Do? No," said Robertson, annoyed to be caught wanting. "Tell me."

"It's a key. Well, it's *part* of a key. There are ten parts. Nine were built into people's homes all around Llandegley, as part of a pact with the Yorebear, when the village was founded a couple of generations ago. He promised to keep the owners safe. But this one, which I retrieved half an hour ago, was buried by the Yorebear himself, so nobody could gather all the parts of the key at once."

"A key for what?"

"The Darkgate."

"A key for The Darkgate?" Robertson repeated, before it dawned on him. "You mean we can turn it *off*?"

"Yes. So I've read. There's a book, just a sewn-up collection of notes really, in the church crypt. It was written by the village leader at the time the Yorebear arrived. He obsessively spied on the Yorebear to learn more about him — he didn't believe the Yorebear's promises but he knew he couldn't fight him in combat. Apparently, the Yorebear pretended the nine stones would give the village his power and protection but, in reality, he wanted to make it hard to re-assemble the key. The village leader risked his life to discover the truth."

"It didn't do him much good in the end, though," said Robertson, glumly. "The Yorebear blew him to pieces."

"Ah," said Pale. "I did not know that. Well, maybe you can make his sacrifice worth something? I have this stone, the one the Yorebear hid, but we'll need to secure the other nine stones from the houses in the village — and that won't be easy because they look like rather ordinary stones, just a little browner, with a strange smooth-rough texture, like this." Pale held out the stone; Robertson stroked it, suspiciously. "Also, you'll need to convince people to take to their houses with a hammer and chisel, to get to each stone, and obviously they risk the wrath of the Yorebear. Looking as I do, I can't do any of that, but I hope Robertson the village leader can."

"You're trying to appeal to my pride."

"I am."

"Well, perhaps it's working," said Robertson, the corners of his mouth turning up slightly. "Now, I'm not saying I believe you, but if we manage to turn off The Darkgate, the Yorebear loses his power, yes?"

"From what I have read, that is correct, yes. Could you get the other stones?"

Robertson thought for a moment, and nodded. "I should think so."

"Good. I imagine some of the families may have their own stories about their stones, and why they were built into their houses, other may not; still others may object to their stone being removed. But, I think it might help if you tell them you've found out how to stop the Yorebear."

"And where will you be, if I do all this, eh?"

"With the Yorebear, waiting to die."

"*With* the Yorebear? Why?"

"Because he is my master."

Robertson stepped back, alarmed, picked up his axe and brandished it at Pale.

"Your *master*?"

"Yes. I have my reasons for him being my master, but the Yorebear is becoming more and more unpleasant and he needs to be stopped."

"Well, I agree with *that*, but how do I know if I can trust you? And what do you mean you're going to wait to die? Will this affect you too?"

"The first answer is that you can't know that you can trust

me," said Pale.

"Well, at least you're honest," shrugged Robertson. Pale continued.

"However, can you read?"

"Yes," said Robertson gruffly. "More than most people."

"Good, then you can read all that I have said for yourself in the church crypt, in the books the rector doesn't even know about, behind the tombstone of Gwenllian of Pen-y-bont. And the reason I'm going back to my master is that it's very likely I will die, or at least fall asleep, because the Yorebear once forced his power into me to keep me alive, as he has done with all of us in The Horde. We all feel that power, and I very much fear that when the power goes, so do we. As it did for many Hordesmen the first time they fell asleep."

"The *first* time?"

"Yes, the first time was over one thousand years ago. The Yorebear himself woke up relatively unscathed, but several of the Horde died when The Darkgate's power to them was cut, others were mutated."

"Like you?"

"No," said Pale, awkwardly. "I've almost always looked like this. The Yorebear came across me a few years ago. He'd been awake for sixty years or so by then; I joined him in 1609. After that, well, you're old enough to know the rest."

"Indeed."

Pale handed the stone to Robertson and backed toward the door, keeping his gaze constant on Robertson's axe. He felt for the door latch behind his back, and in a single movement lifted it, opened the door, and exited the house backwards, yanking the door closed before running off. Robertson didn't chase him. He was too busy trying to process what he'd just heard.

::

For the next few days, Pale stalked Robertson to monitor his progress, using his skills to remain hidden behind trees and bushes, or watching from afar. He observed Robertson visiting the rector at Llandegley church, and leaving with the book. He watched him persuading the villagers to give him the stones from their houses, far more successfully than Pale had feared. After Robertson mentioned that their stone would help defeat the Yorebear, only a few had needed further convincing.

Robertson had arrived to visit the eighth of the nine families when Pale noticed one of the Yorebear's spies, hiding just as Pale was hiding, watching Robertson. Pale crept up behind him, picked up a branch the thickness of a man's arm, and brought it down hard on the Hordesman's head, stunning him. Then, without fuss he lowered it over the creature's head from behind, like a bar, and pulled with the strength of both his arms hard and continuously, using his knee as a pivot in the creature's back, until he had strangled him to death. He buried the body loosely under branches and leaves, took the Hordesman's crossbow, and wrote the dead man's name in his notebook, sighing as he dated and timed the entry so he would never forget.

Late the next night, Pale saw Robertson through the kitchen window, struggling to read the church book: first sitting and studying; jumping up in annoyance, gesticulating and mumbling to himself because of words he couldn't read, and pacing up and down in the flickering candlelight, before sitting at the kitchen table to try again to grasp the words' meaning. Pale walked over and knocked on Robertson's door.

"It's you again," said Robertson.

"You can't read very well, can you?"

"No," said Robertson, tersely.

"I'll help you. I think you now believe me?"

"I do," said Robertson quietly. "You were right. And from what I can read, we need to do something with the stones."

"We need to assemble them. The book says the stones will join when we touch the matching sides together."

"Stones, can't 'join together'!" mocked Robertson. "You read it wrong."

"Let's see shall we?" said Pale, picking up two stones. He examined them both on all their six faces to see if their sides looked like they might match each other. They didn't, so he put down one stone and picked up another. And another, and ... he stopped and looked again at the last stone. He touched two faces together and they dunked to each other like two strong magnets.

Robertson's surprise was obvious, but he came along side Pale and picked up two stones for himself. He soon found two matching sides and joined his stones together.

Between them, they matched two other pairs of stones, so that there were four joined pairs in total and two left unjoined. Pale found that one of the single stones overlapped one of the existing pairs to make a triangle of three stones. The remaining single stone joined another pair to make three-in-a-line, which in turn joined with the triangle of three stones to make a larger triangle of six, offset from each other like the bricks of a wall. A pattern was emerging and the remaining two pairs of stones joined to make a row of four, and then clunked together with the triangle of six blocks, and they had in their hands a rough triangle made of ten stones. It was odd; it felt warm, and the centre of the stone triangle seemed to be browner than it had been. It made their hands tingle when they touched it. They shared a look that acknowledged they had made something special. Robertson pursed his lips and looked at the stone key suspiciously.

"Now what?" he asked.

"To be honest, I didn't really expect to get this far; I think there's something about climbing the Darkgate," said Pale. "We should read the book."

They read that the key needed to be placed in a triangular indentation on the top of The Darkgate and, once in place, the key would allow them to turn the Darkgate off. It simply needed someone to place their hand on the brownish centre stone and imagine the Darkgate no longer working.

"Who's going to do it?" asked Robertson, with a worried look on his face. "Who's putting it in the Darkgate?"

"You," said Pale.

"Why me?" he said, not entirely happy.

"Because, I'll need to go back to The Horde to be with my master at the end. And because you're Robertson, leader of the village. It's your job."

"I *know* my job!" snapped Robertson, moving to sit opposite Pale.

"And *you* know I'm right."

Robertson's glower flicked to the floor, he thought for a moment, and looked back up at Pale's grey eyes.

"Yes, I do."

They sat and looked at each other over the wooden table, to the sounds of the night outside.

"I suppose, tonight is as good a night as any," said Robertson."

"Maybe even the *best* night, if the Yorebear has learned what we're doing," added Pale.

Robertson stood up and went upstairs to say goodbye to his wife. He didn't actually say 'goodbye' he touched his lips to her forehead and kissed her, gazed into her eyes, and left the room without a word. She didn't ask why, she just watched him leave. Robertson rejoined Pale, and the two of them departed the house.

As they trudged towards The Darkgate, everything seemed so much more real than usual: the touch of the night breeze on their faces, the clear shapes of the trees in the moonlight, the feel of their feet in their boots. But soon The Darkgate came into view in the distance and Pale grasped Robertson's arm to stop him walking further.

"I've got to go to The Horde now," he said calmly.

"Hm. Very well. Good luck."

"You too. We'll need it." So they parted: Robertson hastened towards the roughly weathered cone of stones that was The Darkgate, and Pale plodded towards the Horde camp in the wood, now sufficiently far apart from each other that they couldn't both be seen at the same time.

As soon as Pale reached the wood, he walked straight towards the vertical drift of smoke that floated up from the centre, to 'warn' the Yorebear, who was more grateful to Pale than he had been for a year or two. They decamped and crept to the side of the wood that faced The Darkgate. Pale watched the dark shape of Robertson nearing its stones, which glowed orange in the darkness. But Robertson had not been quick enough. Just as he stepped on the bottom stones, to climb to the top, the Yorebear rode out of the wood.

"I know what you're doing, Robertson!" called the Yorebear. Robertson froze. "Nine families lie dead in their homes tonight. They helped you, so my men killed them." Pale gasped. "And when I find out who stole the tenth stone I will kill him myself, just as I will kill you now."

The Yorebear raised his arm so that his hairy palm faced Robertson, who was clambering up The Darkgate in vain, but Pale called out.

"Master, be careful!" It was an attempt to distract the Yorebear, and it worked. A blast of power shot from his palm, harmlessly over Robertson's head, and over the sleeping village of Llandegley.

"PALE! That was *not* helpful!"

"But, Sire, Robertson is nearly at the top!" Pale stated, obviously, but convincingly. And Pale was right. Robertson had used the distraction to scramble to the top and had the key in his hand, poised over the top of The Darkgate.

"Noooooo! Shouted the Yorebear. He fired again, but too quickly and missed by inches. The heated bolt of light roared by, flicked through the air, and blasted a tree a quarter of a mile away. Robertson dropped the key into its triangular hole, and slapped his hand on the centre.

"Turn OFF," he shouted, with his eyes closed.

Before he could fire again, the Yorebear gasped in and yanked his arms back and out behind him. He stumbled forwards, then backwards, trying to keep his balance — lurched forwards again, kept going, and hit the grass, face-first, motionless.

The Horde gasped, and seconds later each of them also began to feel weak. They panicked and stumbled where they stood, Pale included, and started to fall to the ground, dying or asleep, it was hard to tell. Some tried in vain to reach Robertson, to make him pay; others fought to remain standing, but they all failed. The Darkgate's power was off. For perhaps a third of them, their limbs and faces twisted before they turned to dust; for the others, they fell over and became still: one way or another they all succumbed. The field was littered with bodies and remnant dust — and hugging the top of The Darkgate, his eyes wide, Robertson started to breathe again.

- CHAPTER 2 -

Splitting Up

Simon burst into the room, a blur of blue and red, checked pyjamas, aghast and mouthing like a goldfish. Wordlessly, he held out a little piece of paper and swished it left-and-right, horrified. It was a letter just delivered from The Dolls by a pigeon who'd tapped on the window until Simon woke up. Teddy squeezed past Simon's legs into the tiny room, and Joanne stood behind, holding baby Oli to her, looking grim.

"It from Agnes! Dare Muvver's dead!" said Teddy.

"What?" said Gundy.

"She was killed!" said Simon, still wagging the tiny letter. He noticed what he was doing, stopped, peered down at it, and read an extract:

> "... *she was in the garden, hit by a crossbow bolt, and died. It was very quick. The police were investigating Mother's murder, but now they've stopped, saying it was suicide. It's madness and we have no idea what is happening! We saw Mother murdered and we need your help. Things are very wrong. Please bring Teddy as soon as possible ...*"

Teddy looked at Gundy, waiting for a response, but she needed time to understand what she'd just heard.

Simon continued: "I mean we expected the Yorebear to do something, but has he really *murdered* a human?" He looked around the room at everyone; no one said a thing. "But that's not all; it gets worse: The Dolls have had to leave their house and move into the garden, because the bank have already taken control of Mother's house and are clearing everything out to sell the estate! Agnes says she can't even talk to you on the phone because they took all the phones too, before the servants could rescue them."

Suddenly, Gundy knew what to say: "Teddy, my love, you've got to go. You're going to feel conflicted, but it's okay. It's the right thing to do."

Teddy look puzzled. "Um, okay... But I don't want to leave you! I haven't left you since you first Woked up!" And he realised what she meant. "Can you come wiv me?" he asked, with very little hope in his voice.

"I love you, Teddy, more than I can say, but no, I can't go. You have to help The Dolls, and I have to stay to help look after my Bertie — and Oli. As I've said before, if Oli's Mundy were Awake, instead of lying there like a stuffed *idiot*—" Gundy stopped herself. She was frustrated, well aware that if Mundy was ever going to Awake she'd do it at the right time.

So Gundy looked straight at Teddy and shrugged: "We've each got a job to do."

Teddy drooped. "Okay den."

He walked over to her and held Gundy in his soft arms, then they looked into each other's eyes and touched snouts gently.

Gundy realised she was making an assumption and turned to Joanne.

"What are we going to do about the children?"

"I'm not sure," said Joanne. "But we can't stay here and be attacked by a murderer — we need to go somewhere else. Somewhere safe. Now." She was clearly worried but staying calm.

"Whatever you do, I'll help you," asserted Gundy firmly, giving Joanne less of a choice in the matter than might be expected from a soft toy.

"Of course. Good," said Joanne, a bit taken aback.

"Okay, you and the boys need a safe place ... but where?" said Simon.

"Hm ..." thought Joanne, out loud. "I might be able to stay

with Carys Jones in town. She was saying the other day that she wished someone could help her — you know, to cope, after Gareth moved out — and Bertie and her Owen play really well together. It's early, but I bet she's awake, Owen's just as bouncy as Bertie in the morning; do you think we should phone her yet?"

::

Half an hour later they were dressed, the phone call had been made (with much apology for its earliness) and it was agreed. Joanne and the boys would stay with Carys in town while Simon was 'away on emergency business', using their only car. Simon and Teddy would, in fact, drive to Bredwardine although they had realised they needed to be very careful when they reached The Doll's manor house. But they had to do something to help The Dolls because they could no longer help themselves.

So, they would split up: Simon and Teddy would go one way and Joanne, Gundy, Mundy and the boys would go another, and by 8:20am they were saying their goodbyes at Carys' house near the Castle Theatre in Aberystwyth, a hint of early morning summer sea fog still hanging in the air. As the car pulled away from the curb, Teddy kept a low profile but Simon waved one last time, and they set off alone.

They drove down to South Beach, along the front around the castle and the old university, and through the main town. The buildings glided by, shops became houses, and houses became infrequent, and were gone, replaced by trees and hills. They continued inland on the A44, through Capel Bangor, then up into the hills. The day was bright but not quite sunny, with thin white cloud now translucent over the sun's breakfast-time warmth.

After driving for half an hour or so, Teddy had a thought: since they would pass Wrooph, Naystraw and Gwen y Gafr's farm, maybe they should call on them to tell them what had happened to The Dolls? Teddy hadn't been to Gaufron farm for over a year and, more importantly, he could ask them if they had heard anything about the Yorebear. However, Teddy would have to walk alone into the farmyard, so the farmer wouldn't see a car driving up the track to his house. It shouldn't take long and they might learn something useful; perhaps Mother's death was part of a general increase in the Yorebear's activity? Gaufron farm was only seven or eight miles from Llandegley, so maybe the animals would know something? So Simon pulled into a lay-by, opened the back door to get Teddy out of Bertie's car seat, and placed him on the ground.

"Good luck," said Simon, ruffling Teddy's head fur.

"Ffank you!" said Teddy, as happy as usual.

Simon watched as Teddy ran across the road, climbed up and over the metal gate and dropped down into the field.

"I ffink I'm going to get der pooey paws again," he shouted with a smile, pointing at the field covered in cow pats. Then he waved goodbye and disappeared behind the hedge to the left of the gate, to run over the field towards the farm.

Simon waited in the car, vaguely listening to the radio's songs and chit-chat, trying to work out how they might help The Dolls without risking their own safety. Suddenly, the car's windows were shaken by an enormous explosion. A stunned Simon soon located the cause: at the end of the field, the farmhouse had burst apart and the entire structure had collapsed into rubble and raging fire. He gulped, twisted the ignition key with shaking hands and rammed the car into gear. Checking nothing was coming, he doubled back as fast as possible along the road to the farm's track, which Teddy had pointed out as they'd passed by.

It was probably never part of the car's design specification that it should drive down a stoney track at over sixty miles an hour, but that's exactly what Simon did, and very soon he reached what was left of the farmhouse.

If anyone had been in the house they were most certainly dead, and lying on the ground nearby were the bodies of a horse and a goat, surrounded by stones and debris from the house, but there was no sign of Teddy.

"Teddy! Teddy! Are you okay? Where are you?"

There was no answer, so Simon ran around the outside of the demolished house looking for him.

"Simon!" said Teddy's voice, weakly.

Simon looked around and still couldn't see him.

"Simon!" called Teddy again, sobbing.

It was coming from under a piece of wall, and next to it was a black and white dog, leaking blood.

Simon pulled the chunk of wall away to find Teddy underneath, covered in building dust and a little squashed but otherwise undamaged.

"Oh, Teddy! Are you hurt?"

"No, but look! Dare dead, Simon! Wrooph and Naystraw and Gwen! Dare all dead!" Teddy sobbed.

"Is that who these animals are? Oh no! What happened?"

"Der nasty horde man happened," Teddy cried.

"Oh my goodness! How did they know you were here?" asked Simon, before realising something else. "Is he *still* here?"

"I don't ffink so. I saw him walk around der building and kick the animals to see if day were dead, and den came over here to kick Wrooph, and den he left. He couldn't see me cos I pulled my head and paws in under der bit of wall."

"But I guess he was looking for you?" asked Simon, nervously.

"I ffink so."

"So he might still be here! We need to go, right now! I'll carry you."

Teddy nodded, but Simon was already picking him up, and sprinting with Teddy under his arm until they reached the car, engine still running.

Simon tugged open the driver's door, pushed Teddy across onto the passenger seat, and jumped in. He spun the car around, spraying gravel and small chunks of rubble, before he'd even slammed his door, and raced back down the track toward the main road.

But their worst fears were realised. Some distance down the track, blocking their path, stood a mutated human, greenish-brown, with legs and arms of different lengths, and unusual stumps, like half-grown, failed limbs at several locations on his body. He looked like a tree that had been attacked with a chainsaw, and was pointing something at them that looked a lot like a crossbow. He waited until he couldn't miss, and fired.

"It's a bomb, Simon!" shouted Teddy.

Simon didn't need to ask for clarification, he span the steering wheel so the car ploughed into the hedge, breaking off the left wing mirror and smashing all the glass down that side of the car. It was just enough to veer them out of the missile's trajectory, and the bolt missed the car by millimetres. The Hordesman was so surprised that he stood still, mouth open, but Simon had manoeuvred the car back onto the track and was roaring towards him. The Hordesman didn't have time to fire again so he pressed himself against the hedge, and a second later the car's right-hand wing mirror thudded into his longest left arm, spinning him face-first into the hedge. As the car passed, Teddy turned to track their attacker's response: he steadied himself, turned to face them, and in a single action reset his crossbow to fire again. Simon roared up the track but it wasn't going to be fast enough.

"Ohmygoodness, ohmygoodness, ohmygoodness," said Simon over and over again, looking in the rear view mirror.

But before the Hordesman could aim, his first missile hit the ground a hundred metres or so down the track and exploded, destroying the hedge left and right of the impact point for thirty metres in both directions. The force of it tipped the Hordesman forwards and he reacted by gripping the crossbow tightly, in a misguided reaction to steady himself on something. His grasp fired the bolt diagonally into the ground, and the resulting explosion obliterated him in an instant, ripped out another length of hedge on both sides, and re-modelled the back of the car as if it were made of clay, punched by several mighty fists. An instant later, a hard rain of broken glass, followed by stones and hedge detritus, blasted through the back window and showered Simon and Teddy, leaving their ears ringing from the blast.

"Arrrghhh! I dont' like it!" shouted Teddy.

"Should we keep going?!" panicked Simon out loud, to no one in particular.

"I ffink so!" said Teddy. "Dare may be more Horde people around!"

Simon agreed and kept driving. He paused at the junction with the main road, checked for traffic, and they roared off towards Bredwardine.

::

"Bye Carys!" called Joanne as she left the house with the boys, Gundy and Mundy. "See you later, we're off to the swings now."

"Okay, see you," called Carys from inside the house. "I might join you when Owen wakes up."

"Ffwings!" said Bertie, excitedly.

"That's right!" said Joanne, glancing down at Oli. "And maybe Oli can have a go too on the baby swings, when he wakes up."

"Gevver!"

"Yes, you and your brother together!"

Gundy and Mundy rode with Oli in the pushchair while Bertie held Joanne's other hand and walked. It wasn't far, just over the road and through the castle grounds to the gate of the red, metal-fenced play park. Bertie pushed the gate open and ran up to the swings. For a moment, the normality of going to the swings in town had distracted her, then Joanne's mind flashed to Simon and Teddy: she hoped all was well.

In the distance, a small man with round glasses was watching them. He scratched his white-whiskered cheek and thought for a few seconds, straightened his tie, and walked towards the play park.

::

"How the *hell* did they know where to find us?!" asked Simon, his eyes still darting around, looking for danger. "What happened back there, Teddy?"

"Er, I ffink someone tried to kill me. Again. And Wrooph saved my life." Teddy looked at the floor as he spoke, his heart breaking.

"Well, I think it's pretty certain that someone was trying to kill you, but what actually happened, from the moment you reached the farm?"

"Um, I looked around der farm for der uvvers, and I found Wrooph first. He was very happy to see me and I had to tell him to stop lickin' me!"

For a moment Teddy smiled, then he remembered what had just happened.

"Wrooph showed me where Naystraw and Gwen were, and we let dem out because I wanted dem to come up der field to meet you: der farmer and his family are on holiday, so no one would see you."

Teddy shook his head, still not believing what had just happened.

"We were just walking past der house when Wrooph said he could smell someone. Naystraw and Gwen waited by der front door, and Wrooph and me went round der side to have a look. Den I saw der shooty ffings — day went kind of like dis across der farm yard from der bushes and into der house." Teddy indicated with his paw how the missiles had flown.

"Diagonally," helped Simon. "But there was more than one?"

"Yes, dat's it. Dare was ffree, kind of side-by-side and separatin'. Den day smashed ffroo der window at der same time as Wrooph ran between me and der house. Der house blew up and Wrooph was boomed into me and we bowff got blown into der air. Der bit of wall fell on him, and den bounced onto me, but I ffink he got crushed der most … and he's not squashy like me, so it killed him." Teddy started crying again.

"He saved your life."

"He was my ffrend! And he's dead!" wailed Teddy.

"This is getting very, very serious, Teddy. First The Dolls' mother is killed and now this. What is going on? What is the Yorebear doing? This is affecting humans now, and the police will get involved, and who knows what will happen next?" Simon tailed off for a moment to use one hand to comfort and stroke Teddy while he wept.

"Actually, if the police are involved then we'll need to get off the main road. It won't be long before they find the bits that came off our car, and they'll be looking for damaged cars like ours. Damn! This is really serious."

"Do you ffink we can make it to Bredwardine?" asked Teddy, sobbing.

"What choice do we have? The Dolls need us more than ever now. I'm really concerned there's going to be a Hordesman at their house though." Teddy and Simon shared a glance: the danger was clear if Simon was right. "But we can't stop here and wait for the police. Hm. I don't think anyone could have seen us going up or down the track back there because the hedges were so high. And they can only connect us to the bits we left back there if they see the damage on our car. But if they do find us then they'll blame us, or at least question us, and how on earth are we going to explain what happened eh? 'A mutated man with a crossbow shot missiles at us that had the power to destroy an entire house'? I don't think they are likely to believe that, do you?"

"No. I don't ffink so, actchully," said Teddy, taking a deep breath to gain control over his tears.

"So, we might need to keep to minor roads, and find somewhere near The Dolls to hide the car, and I suppose we could walk a mile or two, and we'll have to keep a look out for Hordesmen.

Hm."

"Can you make sure we're on der Dolls' side of der Bredwardine bridge before we stop der car please?" said Teddy, his tears subsiding.

"I'll do my best," nodded Simon, almost smiling.

Simon pulled into a lay-by, to see if either number plate had been left behind. They hadn't, although the rear plate was cracked in two places: he covered both number plates with mud marks to make them unreadable, then he jumped back into the car, put his foot down and they raced towards Bredwardine.

::

Joanne noticed a small, moley man, in a ragged tweed jacket and round glasses, scratching his forehead as he wound his way toward her. She watched him approach, staring directly at him, which certainly didn't ease his nerves. Joanne pushed Bertie on the swing in a steady rhythm as she tracked the man coming straight towards her.

The man finally reached her, doffed an imaginary cap from his head of crazy, white hair and bowed. Then, just as Joanne was about to ask who he was, he turned to face Gundy, who was sitting next to Oli in the pushchair. Gundy took hold of the sleeping baby's warm little hand as the man hat-doffed again, in deference to her.

"Hello, Miss. I am Gwion. May I talk with you?"

"You may, Gwion," said Gundy with a hint of a smile.

"First, a question, to make sure you are who I think you are."

"Okay."

"What was the name of the horse that Teddy woke up riding towards Gaufron?"

Gundy was stunned. How could this odd little human know anything about that? She looked at Joanne for her input, but Joanne was equally taken aback. She shrugged at Gundy as if to say, 'see what happens', so Gundy answered him.

"Naystraw."

"Oh, thank goodness! It's you, Miss Gundy. At last! I'm finally talking to one of you. Oh, at last!"

"I'm sorry, you're not making a lot of sense," said Gundy, flatly.

"Oh, of course, yes. Well, several weeks ago — or was it months? Time passes so quickly — well, anyway, whenever it was, you got the note, yes? About the Third Yorebear?"

It took a second for his words to sink in.

"It was you! Oh my stuffing, it was you who delivered that note!"

"Well, yes, never mind; the point is what have you *done about it*? We're very worried that Arthdu might get to you if you stay at home, and my mistress can't exactly go up to your front door and knock on it can she?"

Gundy's brow furrowed; she glanced at Joanne again who looked equally confused. Who was his mistress? Who was Arthdu?

"Higher! Higher!" shouted Bertie, who had been left to swing limply because Joanne was dumbstruck. Without taking her eyes off Gwion, she mechanically obliged, much to Bertie's glee.

"It's okay," assured Joanne. "We've temporarily moved out to ... another location," she finished carefully.

"Oh, that's very good, very good indeed. Well done!" Gwion clasped his hands together as if in prayer and closed his eyes in gratitude. "But where is Teddy, may I ask?"

"He's ... well, I'm not sure I can tell you actually," said Gundy.

"She's right," agreed Joanne, "We don't know anything about you, or the person you mentioned. Don't take this the wrong way, but we're not going to tell you anything just yet."

"Hm. Fair enough," Gwion nodded. "But perhaps you can tell me this one thing: is Teddy safe?"

"Yes,"confirmed Gundy. "He's safe; he's with a human we trust."

"Oh good. But he's not, you know, anywhere near Llandegley

is he?"

"Um," Gundy looked at Joanne for aid, who replied.

"We're not sure exactly *where* he is," she answered, truthfully. But would it be bad if he *did* go to Llandegley?"

"Oh, yes. Very bad. Very bad indeed."

::

As they passed the village sign for Llandegley, Teddy felt a powerful rush in the depths of his stuffing, and cried out.

"What is it, Teddy?" asked Simon.

"I don't know, it's like I got a hot and a cold feelin' at der same time."

"Is it a good feeling, or a bad feeling?"

"Boaff. A bit of it is like cold water down my back, and I don't like it, and a bit of it is like hot power in my tummy and arms. I don't know if I should like it or if it's naughty power. I ffink it's der Darkgate."

"Really? Oh … Well, don't worry, we're going to keep driving. As long as we don't see any police or crossbows, we'll be okay." Simon lowered his foot on the accelerator pedal.

Teddy wasn't so sure: did The Darkgate or the Yorebear know he was in Llandegley? Could he find them? Or follow them? On top of that, Teddy was still trying to come to terms with the loss of his friends. It was a difficult silence. Simon tried to distract him.

"Um, did Wrooph or the others tell you anything new about the Yorebear?" he asked.

"No, I don't ffink— oh, wait. Yes, he did … kind of. Wrooph told me about der sheep!"

"What about them?"

"Dare killing dogs again, like day killed Wrooph's bruvver. I ffink Wrooph said ffree of dem had died, and day even killed a farmer! But der ffing dat Wrooph ffort was weird was dat day all happened in England."

"Did he say *where* in England?"

"No. He was still telling me when he heard der Hordesman."

"Weird. Why would the Yorebear want to use sheep to kill dogs and farmers? *If* it's him that's doing it. I mean, it's mad! It's like he doesn't care who knows about him now. And what's to be gained by it all? Maybe it's just a sheep virus or something that makes them … vicious. Oh! Unless this is only the beginning. Just imagine a country full of killer sheep!

Teddy looked even more worried.

"Sorry, Teddy. That's not a nice thought, is it?"

Teddy stared at Simon and slowly shook his head. Simon's attempts to help him were hopeless.

They passed the Llandegley village limits and slipped back into the countryside. Teddy breathed out in relief, but somehow it was too easy. He was sure he'd felt something … familiar. Something that recognised him.

"Why haven't we heard about it on the news?" said Simon, cutting across Teddy's thoughts. "I mean, I'd imagine killer sheep would be exactly the sort of thing that news people might like to shout about, but we've heard nothing. We need to get Joanne to check online. Could you phone her, Teddy? Oh, but don't tell her about what happened at the farm yet. I'd like to do that myself."

"Okay den." Teddy picked up the phone and a pen and used the pen to press the '1' button on the phone. It auto-dialled Joanne's number. Maybe this would stop Simon talking about scary things.

"Hello?" answered Joanne.

"Hello, it's me, Teddy."

"Oh, hello Teddy. Um can I phone you back? I'm with someone here."

"Okay, but I just wanted to ask if you could you check sumpffin for us?"

"What sort of something?"

"Could you look up der stories on der news about sheep killing doggies and farmers and ffings?"

"Really? Is that happening? Gosh. I'll definitely look that up as soon as possible, we're at the Castle play park at the moment, so I'll do it when I can get to a computer."

"Ffank you."

"Bye."

"Bye."

Teddy didn't think to ask who Joanne was with.

- CHAPTER 3 -
The Castle

Gundy's paw absent-mindedly stroked Oli's hair while he slept in the pushchair. Joanne ended the call and tossed her phone towards her bag, but it slipped her grasp too early and it fell into the pushchair landing on Oli's legs; his little nose wrinkled slightly as he half-raised one arm.

"Oh! Sorry, sweet pea!" she said, and stroked his fluffy babygrow toes until Oli was soothed, then she picked the phone up again and plopped it into her bag, not minding where it ended up.

"Right, I think it's time … for you to meet Arthgwyn," said Gwion, brightly.

"Who?" asked Joanne.

"Well, hm, I can't really tell you. I have to show you."

"Then we aren't going anywhere, are we Joanne?" interrupted Gundy.

"Gundy's right," agreed Joanne. She gestured to Oli in his pushchair and Bertie on the swing, "We're going to keep these little boys very safe. We're not going to follow strangers around, or meet mystery men."

"She's a woman," corrected Gwion. "Arthgwyn. Well, sort of."

"Well … okay," continued Joanne, scratching her nose. "But it doesn't make any difference. Our main job at the moment is simply to keep the boys safe, so if you want us to meet someone then you'll have to work around that. There's no compromise *whatsoever* on that point," she insisted.

"You need assurances … okay. Give me ten minutes and I will do my best to get them for you, but you really do need to meet my mistress, for your own safety."

"Hm, if you say so," said Joanne, frowning.

At this, Gwion doffed his imaginary hat again to them both and shuffled off towards the castle. Joanne and Gundy looked at each other, confused, and then at the boys. Bertie was still enjoying the swing, with a big smile on his face, and Oli had woken up and was happily bashing a multi-coloured giraffe against the side of the pushchair. Gundy winced, at least it wasn't Alive.

Joanne took Oli out for a few minutes for a play on the baby swing, while Bertie played on the slide.

As promised, Gwion returned ten minutes later. He nodded respectfully at Gundy and Joanne, and took out a rolled up piece of paper from his coat.

"This is from my mistress," he said, pulling on the bow of red silk that was keeping it rolled up. The silk loosened and he slid the bow off the paper tube and un-rolled it. It was a letter, and Gwion began to read it.

Dear Gundy and Joanne,

I am Arthgwyn. Thanks to Gwion, I have been following your lives with interest since Teddy engaged the Yorebear in Llandegley.

Gwion tells me that you are afraid I may harm you, or may be trying to deceive you. I can understand your concerns and I want to reassure you. However, words are cheap, so I have written this letter to swear to you that I will defend you and your children with every drop of my blood.

To prove my promise, I have signed this letter with a spot of blood from my right thumb. If Gundy would be good enough to place her paw on top of the blood, she will immediately be able to verify that I am telling the truth, and that my blood oath to you is real.

Warm Regards,

Arthgwyn.

"If you would be so good," said Gwion to Gundy, indicating the thumbprint of blood to be touched.

There was something odd about it. Although there were clear signs of the swirling ridges of a normal thumbprint, there were also straight lines crossing it in random directions. Whatever Arthgwyn was, she wasn't an ordinary human.

Gundy paused with her paw above the bloody oath mark, and glanced at Joanne for her opinion.

"I don't think it can do any harm," said Joanne.

Gundy breathed in and touched her paw to the thumbprint.

Something seemed to enter her, and she immediately felt like she had been accelerated to an outrageous speed, then slowed to a sudden stop, all while standing still.

"Whoa!" she said. "What was *that?*"

"That was my lady's oath mark," said Gwion. "You and she share ... certain features, and if you ask yourself—"

"Oh my goodness! I know she's telling the truth!" exclaimed Gundy. "How do I know that? How could I *possibly* know that?"

"It's a long story, Ma'am," said Gwion, looking around nervously. "But we should talk about that later, if you please." Joanne was less certain.

"Are you sure, it's okay, Gundy?" she asked.

"Absolutely. I just know it. I *feel* it, deeply. I can't explain."

"And you're sure it's safe for the children?"

Gundy looked at the boys, particularly at her Bertie, the one to whom she belonged, the one she existed to protect. She nodded.

"I have no doubts at all."

"Well, I'm not *totally* happy about it, but I know you, Gundy, and I know you'd never risk Bertie or Oli's safety." She turned to Gwion. "Okay, I'll let you tell us what you'd like us to do, but there are no promises."

Gwion smiled and took a breath: "You need to follow me into the castle. There's a narrow passage and, when we're in it, we will be concealed from view. We will walk along it and make sure we're alone, and I will take you down into the lower part of the castle."

"The *lower* part of the castle?" queried Joanne.

"Yes, it's the only way down, and you need to be someone like Miss Gundy or me to gain access … although, obviously you're very welcome."

"Not like me then," asked Joanne.

"No, Ma'am, you're only human."

"And you're *not*?!" said Joanne, slightly alarmed.

"Er, um, well, not entirely, no," said Gwion, a little wrong-footed. "Not any longer."

"Oh," said Joanne. "And you're saying that if we meet your mistress, she'll help us and Teddy?"

"Absolutely. It's vital we work together. The Third Yorebear will now be focussed on destroying Teddy, because Teddy is a very real threat to him and his plans."

"You know his plans?!" exclaimed Joanne.

"We really should be talking about this with my mistress, I don't think there's anything else I can tell you here."

They stopped talking while Joanne thought through the options. If they went with Gwion she might be exposing the boys to danger, whatever Gundy felt. On the other hand, if she stayed here and didn't meet Gwion's mistress, there was the very real possibility that Teddy and Simon might be in even more danger, perhaps from the Yorebear himself. Joanne looked at the boys that had come from her own body, at Gundy who looked back at her with hope in her eyes, and finally at Gwion.

"We'll come with you," she said, surprising herself.

"Oh, thank goodness," said Gwion with obvious relief. "Please, follow me."

::

It took a minute to convince Bertie that it was time to leave the playground, but soon enough they were marching up the slope and into the castle, walking between the broken remnants of castle towers, walls and rooms that had been ruined hundreds of years ago, left split apart and cracked ever since. Anyone watching would assume Joanne was out for a stroll with her two children and short little father, but the atmosphere between them was far from being that of a lazy family day in the weakening sun.

Gwion walked directly towards a small arch that led to a narrow passage. He stopped, straightened, and turned to look back to the family following him.

"Hm. We'll need to fold that up," he said, pointing at the pushchair. "Do you mind?"

"Can you carry it for me?" asked Joanne.

"Certainly, Ma'am," nodded Gwion.

So Joanne lifted Oli, Gundy and Mundy out of the pushchair and directed Gwion on how to fold it up. She bent down in front of Bertie and gave him Gundy. "Can you hold on to Gundy please, Bertie? She needs a big boy like you to carry her."

"Okay, mummy," Bertie beamed, pleased to be appreciated.

Having completed their preparations, they walked under the arch and into the passage, plodding along its length until it turned to the right to join a spiral stairwell, where Gwion stopped to make sure they were alone.

"If Miss Gundy would like to do the honours, we will go down now. Please touch your paw here." He indicated a stone in the middle of the wall that was slightly browner than the others. Gundy turned to Bertie.

"Bertie, can you put me next to that stone there, please?" she pointed.

Bertie complied a little too readily and accidentally squashed her head and body into the wall.

"Mmff!" said Gundy. But it worked. As soon as she touched

the stones, they began to change their appearance, becoming less like stone and more like wet clay. The phenomenon spread until it covered an area the size of a large door, and a hole formed in the middle. The clay seemed to fold and slop inwards, flattening against the walls of the stairwell that the opening revealed. It only took two seconds at most, and they were standing in front of an archway through which was an orange-glowing flight of steps, descending into the ground. The steps were not lit, it was the stairwell's stone itself that was glowing dull orange. It was unexpectedly cozy.

"Someone's coming; we must hurry before they see us," said Gwion, not explaining how he knew.

One by one, they walked down the steps. First Joanne, carrying Oli and Mundy; next Bertie and Gundy, and finally Gwion carrying the pushchair. He checked to make sure no one had seen them and touched a brown stone on the glowing wall. The 'clay' door filled up behind them and reverted to its rocky appearance.

Having descended five or ten metres, they came out into a chamber the size of a small hall in a house. Gwion placed the pushchair in one corner of the entry hall and indicated for them to walk through the room's other doorway, immediately opposite where they stood at the bottom of the steps.

They went through and found themselves in a much larger room, clearly a 'neuadd fawr' (big hall), with two battered arm chairs, an old oak table and some hangings on the stone walls. Someone was sitting in one of the chairs, wearing a cloak, with a hood pulled forwards to hide their features underneath. The figure stood up, lowered the hood and Joanne let out a little scream. Standing in front of her was a woman, but her hands, her face and her feet were covered in a thin layer of hair, and her nose was snout-like. Joanne had a very good idea what kind of person she was looking at.

"Don't be afraid. I know I look a little odd to you, but I can assure you I used to be just as human as you are now. I was young and beautiful. But that was an age ago — two ages, from my perspective — and I've looked like this for both of them. I suppose I should be grateful that I never really grow old, perhaps that's the only benefit of being a Yorebear."

::

Gwion came back, from wherever he'd gone, with two extra dining chairs. One was for Joanne and one was for Bertie, and he went to get the pushchair for Oli and Gundy. While he was out of the room, Arthgwyn walked over to Bertie, who was looking at her uncertainly, and knelt down in front of him with a smile.

"Bear!" pointed Bertie. "Really bear! Like Teddy!"

Arthgwyn's hairy face burst out laughing.

"I haven't seen a child this close for hundreds of years; he's adorable!" But almost immediately she became solemn and stood up, perhaps because she'd just reminded herself what a cut-off life she was living, or how childless she was.

"In some respects, it is sad that we have to meet at all. It would be better if life could carry on as it did three, four, five years ago. But Teddy met 'the Yorebear', amongst other things, and now he has re-awoken, so we need to work together."

Joanne nodded to show she was listening.

"The Third Yorebear has a name, Arthdu. As for me, Arthgwyn, I was the First Yorebear ... and there was Arthllwyd." She sighed and looked pained. "He was the Second Yorebear, who quietly died centuries ago. However, I'd prefer to focus on the present, and talk about how we can keep you, Teddy and your children safe from Arthdu."

Joanne blinked and swallowed quickly.

"So you *know* the Yorebear — the Third Yorebear, that is?"

"Yes, I know him, or at least I did. As I said, his name is Arthdu. Well, that's not his real name but ... no, I'm not going to talk about the past. Arthdu is out there and from what I hear and feel, he is more awake, and more dangerous, than he's ever been in all the centuries we've been alive. It's up to us to stop him."

"How do we do that?!" asked Joanne, hoping the answer wouldn't involve her family.

"I have no idea, whatsoever."

"Oh," said Joanne, now feeling a tang of worry and adrenaline.

"However, Joanne, I think Teddy can help us, because he is a bear and because he was able to put Arthdu to sleep last time — which is, of course, exactly why Arthdu will be trying to kill him. We need to help Teddy, so let's go over what we know, starting with Pale."

"You know Pale?" asked Joanne, surprised.

"By reputation, yes. He also put Arthdu to sleep, a long time ago. We've had quite a while to find out what he did, although some of it is guesswork of course ..."

"We have Pale's notebook."

"Show me!" said Arthgwyn, her eyes widening, just as Joanne's squeezed closed with a sigh because they were obviously going to have to go through the whole of Pale's book again. She shrugged and reached to retrieve it from her handbag, and had just set it down on Arthgwyn's old oak table when Bertie grabbed it.

"Story!"

"No, Bertie, not a story. This is not a story book."

"Want story mummy!" he insisted and held the book tightly.

"No, *mummy* really needs this book now; we can have a story later."

Bertie pouted and threw the book to the floor. It landed on the lower corner of its back cover, with its pages wide open, and the corner split.

"Oh dear, Bertie, look! Oh *dear!*"

Bertie looked to his right and dropped his head, but Gundy had noticed something. The corner of Pale's book had slightly peeled back, and there was something underneath. She ran over to the book before Joanne could reach it, picked it up, and stroked the raised corner with her paw, intrigued. It tickled across the fur of her paw pad and, as it did so, the corner lifted up a little more, revealing the diagonal bottom half of the word '*death*'.

"Arthgwyn! Joanne!" she shouted. "Look! Words!"

They scurried over to kneel down next to her and Gundy pointed to what she had found. Joanne glanced at Gundy and Arthgwyn, and she gently, carefully, pealed back the loose corner of the book. As she pulled, it revealed a hidden message underneath, written on the actual back page of the notebook, concealed by a false cover, stuck with something like the glue used on a post-it note. She pulled it off completely, and read what Pale had written:

> "*You have found my secret. If you have been reading my book then you have earned it. If not, there is nothing I can do; I am probably dead. Know this: the rector of the church in Llangurig owns a book, written by Robertson. I discovered what happened to him, and the existence of his book, when He awoke us. It is supposed to contain all you need to know about how to defeat the Yorebear forever. Although I am no longer convinced there is any point trying to stop Him, do what you will. I find myself wishing you good luck; I'm not sure why. After a while, life is no more than acting, aching, waiting for death.*"

"This man may have saved us all," said Arthgwyn steadily.

"But he also tried to kill Teddy three times," reminded Gundy.

"Perhaps this is some reparation?" Arthgwyn mused, and shrugged at the conflict. "Is there anything else in that book?"

"You should read it. We've been over it a hundred times. There's a lot about the plants and animals and people he killed, some depressing philosophising about life, just before *he* was killed, and an account of how Pale and Robertson put Arthdu to sleep in

1618. Have a look, if you like?" said Joanne, offering the book to Arthgwyn.

"I will, thank you," she said, with a nod, taking it in her somewhat furry hand.

"So, what are we going to do?" asked Joanne. "Do we just go and *get* Robertson's book? Is it really that simple? Sort of 'stopping the Yorebear by numbers'?"

"Well, I've found it's often worth trying simple things first," said Arthgwyn.

Joanne's thoughts flashed to Simon for a moment, and she remembered what Teddy had asked.

"Oh! There's something else!" said Joanne.

"What's that?" asked Arthgwyn.

"Have you heard anything about sheep killing sheepdogs and farmers?" Arthgwyn shook her head and shrugged. She looked over to Gwion, who also shook his head.

"Do you have a computer? Could we look it up?"

"Of course," said Arthgwyn. "Gwion works in the Physics department in the university you know! I believe you work in the university too? In Computer Science?" Joanne nodded. "You may have seen him around?" Joanne hadn't but she half-nodded because she didn't want to disappoint Arthgwyn, whose warmth for, and pride in, Gwion were suddenly obvious. He dropped his gaze, smiled shyly and gestured towards a corridor. "Let's have a look."

They all moved to Gwion's room to use his laptop. It was a small room with space for a bed, which was covered in research papers and a few aged cushions, and a roll-top desk, on which the laptop sat. It was plugged into a slatted metal box that sprouted tubes and was half buried in the wall; for ten or fifteen centimetres around the contraption, the wall glowed orange.

"I've used the Darkgate to hack into the university's microwave link with Swansea: great bandwidth!" said Gwion, proudly.

"Never mind that, Gwion, let's do some searches," said Arthgwyn.

Gwion looked a little crushed as he sat down in front of the laptop.

Twenty minutes later they had the information they needed. There were three strange things: First, there were indeed reports of killer sheep; they had not only killed several dogs but, in at least three cases, farmers had been killed too. It was a cause of great fear in some farming communities; indeed, some farmers had been selling or culling sheep. Second, while they were looking, they also came across reports of Live toys being ejected from people's homes — teddy bears, cuddly pandas, fluffy dogs — all thrown out by owners who were, for some inexplicable reason, suddenly terrified of them. The toys had started gathering together into groups, which caused even more fear, and the groups were moving towards Wales. Third, none of the details were in the national media; weirdly, the reports were solely in blogs and local newspapers, in and around the West of England and Welsh border.

There was a pause while they considered what they'd learned. Joanne spoke.

"I'd better phone Simon and Teddy, to tell them what we've found."

"Very well," said Arthgwyn.

Joanne stood up to leave, to phone from the surface.

"No, Joanne — you can phone from here. Gwion's rigged up a … um …"

"… repeater," said Gwion, finishing Arthgwyn's sentence.

"Yes, that. So you don't need to leave the Darkgate!" Arthgwyn smiled. Joanne smiled back, reached down into her bag to extract her phone, and rang Simon's number. Teddy answered.

"Hello."

"Hello, Teddy; it's Joanne. I've got the information you wanted. But there's some other really important news. Can you repeat everything I say, so Simon can hear it? ... well, unless you can remember how to turn on the speakerphone?"

"Oh, um, no, um, I ffink I'd better just repeats evreeffing."

In this manner, Joanne told Teddy and Simon about meeting Gwion, the existence of the Darkgate under Aberystwyth castle, and meeting Arthgwyn. It was all ver unexpected, but it seemed like good news. When she had finished, she told Simon what he needed to know about killer sheep, and shared with him what they'd discovered about Live toys being ejected from homes and forming gangs to protect themselves, and how all these things were only happening in West England, not in Wales.

Teddy was upset to think about those like himself having to live a nomadic existence; he, Simon and Joanne discussed what they could do about it, which was almost nothing. If Simon and Teddy saw a group of Live toys, they might be able to help them, but there was no room in the car to carry more than one large group, and there was no place near The Dolls to which they could be taken that would give them safety — certainly not The Dolls' manor itself, since The Dolls were having enough trouble of their own.

Simon Joanne and Teddy talked through a few other possibilities but none of them would have worked. Eventually, after a pause, Joanne moved on to tell them about the message in the back of Pale's notebook that detailed the location of Robertson's book, adding that Gwion was planning to travel to get it from Llangurig. By now, Simon was excited that Arthgwyn might be the ally they needed to help stop Arthdu for good ... but he wanted to talk to Joanne, in person, about his and Teddy's experience at the farmhouse.

"Oh, just a minit, Joanne. Simon wants to talk to you. He's stoppin der car."

Joanne waited, and soon Simon came to the phone.

"Hello... um, we've had a few problems. Quite nasty ones, I'm afraid."

"Oh no! What happened?"

Simon described what had taken place at Wrooph's farm: the Hordesman with the exploding crossbow bolts; the damage done to the car, and their fears of police investigation. He explained how they would park and hide the car somewhere in the trees near Bredwardine, so it wouldn't be found by the police, then they could focus on helping The Dolls — and he tried to reassure Joanne, told her they were safe, promised it would all be okay. However, he couldn't help feeling all he'd done was re-iterate just how dangerous things were: it was hard to be convincing.

Simon was aware that he couldn't stop the car for long, so he pressed the speakerphone button, gave the phone back to Teddy, and continued driving towards Bredwardine.

"I don't mind saying, I'm a bit scared by all this," said Joanne.

"Me too," added Teddy. "But I did lots of der scary ffings before, and day all worked out okay, so maybe we will be okay dis time too, actchully?"

"I hope so, Teddy," mused Simon. "I'm a bit concerned there might be a Hordesman waiting for us … but if we go round the back to meet them, I'm sure we'll be fine; that way, we can find out more about what's happening." Whatever his words, there was worry in his voice. "Joanne, I'll phone you again to let you know how we're getting on, okay?"

"Okay. Be careful," agreed Joanne. "Really careful."

"You too," said Simon. There was a pause, then they said their goodbyes.

Joanne looked at her phone slightly longer than usual and pressed the 'end call' button.

"Cup of tea?" asked Arthgwyn.

Joanne had just learned that she and her family were under greater threat from Arthdu than she'd ever expected … and yet a cup of tea was exactly what she needed.

"Yes please," she said slowly, with a wide-eyed smile at the insanity of it all. Gwion stood up from his desk to make the tea but Arthgwyn indicated, with a downward motion of her hand, that he should stay seated.

"It's okay, Gwion, I need to *do* something. Shall we move back to the main hall?"

Five minutes later, Joanne, Arthgwyn and Gwion were taking tea while the children played noisily, rolling on the ancient rug on the stone floor. No one over the age of three uttered a sound, they just sipped tea and thought. Gundy had never cared for tea, so she joined the boys' fun on the floor, interspersed with the sounds of clinking china.

::

"So why are people in England suddenly throwing out Live toys?" asked Joanne.

"Are you asking why it's happening in England but not in Wales, or asking why they're suddenly scared that toys are Alive?"

"Um, both I suppose."

"Well, I can't really answer either question with absolute certainty, but I think Arthdu is beginning to destabilise England, for a reason — a reason I can guess — and I think there's something about a toy being Alive that, until recently, has innately calmed its owner. Now that calming effect has somehow been removed, their owners are panicking."

"And what's Arthdu's 'reason'?"

"He wants to restore power to the Britons."

"He wants to take over Britain?"

"No, Briton. The old country before the Saxons and others invaded. But I have no idea how he thinks he's going to succeed, given the military resources of twenty-first century England. But that's my guess and, knowing Arthdu, I think it's a pretty good guess."

"Okay, but how can Live toys be stopping their owners from freaking out? I mean they don't seem to be doing it deliberately, and there's no other connection between a toy and its owner … is there?"

"There is, actually," interjected Gwion. "May I tell her?" he asked Arthgwyn. Arthgwyn weighed something in her mind for a moment, closed her eyes and nodded.

"Picocells," said Gwion, with a boyish grin at least sixty years younger than his age.

"What?"

"Picocells, or 'lifedust' as Arthgwyn puts it. They are very, very small processing units that act together, in concert."

"Well, I've heard of nanobots, because of my university research, but I've never heard of 'picocells'. Presumably they're smaller?"

"Yes. And completely impossible for us to make! Fascinating, isn't it?!"

Joanne's eyebrows lifted, although 'fascination' wasn't quite the right word to describe her expression, 'alarm' was more accurate.

"But how can these picocells be responsible for this calming effect, or anything else, if they can't exist?"

"I didn't say they couldn't exist, I said we cannot make them. Not the same thing at all. They're responsible for the 'calming effect' alright, and a lot more besides; they emanate from a Darkgate according to a Gaussian distribution, so even at a distance there's some small effect. I've spent a lot of time up in the physics department, late at night, working on this. My research suggests that picocells are actually quite simple, in principle. They are machines made from hierarchically organised groupings of subatomic particles. Well, particles isn't quite the right word, but … hm, the point is that they're held together by exquisitely balanced forces, and activated and connected by radiation and absorption processes, in such a manner as to make an internally communicating, collectively-sentient entity. Thus, in the end I found they were quite easy to understand, just impossible to build."

"What? That's *easy* to understand? I mean I have a PhD in robotics and my best guess is that you're saying a Live toy's personality — Teddy's for example — is created by lots of tiny things inside him that are sending signals to each other, like a brain's neural net?"

"That's a *bit* simplistic, but basically, yes. Just as our brains are collections of neurons, organised in groups that talk to each other, from which sentience and personality emerges, so Live toys contain collections of picocells. And although there's no lab on this planet that could make even the simplest picocell collective unit, I *have* managed to work out *what* they did, and it's beautifully elegant."

"It sounds almost like you're saying picocells are not from this planet!" laughed Joanne.

"Yes, absolutely. Didn't I say?"

Joanne shook her head slowly, with eyes like saucers.

"Oh. I thought it was obvious. They were in the meteoroid that crashed, back in September 571: the one that transformed my mistress and—"

Arthgwyn cleared her throat and Gwion knew exactly what she meant. He changed tack smoothly.

"My mistress saw them in their *rawness*, before they'd had a chance to form the Llandegley Darkgate; they flooded into her and she was changed by them almost immediately."

For a while Joanne just stood there, trying to take it all in, trying to break down what she'd just been told into smaller, more understandable chunks. She gazed at Arthgwyn anew, and Arthgwyn looked back at her like a damaged little girl. Joanne looked at Gundy, who was also wide-eyed, struggling with the implications. And she turned back to Gwion, who seemed overjoyed to be able to share all this with someone other than Arthgwyn.

"This Darkgate is stable now. You could hit it with a demolition ball and nothing would happen. But the fascinating thing is that your Simon's report about the exploding farm suggests someone has chipped off parts of the Llandegley Darkgate, fixed them to the tips of crossbow bolts, then deliberately made the tips unstable — the energy from a sharp impact would be enough to a cause a cascade destabilisation, a near-instant explosion in which a tiny portion of the flint's subatomic matter would be completely converted into energy. Someone's done it deliberately, someone clever enough not to let *all* the matter convert to energy, which is a very, very good thing because the energy in even a chipping-sized piece of Darkgate matter would be enough to remove Wales from the world map. Einstein, you know. Simple."

Joanne was more and more alarmed. Her physics was rusty but she had no trouble remembering that the conversion of matter into energy was the basic principle behind an atom bomb.

"There's a good side too, though. Did you know people with high picocell counts can live indefinitely, because the picocells manage the length of the body's telomers? *And* they directly maintain life, so their 'owners' don't even need to eat or drink!" Gwion's excitement made him forget to explain at a level Joanne would understand, but this last point was something that Joanne had seen for herself.

"... but Live toys *can* drink, if they want to, that's how Teddy and Gundy can do it!" she smiled. "Let me guess, the picocells break down the food and drink — into oxygen, hydrogen and carbon dioxide, I suppose — so it's all turned to gas? Of course! It makes sense now!" she exclaimed, but soon looked puzzled. "Still, I don't see how that can explain why Live toys are suddenly being rejected by people in England."

"Well, picocells give off a field that allows them to communicate with each other, whether inside a Live toy, or in us."

"Inside ... *us*?" questioned Joanne, licking her lips nervously.

"Well, yes. I mean, picocells are everywhere in small quantities. I've shown that in the lab. After all, they've been here a long time — at least fifteen hundred years, maybe more — and during that time they've been carried all over the world by wind, and people, and animals, on wings and fur and shoes. We've ingested them too: they're inside us, in our brains, our muscles, our bones. I suppose, picocells are a little like water vapour that diffuses from places of high concentration to places of low concentration, though it's a controlled kind of diffusion. If a Live toy is like a pool of picocells, a Darkgate is like an ocean, and this picocell 'vapour' has been gradually leaking from them into the rest of the world … therefore, to answer your question from a few minutes ago, the picocells can have an influence on us to some extent, maybe just enough to dull or enhance any reaction we'd normally make, but certainly enough to prevent someone from 'freaking out', as you put it, about a Live toy. Presumably Arthdu is interrupting that influence, so people are no longer calm about the idea of a Live toy in their house. In fact, I'd guess he's actively *reversed* the effect of that link to make people fear Live toys."

Joanne nodded slowly, beginning to understand the general idea, but was puzzled about something.

"So, why are there two Darkgates? There's Arthdu's Darkgate and there's this Darkgate *here* in Aberystwyth — Oh! I've just realised! The main street is even named after it! Great Darkgate Street! — but where did this Darkgate come from?"

"The meteoroid broke up and landed in chunks across Wales, or 'Briton', as it was. One chunk in Aber', one chunk in Llandegley and—"

"Gwion, that's enough for now," interrupted Arthgwyn.

Gwion stopped talking and looked around awkwardly. Joanne was thinking over what had just been said. Arthgwyn was trying not to look guilty for being sharp with Gwion.

"Will this Darkgate change *us*?" asked Joanne, serious again.

"It might. Eventually," admitted Arthgwyn. "But it's safe for now. Gwion's been affected, but here's been here years, decades. It's not remotely as active as it was when I found the meteorite."

Joanne clenched her jaw. Then she spoke.

"That's it. We can't stay here."

"Really? It took *months* before Gwion noticed even the slightest change at all."

"Actually, it's not that," said Joanne. "Not *just* that … I thought staying with Carys in Aber would be safe, but now we've found out you're here, and either you or we could be targeted, and that wouldn't be fair on anyone. We need to leave … perhaps my mum and dad's house in Somerset would be a sensible place to wait for things to calm down?"

Joanne looked at Arthgwyn to gauge her reaction; other than a furrowed brow, there wasn't much to go on. Joanne continued:

"This picocell/Darkgate thing is just the final straw. Any change to my boys, however small, is not acceptable." She sighed, realising how this must sound. With a gentler tone, she persisted: "If Gwion's going to Llangurig to retrieve Robertson's book, then maybe he can give us a lift? We could catch the bus from Llangurig to Caersws station and get a train from there. And, I suppose, I could also check on our house as we drive by."

"Your house, why?" asked Arthgwyn.

"Well, they blew up Wrooph's farm; what might they do to our house?!"

"I wouldn't worry, I'm sure they only blew it up because they saw Teddy was there."

"But will they blow our house up when Teddy returns to it? Is there a Hordesman waiting outside our cottage, somewhere in the woods? Are they watching my *home* right now?" Joanne began the questions calmly, but there was a rising anger in her tone.

"I see what you mean," agreed Arthgwyn, diplomatically. Joanne continued.

"After all, Gwion was able to deliver your message to us without us knowing he'd ever been there."

Arthgwyn frowned at something in her words; Joanne didn't notice.

"I imagine Arthdu could harm us or our house with equal ease, if he wanted to — which I assume he does."

"Hm. It's possible, but I can't see why he'd bother blowing up your home if you're not inside."

"I want to know our house is in one piece, and I want to take my children to my parents, to safety — that's all."

Arthgwyn sighed. What could she do? These weren't her soldiers, and arguing with a mother about her children's safety was clearly pointless. However, there was one other thing to try.

"It doesn't look like Gundy will be very welcome in England."

"Maybe not, but I know what I need to do." Joanne's lips were firm, almost pouting. Gundy was shocked at the implication that she'd either have to come along and risk being attacked by mad English people, or would have to leave her dear Bertie's side, but Joanne was not going to change her mind.

"When will you go?" asked Arthgwyn.

Joanne thought for a moment.

"I'll need to talk to Carys first, but after that we'll—"

"I'm not going," said Gundy in a low voice.

"But you ... I mean ... really?" said Joanne.

"Really. I desperately want stay with Bertie and make sure the boys are safe, but Teddy needs us too. Arthgwyn needs us. You're looking after the boys, so I have to stay to help her, to help Teddy. To some extent, it will help you and the boys too."

Joanne felt a little guilty and, even though her entire being had only one biologically-driven concern, for the sake of the others she could see she needed to talk this through. She sat down.

For Arthgwyn, it was a painful reminder of her own past.

"You know, I've seen this totally understandable, panicked fear before."

"You have?"

"Yes. This time it's you, afraid about what might happen to your children, but there's nothing new under the sun. I've caused this kind of fear myself. One minute I was a seventeen-year-old young woman, with my whole life in front of me, well-liked by the men of the village, with a gorgeous man courting me," she smiled. And her smile vanished. "The next, I was altered, changed, mutated." A lot of things happened after that, many of them painful, but one of the worst was having to leave my village, my friends, my home because of the fear I struck into people's hearts. The kind of fear that's in you, and the same kind of fear that's in England at the moment. For a long time after that, my life became a painful trudge: for which Arthdu is partly responsible."

Arthgwyn was opening up to Joanne and it wasn't something Joanne was expecting. She didn't know what to say. Arthgwyn continued.

"The last time I saw my parents was when I'd broken into my own home to get my hooded cloak. All I wanted to do was hide myself, my face, from others. I'd never felt like that before. I used to walk into a place and enjoy the men looking at me, but now they would shake their fists, or take up weapons, and jeer at me to leave.

"I still have that cloak. I can't wear it now, after all these years, it's much too delicate, but I still have it, preserved under glass. It's proof that I used to have a life before being *this*." She indicated her face and body.

Joanne had had time to think. "I don't see you like that. I see you as a strong woman, someone I admire."

Arthgwyn smiled sadly.

"My name was Gwynyth you know. It's funny isn't it, I was Gwynyth for just 17 years and I've been like this ever since, for over 1,500 years, and yet I still think of myself as that young woman. I suppose that's the real reason I wear a cloak: it's not to hide my features from others, it's to hide them from myself, so I can carry on believing I'm the beautiful Gwynyth from Llandegley." A single tear tracked down Arthgwyn's lightly furry cheek, collided with a hair and spread along its shaft. She breathed in and changed tack. "So I know why you're afraid of the Darkgate, and in some respects you're right: it can do horrible things to people. But I promise you, this Darkgate is safe now. Your boys could stay here a week and nothing would happen."

As much as Joanne appreciated Arthgwyn's openness, she remained unconvinced.

- CHAPTER 4 -

The Dolls and the Gazebo

Teddy stopped talking at the sight of the Bredwardine bridge looming up in front of them both. It was from this bridge that he'd fallen three years ago, punched into the air and over the side by the troll who lived underneath. He half-expected to see the troll thundering towards them from the other end of the bridge. He found he was holding his breath. Simon glanced at him, concerned; he was like this every time they crossed over to Bredwardine.

The car rolled onto the bridge and Teddy grasped his seat belt. Parapet after parapet passed by and Teddy looked left and right defensively for any sign of the troll. All he could see was the river below, flowing has it had done for long ages past. He thought of the otters who had saved his life, dragging him, while Asleep, from the river to safety on the river bank.

There was a bump where bridge met land, and they were on the other side. Teddy breathed a sigh of relief.

"Simon, why do we get afraid?" asked Teddy.

"Well, hmmm, I suppose it's useful because it stops us doing things that could hurt us?"

"Like walking over dat bridge?"

"Yes, just like that," said Simon said. "But we're quite safe in this car — well, what's left of it."

"So fear is good den?"

"It can be, yes."

"Why does it feel so nasty den?"

"Um. If it wasn't, I suppose we might ignore it. Fear tells us to act *right now* to keep out of harm's way."

"Like when we're worried dat someone's in trouble, and we

have to help dem right now, but we don't know how, or if it's safe?"

"Yes, Teddy, just like us helping The Dolls," reassured Simon. "But we're going to be *very* careful."

They drove into the village, bore left at the junction, as they'd done many times over the past three years, and rolled towards The Dolls' manor house. But, instead of stopping to let Teddy out, they kept driving — it would not be safe for Teddy simply to crunch up the golden gravel drive today; they'd have to park somewhere else and walk.

For a minute, they headed toward Moccas but soon turned right, up a narrow, overgrown lane signposted 'Dorstone Hill', one of a ridge of hills rising up behind Bredwardine.

Wind flapped through the damaged car as they climbed the incline, searching for somewhere hidden to park it. They began to feel haunting panic rising that it might be impossible to find such a place, and the car would be seen and reported, and they would be found and arrested and charged with murder or, at the very least, the destruction of a farm and several of its animals.

For ten minutes they drove around but found nowhere. It was extremely frustrating. Then they saw a derelict house.

Simon turned sharply, still at speed, into the fronded drive, with its dehydrated tracks sunken into dried broken stones, as cracked as the house in front of them. It was a wreck: roof caved in, all the windows fractured, moss, ivy and plants everywhere out of control. Their car and this house were made for each other. Around the back, they parked and Simon quickly took Teddy out and placed him on the stony ground.

As they stood Teddy looked up at Simon, quizzically.

"What's wrong Teddy?" asked Simon.

"I'm not sure, actchully," began Teddy. "I ffink it feels a bit like it did at Llandegley, but wivout der scareyness ... but I don't understand how it could feel like dat here?"

"Do you think Arthdu or his hordesmen are around?"

Teddy thought and felt for a moment.

"No, no, I don't ffink so. It just feels … fizzy."

"Fizzy?"

"Yes. Dat's what it feels like. It's funny."

Simon looked around, listened, concerned: the leaves were rustling in the light breeze; everything about the house was fixed and still; the drone of a far distant car; the shush of waving grass over the road; occasional birdcalls; nothing more. What option did they have except to persevere on their course to The Dolls?

"Hm. Come on, Teddy," said Simon, quietly.

The sun was shielded by white cloud, but it was a fairly warm, summer mid-morning with only a gentle breeze, so there was no need for a coat. Simon reached into the car, unplugged and extricated the window-mounted sat nav; thunked the door shut. Then Simon and Teddy walked off towards The Dolls. Later, maybe, they could locate a car glazer who didn't ask questions.

The sat nav's display showed they needed to travel towards a track, then cross-country, over a field, and into a wood. Although the screen showed none of these things as an ordered route, it indicated where they were now, and where Teddy and Simon needed to be, and it was easy enough to keep on target as they walked through the blank space in between.

They plodded along, mostly in silence, stepping quietly, listening for attackers, looking around for danger — then they dropped down into the wood, pushing aside branches and stepping over brambles. Teddy soon began to struggle to make his way through the thicket, so Simon carried him. He stepped slowly, not wanting to crack a branch or even rustle against leafy branches, hardly breathing, but they made it to the fence at the back of The Dolls house; it took twenty minutes and Simon was warm from walking.

::

Now that they could see the house through the garden trees, set out in the the estate grounds below them, the question was how to reach The Dolls without being seen by a Hordesman — if, in fact, such a person was in the vicinity. Then again, it seemed likely one might be, since one had even been waiting at Wrooph's farm. Teddy and Simon shared a glance. This was not going to be fun, but they were on a mission.

They knelt (at least, Teddy tried to, then simply sat on his bottom) while Simon stowed the sat nav in his messenger bag and retrieved his binoculars. For a few seconds he scanned the grounds with them, saw nothing except plants and trees. He felt stupid and re-bagged them with a huff. This was silly; however much he wanted to pretend otherwise, he was not a professional infiltrator who could penetrate the horticultural complex below to meet their clients, unseen. He was a balding, 41-year-old father-of-two, kneeling next to a talking teddy bear, trying to find some dolls. If there was a Hordesman down there, he and Teddy were in serious trouble. Simon sighed. They'd have to take the risk.

"Come on, Teddy. Let's go." Teddy's pained look made it clear he had similar worries. They stood up and climbed over the fence into the garden.

For a few minutes they carefully crept about, from place to place, trying to make as little noise as possible, while searching for some sign of The Dolls. Occasionally, they thought they heard a noise but it was always a bird or animal hidden in the undergrowth. No crossbow bolt shot out and blew them up, and there wasn't the slightest sign of The Dolls. The odd couple peered around, with no idea where to go next, gave up and looked at each other for inspiration.

"Good afternoon, sir," said a small, calm voice from behind them, making them both jump.

"If you'll follow me, please ..." said the tiny servant with a shock of black hair shooting straight up out of the top of his head. "... I'll take you to The Dolls. They are expecting you." The servant's voice was deeper than most people would expect from something only ten centimetres tall. He led them through the garden, down narrow paths, and across lawns: all a little unkempt, and they stopped in front of an old red-brick wall covered in ivy, bricks cracked by a hundred icy winters and hot summers. Two thick leafy bushes grew left and right of the wall, both madly sprawling in all directions, reaching high above the barrier. The servant turned left and indicated that they should squeeze between the trunk of the bush and the brickwork. Simon had to scrape himself against branches and brick to ease through, but they both found themselves on the other side of the wall in a Victorian secret garden that, apart from a reasonably well-kept grassy area, had clearly not been tended for some time. At the back of the square-walled space, was a gazebo.

"They're in there, sir. Perhaps you'd like to go ahead, my legs are short and I would not want to delay you."

"Thanks, we'll do just that," said Simon. He picked Teddy up, hurried over to the gazebo, his feet shooshing through the grass. When he reached the gazebo he knocked on a wooden pillar to attract attention and placed Teddy back on the ground.

"Teddy! It's you!" cried Agnes. "Oh it's so good to see you! So good!" and she burst into tears, along with the other dolls, all exclaiming their happiness at seeing Teddy again.

"Hello, yes, it's me!" said Teddy, above the din, a little too happily given the circumstances. "And dis is Simon, my owner, you can trust him."

The Dolls and Simon had never actually met over the past three years, although they had spoken on the phone. They nodded and smiled greetings at each other.

"Where's Rufus?" Teddy asked, referring to the fluffy dog who lived with The Dolls.

"He's gone to see what's wrong with the Dwarves. We've sent messages to them but heard nothing back, and some of the pigeons haven't returned. It's not like them." Agnes was worried. "But, you're here now! And we are so very grateful that you're going to try to help us!"

"So, what happened to Muvver den?" Teddy asked.

Agnes took a breath to compose herself. "Mother was gardening by the rear of the house and someone shot her in her left leg with a crossbow bolt. One of the servants saw it happen from the downstairs kitchen window. To begin with she looked shocked and annoyed; then she just wobbled and fell over, and she died."

"Dat's *not* nice," understated Teddy, leaving his mouth open.

"We think the bolt was poisoned. There was nothing we could do. We couldn't phone for an ambulance; we couldn't help her; we couldn't move her; we couldn't pull the crossbow bolt out. Even if we had, she would still have been dead."

"But, um, she's not there now," said Simon, gently. "Who moved her?"

"The ambulance men, when the police came to make their 'investigations' — but that was days later. Mother just lay there until someone missed her. It was heartbreaking that it took so long. It rained one day. Her hair was a mess. She would have hated that." Tears welled up again in Agnes' eyes and Teddy poddled across to hug her. Hattie and Dora came over and looked at Teddy with big, sad eyes; he opened up his other arm to them, and they nestled in. The remaining Dolls snuggled up to Teddy's sides and were comforted. Agnes regained her composure and continued.

"The police arrived. The servants overheard them talking about doing tests on the crossbow bolt, and they seemed to be working out where the assailant had been standing when they'd fired the bolt. Then the strangest thing happened. Within a few minutes all, except one of them, stopped moving and stood still. The one, who wasn't affected, moved among them, talking to them, apparently trying to revive them, without success."

"Really? How odd! What were they doing?" asked Simon.

"Nothing at all! But they gradually started moving again, and they all agreed that there was 'nothing more to be done' here, Mother had killed herself and the case was closed. Two minutes later they were all gone."

"Weird ..." began Simon. "What about the ambulance people? Were they affected too?"

"Yes. They both seemed to be influenced. They took Mother away, the police left, and it went quiet."

"And no one came back?"

"Not from the police, no. But there's something else. The policeman who wasn't affected looked unusual. I saw him myself, and he was shorter. I mean too short for a policeman, and he was wearing plain clothes with a dark raincoat over the top. I don't remember him arriving with the others either. I believe it's possible he did something to the police and ambulance crew."

"Oh dear. I'm thinking 'Yorebear involvement'," said Simon.

"Exactly," agreed Agnes. "Perhaps a Hordesman? But there's more."

"The house?" winced Simon.

"Yes. Three days after that, a man and a woman arrived. The back door was still unlocked from when Mother went into the garden, so they simply walked in. The police had left so quickly, they hadn't even locked up! Well, the point is, the man and the woman went around the house, into each room, and discussed what they could sell, and what they would have to throw away. These were Mother's things! They had no right!"

"Oh dear, Agnes; poor you! Dat's horrible!" sympathised Teddy.

"They talked about how they would have to ignore Mother's will because she was 'obviously mad', since she'd left everything in trust to 'a bunch of dolls', and Mother was going to provide a person to look after us. It's the most caring thing Mother had ever done for us and they just overruled her!" Agnes was livid. She snorted through her nose.

"So they took everything, and would have taken us too, if we hadn't decamped here. They plan to sell the house and all the belongings, and give the money to the nearest relative they can find. We are left with nothing, except what we could gather from the house before they came back with the removal men the next day. We *thought* we'd be able to get back into the house using the key Mother had given to the servants, but they'd *changed the locks*." She was steaming. "Why would they do that? THIS IS OUR HOUSE, DAMN IT!" she yelled, her habitual calm cracking for a moment.

Teddy put his arm out again and she accepted it around her.

"Simon, do you ffink we could give her der ffingy now?"

"Oh yes. Well, now is as good a time as any. Agnes, we've got a small present for you and the other Dolls," said Simon.

Agnes, tried to smile. "Thank you. You are kind."

"I'm afraid it's a bit of a practical present, but hopefully you'll like it."

"These days, we're appreciating 'practical' over 'elegant', so your present sounds ideal already."

"Here we are," said Simon, pulling the present, wrapped in a plastic carrier, from his messenger bag. He handed it to her. "I saw it in a garage when we were filling up with diesel." She un-wrapped it and found a phone and a solar charger inside. "That's just my old phone," pointed Simon. "It's still got credit and I'll keep it topped up from home, so you can always call us. I've programmed our number into the phone, just press and hold the '1' button. But the charger we bought should be able to charge the phone even on a dull day, as long as you wait long enough."

"Oh, that's wonderful! Thank you so much! I think one of the worst things about living here like this has been that we've been cut off from Teddy. Thank you!"

She held the phone to herself with both arms and closed her eyes. As she opened them again, her expression fell.

"There's something else though."

"Not more?!" said Teddy.

"Cordelia's dead," said Agnes.

Teddy gasped.

"She didn't want to get her feet wet on the grass dew as we made camp here, so she got the servants to carry her on a plate from the kitchen." Agnes sighed. "A cat saw Cordelia, apparently gliding above the grass, and it ran over to her. She panicked and tried to beat it off, so it bit her." Agnes winced at the thought. "Then the cat took her in its teeth and ran off, over between the wall and the garden shed and, well that's enough information I think. By the time it had finished playing with her, she was dead and in pieces."

Many of The Dolls had their hands over their mouths, queasy and upset.

"But ... there is some good news too." Agnes tried to brighten a little. "Ffion and Ayee are now married!"

"Who's 'Ayee'?" asked Teddy.

"Servant A, our lead servant — 'Ayee' for short." At this Ayee smiled and gave a deep bow to Teddy and walked over to comfort Ffion, who was still upset about the talk of Cordelia's death. He held her hand and looked up at her reassuringly.

"Now," said Agnes. "Tell us what's been happening to you ..."

Some time later, after Simon and Teddy had described their journey and conveyed their news, the conversation returned to the strange behaviour of the police after Mother's death. Agnes mulled over what they knew.

"Right, so we think that smaller man was in fact working for the Yorebear ... who you tell us is called 'Arthdu'? If Arthdu can control the police, you could be in a lot of trouble because they could find a reason to arrest you."

"The main one being the death of the Hordesman back in Gaufron," said Simon dryly. "Although, I don't think there's much of a body left for them to examine."

"If they are on Arthdu's side, they'll use any excuse they can find ..." She paused. "Now, I don't want to belittle your problems but I'd still like to sort out this business of Mother's murderer."

"Of course," said Simon.

"Okay. So, those of us who were here need to remember each of the people we saw that day, and when and where we saw them. In that manner, we will work out who arrived and left in which vehicle, what they were doing while they were here, and so on."

Everyone agreed and Simon wrote down their recollections and assumptions. When they'd finished, and distilled it all down, they found they'd agreed on several points:

(1) There were three police, two men and a woman. One of the men was guiding the operation.

(2) There also was a man who seemed to be gathering forensic evidence from the body, and he might have been a doctor because Ffion had heard him using technical terms to describe what the crossbow had done to Mother's leg.

(3) There were two ambulance men who arrived a few minutes after the police.

(4) There was the mystery man, who no one remembered arriving at all; he certainly didn't seem to arrive or leave in a car.

(5) After the weird 'standing-still', which seemed to have lasted about five minutes, every single one of those people had suddenly agreed Mother had committed suicide — she had deliberately stabbed herself in the leg with something poisonous and died.

(6) As a result, the crossbow bolt itself was ignored or forgotten, and the case was closed.

"What about der Moccasins doh?" asked Teddy. All the talk of a crossbow bolt had led everyone to assume Arthdu and the Horde were responsible.

"That's a good point, Teddy," said Simon. "What do you think Agnes? I mean, we know The Servant Master hates ... isn't friendly with—"

"Simon, it's okay; thanks for trying to save our feelings, but we all know what he thinks of us," said Agnes.

Simon felt a bit foolish but carried on. "Given the way the Moccasins were under some sort of Yorebear control, even after the Servant Master had been thrown out, I don't think Arthdu would give up control over them; he may even have sent some sort of leader from Llandegley. But, whatever the case, I bet Arthdu still has influence in Moccas — the way Teddy described him, he doesn't sound like someone who'd simply give up."

"This is all very important, Simon," said Agnes. "And I agree with what you're saying, but I believe I would be neglecting my duties as hostess if I didn't point out that it's time for something to eat and drink!" Simon smiled. "Will you take tea with us? We managed to rescue some biscuits."

Simon agreed: "Thanks, that would be lovely."

::

After one of the best cups of tea Simon had in ages (coaxed from an old kettle plugged into the gazebo's rusty garden socket, some milk provided by The Dolls' local supporters, and a bowl to act as a teapot) they decided to consult Arthgwyn and Joanne about The Dolls situation: Simon called Joanne, she answered, and both set their phones to speakerphone.

At first, Agnes was somewhat stilted with discussing their needs with Arthgwyn, who was not only a stranger, but also a yorebear; however, Joanne convinced everyone to introduce themselves, and one-by-one, they opened up, and shared their thoughts, and brought each other up to speed on their news.

Joanne revealed that while Simon and Teddy had been treking to The Dolls, she had begun to look into The Dolls' need of a new mother, and was planning to meet a woman called Emily who had been caught helping Live toys. The Dolls were interested in this possible new 'mother', but refused to get their hopes up at this stage.

Since there wasn't much more to say until Joanne could report back on her meeting with Emily, the conversation soon turned to who had killed Mother and why she had died.

"That was, without doubt, poison," confirmed Arthgwyn. "Arthdu has used it a lot, over the centuries; it's an old, forgotten skill we learned, but it works well ... then again the manner in which he affected the police is a little unlike him. He's normally much more direct than that. That sounds like some sort of gas, something subtle. Perhaps I'm underestimating him, or perhaps there's someone else with him behind the scenes, but it could easily be him. What I don't understand is why the gas didn't affect the mystery man who seems to have been responsible for Mother's death. Hm. Perhaps they're immune for some reason..."

Simon's eyebrows raised when he visualised the image of Arthgwyn and Arthdu 'brewing' things up together. How close had they been? And what had they been doing?

"I never was as good at brews as Ce... Arthdu, but it must be something like that. The sleeping drug could have been made up almost anywhere and transported, but poisons almost always have to be made up with *very* fresh ingredients, newly plucked, so it's likely that there's someone nearby who's involved in this."

"Perhaps that means Moccas *is* likely to be involved?" mused Simon.

"If there are those with that kind of knowledge in Moccas then I would say so, yes," agreed Arthgwyn. "Moreover, you mentioned these Moccasins live in a wood, which would be perfect for gathering the ingredients for a brew like that." She sighed. No one spoke. "Well, I have to go. Joanne, Gwion and I need to discuss their journey, and I'm going to cook pasta for the boys!" she sounded as joyful as Christmas at the idea.

"Goodbye, Arthgwyn, all the best; nice to have talked with you," said Agnes. The other dolls murmured their goodbyes too.

"Thank you; hope to talk to you soon. Bye."

Teddy and Simon said their farewells, and Simon ended the call and pocketed his phone again.

There was a moment of silence in which they all looked around half-smiling at each other; Simon broke the unexpected awkwardness.

"Well, if Mother's death was ordered by someone based in Moccas, I suppose we need to know what's going on in that wood. Do you know who's in charge in Moccas now?"

Agnes sighed. "It's hard to be sure these days, especially with *this*." She threw her arms up at the gazebo around them. "But the last we heard, there were signs that Ess, your so-called 'Servant Master', is back. One of the otters was in the Moccasin's field, a week or so back, and he heard the Moccasins talking about him, and they weren't talking about three years ago; it seemed to be current."

"Okay," said Simon. "And there are up to a thousand Moccasins?"

"Probably not *that* many. Several hundred, I'd say."

"Anyone else? Teddy saw other Masters the last time he was there."

"No, we think they've gone. There hasn't been a hint of anyone else over there, other than Ess. If there *is* someone else there then they're good at keeping themselves hidden, and out of gossip."

"Right," said Simon firmly. "What's to stop me from simply walking up to the Servant Master and asking him what he's up to?"

Agnes' head jerked back a few millimetres and she smiled at the surprise. "Nothing, I suppose — but you can't simply assume you're right. Especially after your experience at Gaufron farm. It would only take one Hordesman with a crossbow to kill even you; you need to be careful. In fact, Bee saw a Hordesman stationed in the bush over the road from our gates yesterday — we were concerned we'd drawn you into a trap! Luckily, you had more sense."

"Really?! Woah. I'm glad we arrived through your back garden then!" Simon had a thought. "Nevertheless, do you remember the Servant Master was annoyed when he thought Teddy was from Llandegley, and had come to mess up his plans? That suggests Arthdu *isn't* totally in control in Moccas wood."

"I don't agree; it suggests he *wasn't* in control, three years ago. A lot can happen in that time."

Simon marvelled at the wisdom of the 35 cm-tall talking china doll in front on him. "You're quite right, I stand corrected," he smiled. "Still, if we don't go, and if they are responsible for Mother's death, who knows what will happen next? Rufus and your servants protect you well but, although you have many friends around here, I wouldn't be surprised if several of them are less sure about helping you after what happened to Mother. If we can root this out now, it might be better for you."

"Hm. True. It's a concern. I'm not saying I don't want you to go, I just don't want you injured or killed on our behalf while we simply *sit* here."

"It's not your fault," reassured Simon. "This sort of thing is not your strength; I'm not sure it's mine either! But, equally, I *am* sure Teddy and I can't leave here only to get a letter from the Dwarves or Ramgar next week, or next month, or next year, telling us you were all killed, because we didn't help when we could." Several of The Dolls gasped in shock and fear at the suggestion. "Sorry. Didn't mean to upset you. I'm just saying, I'd like to go."

"And I'll come too," said Teddy, touching Simon's hand with his paw.

Simon smiled. "What do you think, Agnes?"

"Hm. Well, if you're sure you want to take the risk … very well, go with our deepest thanks and appreciation — but be careful! I would send Rufus after you when he returns, but he has no transport and it's dangerous for a Live toy to be outside these days."

Simon could see she was concerned about her partner's safety.

"He'll be okay, Agnes. He's a clever dog,"

Agnes half-smiled, wanting to believe.

- CHAPTER 5 -

Cracks

An hour before Simon and Teddy succeeded in meeting The Dolls, Joanne was trying to cope with the clawing panic that was rising inside her. It wasn't just that her boys were playing on the floor of a Darkgate that had the power to alter them, next to two already-changed strangers, she felt as if things were unravelling: her family was under threat, her husband was miles away, and she felt alone and uncertain. Joanne's face was fixed and grim. But there was one thing she *could* do, and she was going to do it.

Her decision to leave Aberystwyth — to seek the safety of her parents' home in Somerset — had caused waves of disharmony throughout the small group inside the Aberystwyth Darkgate, but she wasn't going to be persuaded otherwise. Unfortunately, by now Bertie had become bored and grumpy, and Oli was screaming for a feed, so they couldn't leave yet.

Joanne lent down to pick up baby Oli. Cradling him in her left arm, she began to feed him, and as he did, she realised he'd need somewhere to sleep. Both Arthgwyn and Gwion were looking in any direction except hers, but she attracted their attention and explained what Oli would need in a few minutes. A blushing Gwion offered his room. He shuffled off, faster than necessary, to prepare things for Oli, followed by Joanne's thanks.

When Oli was full of milk, and settled on the bed with Gundy stroking his hair, Joanne turned her attention to Bertie. They read the book she had promised earlier, scribbled some drawings, played peek-a-boo, and had cuddles and tummy raspberries. Joanne almost relaxed.

Bertie and Joanne were still playing when Oli woke up after

only thirty minutes sleep. It was unexpected because he usually slept for at least an hour, but he seemed totally rested. So Joanne held him and let him lie in her arms, as he played with his giraffe, while Bertie sat next to her lifting the tabs on his 'Where's Maisy?' book.

Gundy had continued to rest on Gwion's bed, after her poor night's sleep, then she too awoke feeling rested, and unusually Alive, and joined the playing and reading and hugging.

Intermittently, while all this was going on, Joanne used Gwion's laptop, now on the table in the *neuadd fawr*, to search for The Dolls' new mother. She hoped to set up a meeting with someone on the way to Somerset. It would be a positive thing, a contribution from her towards the cause before she escaped with her boys to keep them safe. It would help her feel a bit better about leaving.

::

As Joanne had imagined, searching for 'New mother Live dolls West England' turned up no results of any value. She pondered: perhaps she needed to think more laterally? What they needed was simply a person who had no problem being around Live toys. On the face of it, that was the very last thing that she was likely to find while a significant proportion of England's population was alarmed by them. She had seen the pictures of teddies and pandas and rabbits and dogs, running away from their towns and villages, in a fluffy refugee outflux — but perhaps that was it: she needed to search the news coverage for someone who maintained there was nothing to fear from Live toys, maybe even someone who was being persecuted for helping them.

Within fifteen minutes she'd found several news stories, but one in particular, about a woman in Tewksbury, fitted the bill perfectly. *'Top toy shop owner admits to harbouring "Live" toys'*, was the headline; Joanne studied the story and a smile spread on her face.

The toy shop owner, Emily Braxton, was a bubbly, well-known, wealthy figure in Tewksbury. She had started her toy shop back in 1993, and grown it into the largest soft toy shop in the West of England. More importantly, she'd made millions setting up other shops and selling franchises around the UK, US and Europe. She was rich and she liked soft toys, and that included Live toys.

But Emily Braxton had made a mistake. She had assumed that, because she was rich, she could stand up for Live toys and remain safe. She was wrong. The writer of the news story had made a vague attempt to be even-handed, and yet had written, '*Once-respected Emily Braxton has disappointed, if not horrified, the people of Tewksbury by taking sides with the disturbing armies of Live toys that threaten us all.*'

It seemed Emily was exactly who The Dolls needed — but surely she'd be impossible to find because she'd need to lie low? Maybe not: Joanne opened a new tab on Gwion's computer and began to search all the social networks she knew for 'Emily Braxton': it wasn't hard to find her because she was using several of them to promote her shops, even if some of them now reported that the shops were 'closed until further notice.' Joanne drafted a personal message:

> *Dear Emily,*
>
> *I saw the news story about you and I imagine you are having a rather hard time at the moment. I live in Wales, where there is much less fuss about these things and I would like to buy a Live toy to look after. It would be one less for you to worry about, so I think it would help us both.*
>
> *I attach a video of me and my friend Gundy, a Live bear, so you can see we are friendly and on your side. We would be willing to take a risk and meet you in Hereford later this afternoon if you like.*
>
> *Warm regards,*

Joanne.

They made a short webcam video, in which they waved and said hello and wished Emily well, and Joanne attached it to her message, sent it to all Emily's active accounts, and waited. Only twenty minutes later a reply appeared:

Dear Joanne,

Yes, times are hard, but onwards and upwards! Silly people and their silly ways, worrying about a few happy toys!

Would love to meet you and Gundy in Hereford, assuming the Silly People don't try to stop me! Do you know the town? There's a coffee shop down a passage near M&S. Could meet you there. My daughter Sophie will join us for moral support! Can you make it to Hereford by 4:30pm? Got a few 'errands' to run this afternoon. Tell you more later!

Best,

E. x

Joanne knew Hereford well and replied that she could just about make that time, and not to worry if she was a few minutes late because she'd be arriving by bus.

::

Joanne smiled to herself, glad that she was doing something positive … then she realised it was time to re-start the conversation about leaving with Arthgwyn.

Joanne mostly wanted to work out how to safely spy on her home and make it to Somerset by evening, but she was open to helping Arthgwyn recover Robertson's book from Llangurig. Arthgwyn took a breath to reply just as Joanne's phone rang: it was Simon and The Dolls calling to ask Arthgwyn about the use of poison in Mother's death. Arthgwyn contributed her knowledge, Joanne told them about her plan to meet Emily, and she placed her phone back in her bag and turned to face Arthgwyn again, who was still excited to have been involved in the machinations in Bredwardine.

"Well, *that* was interesting!" said Arthgwyn. "It's good to be able to hear what's happening 'on the front line' as it were."

Joanne shifted in her seat at the thought of her husband at war. Arthgwyn noticed and changed the conversation.

"I'll make us lunch in a minute but, before then, can we have another go at working out how to secure this book from Llangurig," she said. Then, with rather less enthusiasm, she added, "And to get you to your parents."

Joanne and Arthgwyn calmly discussed the pros and cons of various permutations of people and toys who could retrieve the book. Joanne now wanted to hire a car; Arthgwyn said that was silly, Gwion would drive them. The conversation knocked back and forth and, eventually, they began to make some progress.

All the while, Gundy played with Bertie and Oli on the rug on the floor. Gundy was moving Mundy's arms around and pretending Mundy was speaking to Oli. "Hello Oli, you're my boy! Would you like a cuddle?" And she gave Oli a big hug with Mundy's arms. Bertie laughed like it was the funniest thing he'd ever seen, and Oli smiled and gurned the way happy babies do.

Joanne had realised that her idea to look at their home as they passed by in the car wouldn't be enough. She wanted to make sure the cottage hadn't been broken into or occupied, but she couldn't see how to do that without putting her children at risk. Arthgwyn suggested a direct approach — parking nearby and walking to the house — but Joanne rejected it as too hazardous, and the conversation became frosty once more. They lulled into silent thought, or rather it would have been silent if Gundy hadn't been pretending to be a dinosaur.

Arthgwyn and Joanne were getting nowhere. After a couple of minutes, Joanne broke the silence and said she really did appreciate all that Arthgwyn was trying to do, and suggested they talked again after lunch ... but they would eat back at Carys' house because Carys might be worried by now. She would tell Carys that they were leaving, and they'd re-group with Arthgwyn and make a final decision about what to do. Arthgwyn shrugged with cold displeasure, now that she wouldn't be allowed to make lunch for the boys, but agreed. So Joanne gathered their things, and they waved a temporary goodbye.

Gwion led them to the top of the stairs and instructed Gundy on which stone to press, so they could re-enter the Darkgate on their own — but he emphasised that they must ensure no one was around, otherwise they'd need to make up a batch of Arthgwyn's 'forgetting' brew, which left people disoriented, with very bad headaches. He joked that students would probably like to get their hands on the recipe, but Joanne's face showed she wasn't in the mood for jokes.

Just before he opened the door, he took out a hammer and chisel from the bag he was carrying over his shoulder, and used the tools to attack the wall, breaking off a chipping from one of the stones that lined the stairs. He gave it to Gundy; it was slightly smaller than one of her paws. The weight felt good and it tingled in an encouraging manner.

"If you should get into trouble, just hold it in one paw, and put out your other paw in front of you, and think, 'defend me' and you'll be okay."

"Well, I hope we don't need that, Gwion, but thank you."

"Just in case," he reassured her, then he touched his hand to a particular stone and closed his eyes, as if checking something. All must have been well because he opened his eyes and quickly touched the stone to open the door.

A minute later, Joanne was walking back down the path from the castle with Oli, Gundy and Mundy in the pushchair, and Bertie holding hands alongside. They strolled past the flowerbeds, up towards the road on which Carys lived. Bertie was singing to himself while pulling and bumping his mummy, which made pushing the buggy non-trivial, but Joanne was used to this. As they ambled along, she thought about what had just happened. It was one thing to have heard Teddy's stories; it was quite another to have had similar experiences herself. If she was honest, there was something a little exciting about it, but she knew 'exciting' could turn into 'deadly' very easily.

They reached Carys' doorstep where Joanne retrieved the key from her handbag and opened the front door. Bertie went in first while Joanne turned the buggy round and pulled its back wheels up and over the outside step, then up again into the house. Once into the narrow, Victorian hall she reached over the top of the buggy and gave the door a push so that it slammed shut, then struggled to turn the buggy around in the narrow corridor.

"Carys! We're back!" Joanne called. There was no answer. "Carys!" Joanne called, leaning down to get Oli out of the pushchair, un-cliping his restraints. Oli reacted to something and, for an instant, Joanne was absolutely sure that both his palms glowed … and Mundy's arm moved to hug him. Joanne gasped. Mundy wasn't Awake yet, but she had moved, and what had just happened to Oli?

"Maybe dat man knows where the lady is?" suggested Bertie. It took only a moment to register what he'd said and she span round on the spot to see a short, mutated man, with apparently electrocuted black hair and vicious-looking metal gloves, pointing a crossbow at them from the other end of the hall. "He's a baddie, isn't he mummy?"

"Arrrgh!" she screamed.

"Don't get the baby out," croaked the Hordesman. "We're goin' for a little drive. Don't worry, yor friends are havin' a sleep for a few hours, so we *won't* be disturbed."

Joanne wasn't sure what shocked her more: the fact that she was facing a hordesman in Carys' hall, the weird thought that this creature could drive a car, or the dread that Carys and her son might have been harmed. She complied and placed Oli in the pushchair, but picked Gundy up and turned back to face the Hordesman, her arm around Gundy's middle, so her paws were free.

"Put the crossbow down!" screamed Gundy, "I've got a Darkgate stone here and you've made the mistake of endangering my boy," she indicated Bertie, who had backed into his mother's legs, a little afraid. Gundy wrinkled her snout and pointed her palm at the Hordesman.

The Hordesman's eyes widened. "Now, let's not get hasty—" but Gundy had no idea what she was doing with the stone. Somehow it was connected to her feelings: it could feel her needs and she could feel its presence and availability for her use, but it was all ill-focussed and unclear — in her fear she accidentally triggered a release of power from the stone, a tendril of hot, white light crackled and leapt from her outstretched paw, flashed down the corridor and seared into the crossbow. It was a weak, uncontrolled effort, but it damaged the crossbow enough for it to shatter itself under the stress of the bow string. The Hordesman yelped and held his string-snapped left hand under his right arm, which still held the remnants of the crossbow.

"I'm being nice!" Gundy lied, embarrassed at her lack of control. "Now tell us why you're here."

The Hordesman licked his lips nervously, deciding what to do. He studied Gundy's serious, furry face, there was a vicious flash of orange in her eyes. The power of the stone felt good, and it was teaching her what to do, and Gundy liked it. But the Hordesman decided to take a risk, darting back into the kitchen behind him, and he was right: she didn't fire.

"Go after him Joanne!" Gundy urged. Joanne didn't want to but maybe this Hordesman was running to get help … she moved Bertie to one side, hastened down the corridor into the kitchen, and nearly tripped over Carys and her son lying on the floor.

Joanne cried out. But Gundy was too busy tracking the Hordesman's escape through the kitchen window.

"THROW ME AT THE WINDOW, JOANNE!" shouted Gundy. "NOW!" Joanne didn't have time to think this through — and launched Gundy. The Hordesman was running towards the end of the small garden, making for the door in the wall he'd previously forced open, judging by the splintered wood. While in mid-air, Gundy fired a blast at the window and shattered it, immediately followed by another blast through the empty window frame at the ground in front of the Hordesman. She wasn't a great shot but it was violent enough, and near enough, to throw the attacker backwards so that he fell painfully on his lower back, just as Gundy landed on the window sill and nearly slid out into the garden.

"Stay exactly where you are!" she shouted, steadying herself against the jagged window shards. She stood and pointed her paw at the creature. Conflicted, the Hordesman looked at the nearby gate, and then back at Gundy. He weighed up both possibilities twice but it was obvious he'd never make it through the gate alive, if Gundy fired.

"What you want, teddy bear?" he sneered.

"You will tell us how you found us. Talk now," and she fired another blast at the ground next to him.

"Okay! Okay! Wait!" he urged. "I'm talkin'! I followed you from yor 'ome! I saw you goin' into this woman's 'ome, so I broke in. By then you'd gone to the Darkgate and I couldn't follow you ... so I waited until I saw you coming ffroo the park. When I ran round the back 'ear, I broke ffroo the gate and crept into the kitchen, and smuvvered a 'night-night' pad over them when they came to see the noise I'd made. Just made it before you came in ffroo the front door."

Mundy looked stern.

"You really have a car?"

"Yeah. It's rubbish but, yeah. Now, let me go. If one of His spies 'as 'eard us then you've basically just killed me, but I swear that's what 'appened."

"Okay, go. Tell Arthdu that we will not back down. We will not let him do what he's doing," and Gundy fired one last time behind the Hordesman to hurry him along. He disappeared through the gate and she counted to ten. Only then did Gundy look down at the floor. "Are they dead?" she asked quietly.

Joanne was kneeling next to them, feeling Carys' pulse, having already checked little Owen.

"They're both alive," she said. And breathed.

"We can't have lunch here, Joanne," said Gundy. "It's too dangerous for us, and it's not exactly safe for Carys and Owen either." Joanne closed her eyes and nodded with a sigh.

"Not to mention I destroyed their kitchen window and made three burnt holes in the garden. Hm. Before anything else, we need to ask Arthgwyn what to do."

Joanne phoned the Castle Darkgate; Gwion answered. He guaranteed to make it all better, and not to worry: Carys and Owen had only been drugged. By the time they awoke, Gwion promised there would be a new window and no sign of the holes in the garden. Joanne had no idea how Gwion would manage those feats, but it was a relief all the same.

"I'd better write a note," she said to Gundy, who had jumped down to give Bertie a hug around his neck. Joanne found a pen and some paper:

Dear Carys,

We came back from the swings to find you, but you were fast asleep and I didn't want to wake you. Hope all's okay? Just to say that my brother has asked us to go to stay with him and his wife in Manchester, and I said we would, but he wants us to get to him by this afternoon! I'll pop round again when we're back, with a bottle of wine to say thank you so much for having us at such short notice! You're really kind!

Love, Jo. x

She read it out to Gundy who nodded in agreement. She particularly liked the misdirection: Joanne had no brother, in Manchester or otherwise.

Before they left, Joanne dragged Carys onto the sofa in the lounge, rested her son Owen on top and wrapped Carys' arms around him.

Joanne grabbed their suitcase, still packed and upright in the back room where they would have slept, and struggled to guide it, the buggy and Bertie down onto the pavement, across the road, through the park and back into the Darkgate.

::

On their return, Arthgwyn listened to what had happened, hugged Joanne, and assured them that Gwion was very good at 'tidying up'. He'd done it several times before over the years and had his own Darkgate stone for the purpose; she stopped talking and it went quiet.

Joanne sat down with her cup of tea and the reality of what had just happened began to hit home; her hands began to shake.

"What do you think he wanted with us?" she asked Arthgwyn.

"I should think he wanted to kidnap you, to put pressure on Teddy and Simon."

"He could have killed my boys, Arthgwyn! I *hate* this!" She glanced at Bertie, who was happily agreeing to a big portion of pasta and tomato sauce from Arthgwyn, and down to Oli feeding again. "My body made these boys; they are mine, from me. What else can I do except run as far away as possible from all of this?"

Arthgwyn paused and breathed before continuing. "What just happened to you is a shock, and is a reminder of times past for me too. While you were gone I was thinking about what we discussed and I realised I was a bit hard on you. I've never had children. I have no idea what you're going through, but I have seen your expression on dozens of women over the years. I've also seen mothers weeping and wailing. I don't want that to happen to you. Just because I've never felt what you're feeling, it doesn't mean your feelings are not valid. I apologise."

Joanne half-smiled.

"But I do want to suggest one thing," added Arthgwyn. Joanne looked up, wondering what it could be. "We need to wake Mundy."

"No!" said Gundy immediately. Both Arthgwyn and Joanne were taken aback.

"Why not?" asked Arthgwyn.

"Because she should Wake up naturally. I don't know what you're going to do but I'm fairly sure it's not going to be anything like the beautiful, natural experience Teddy or I had when we Woke up. In any case forcing things might hurt her."

"Gundy," said Joanne gently. "I think Mundy's Waking up anyway."

"She is?"

"Yes. She tried to protect Oli, back at Carys' house. She put her paw around him."

"Oh my goodness," gulped Gundy, and she ran over to where Mundy was lying with Oli on the floor and nudged her with a paw. There was no response.

"I can see this is important to you, Gundy," said Arthgwyn. "But you need support. There's only one of you, but there are two boys. Joanne needs *both* you and Mundy to help her."

But Gundy wouldn't listen. "No, it's really not right. Joanne doesn't want you to change her children, and *I* don't want you to change Mundy." Gundy realised she had been rather forceful, so she added, "Please?"

Joanne attempted to mediate. "On the one hand, I agree with Arthgwyn that Mundy would be useful, Gundy," she began. "On the other, I'm not sure it makes much difference now: once we're on the train at Caersws, we should be safe from Arthdu. But, Mundy would then have to hide with you almost the whole trip back to my parents because of the anti-toy feeling in England at the moment, so there's not much point."

She turned to see Gundy stroking Mundy's forehead, looking concerned and whispering in her ear.

Joanne's face dropped: "Oh dear. Actually, It's worse than that. If we don't wake Mundy up now, what if she Wakes up at my parents' house? I'm not sure how I'd explain it to them, especially with the weird fear of Live toys in England. I'm beginning to think she should stay with Arthgwyn and Gwion."

"No," said Gundy. She stared at Joanne and Arthgwyn in turn.

The conversation lulled into another silence, except for the sound of Bertie eating with his mouth open, which almost drowned out the gentle sound of Gundy brushing Mundy's fur.

::

Gwion arrived back from his mission and walked back into the *neuadd fawr* with a smile on his face.

"I used a brew on Carys and the boy, so they'll forget the Hordesman, and got rid of Miss Gundy's really rather good blast marks! They'll never know anything happened, except that the kitchen window is lovely and clean. And I checked: their neighbours were out so I don't need to use any brews on them."

He looked around, and realised he'd missed an entire conversation; one that obviously hadn't gone too well.

"Well done," supported Arthgwyn, quietly. "Nicely done." Gwion thought that it might be best to sit at his laptop and keep his head down. With a last glance around at the silence, he refreshed the news webpages he'd opened earlier.

After a couple of minutes, Joanne spoke.

"So, Gwion, can you give us a lift to Llangurig?"

But Gwion wasn't listening, he was looking at something on his laptop. "Ma'am," he said to Arthgwyn. "I think you should see this."

Arthgwyn and Joanne gathered behind his chair to see what was bothering him. Gwion read a story from the BBC news website:

"Breaking News: Calls for Troops on Welsh Border

"*Far right organisations today called for the Welsh border with England to be closed and defended by armed forces. The calls were made after the inexplicable rise in the number of Live toys and violent sheep in the West of England.*

"*There are reports that families have thrown out their children's soft toys, particularly those that have spoken or moved on their own, and several farmers have culled their sheep.*

"*Fears have arisen about the stream of refugee toys that have crossed into Wales, which are gathering on the other side of the Welsh border.*

"*Despite widespread concern in the West of England, most residents in Wales seem unworried about the groups of toys. The 'killer sheep', however, have remained in England and often attack dogs and farmers that attempt to move them.*

"*Lee Stainer of the ultra-nationalist group 'Stone Fists of St George' said, 'We're not just going to stand here and wait to be attacked by these freaks. Whatever's going on it's got to be the Taffs that are doing it, otherwise why are all those toys just waiting on the border? Why are there no killer sheep in Wales? Stands to reason. And what's next? Killer cows? Pigs? The people of England can't afford to find out! Get the army in there, now!'*

"*This morning, even moderate voices were suggesting that the Government should make preparations for a response by the armed forces, should it become necessary.*"

"This is making me very nervous," said Joanne.

"Hm. I think it's supposed to. I think that's the point of what's going on. It reminds me of when I first came to Aber, a very long time ago — I think it was 572 — I saw a group of people being attacked by some soldiers, invaders from down the coast. I fired some warning shots and they left. The people I'd saved told their families and friends what I'd done, and soon, I was a hero, defending the village that used to be here, where the castle is now. It was good to be wanted after having been an outcast for a year. We built a stockade, with a strong wall and a vibrant community within. Of course, it was only a matter of time before someone challenged us. I had to kill attackers to defend my people. It changed me.

"Then the attacks stopped, and the war was no longer about arrows and swords, it became about whispers, fears and rumours. Our enemies realised they couldn't beat me by strength, so they attacked me on another front, and it worked. They encouraged factions in our village, sowed stories, and lies, and fears, which grew and took hold, and eventually the groups in our own ranks began to fight each other!" Arthgwyn sighed. "We were divided, and my best efforts to stop it only made matters worse ... both factions accused me of siding with the other. Do you know what I did?" Joanne shook her head. "I gave up hope and retreated into the Darkgate. I was pathetic ... Hm. I'm rambling. The point is this: the fear in England, and the lack of fear in Wales will cause division, because fear makes us question and mistrust each other." Arthgwyn cleared her throat. "I suppose there are hints of that between us today, aren't there?"

Joanne nodded, a little ashamed.

"But what happened next? After you shut yourself in the Darkgate?"

"Oh. Well, I suppose I can tell you," said Arthgwyn, shyly. She dropped her gaze and took a breath before peering up at Joanne. "I was alone and found I could communicate with the

Darkgate. It was a revelation. I learned it could put me to sleep and make people forget me. So I told the Darkgate to send out a huge pulse to stun everyone near by, so they wouldn't remember me when they woke up a few minutes later, and it was supposed to put me to sleep forever. It failed. Instead, I slept for exactly a thousand years. Later, I discovered The Darkgate counts the rotations of the earth around the sun, and it will remain dormant for no more than one thousand rotations. When I awoke, in 1575, there was a Tudor town here, and the marcher lord had built a castle on top of the Darkgate! To this day, I have no idea what happened to my village, but I imagine the factions attacked each other before being taken over by the attackers from down the coast. And the attackers themselves were probably defeated by other attackers, and so on until Wales was attacked by the English. All I'd known had gone; I had to start again, and I don't think I really felt a part of things for a good thirty or forty years.

"I've been through a lot, and now you're sharing some of that. You're learning that to be strong — to really protect people — you must minimise the fear you feel, you stay strong and calm. And, actually, that's what you are, Joanne. You were scared but you didn't fall apart after the attack at Carys' house. You are a strong woman, and we are side-by-side in this fight. Let's do all we can to help end this division, even if we do have to go our separate ways?" Joanne smiled and reached out to touch Arthgwyn's hairy hand, and Arthgwyn smiled. She stood up, gave Joanne's arm a quick squeeze, and disappeared down the corridor for a moment, returning with a large box of knock-out darts and a dart gun.

- CHAPTER 6 -

The Servant's Return

When Simon thought about it, driving to Moccas wasn't a good idea. Although the car was nearer, Simon didn't want to use it again until they had no choice; in any case, they'd have to find somewhere inconspicuous to park when they reached Moccas, and then they'd have to walk from there to the Moccasins' wood — it was simpler, and probably faster, not to use the car at all.

For Teddy, the walk to Moccas was not a happy one. Memories flashed into his mind at unpredictable intervals of a dead fox and murdered blacksheep. The images dug at the pit of his stuffing and troubled him: creatures had perished because of his actions. It may have saved his life but that was hardly the point: his actions had caused a chain of events; as a result, they had died, and it was horrible. And another death came to mind: the limp moccasin lying on a hot summer road. He felt like a murderer, an invader, a herald of what was to come, and now he was returning — and the fact that he was leading a human toward the demented footwear collective, exactly as predicted by the Servant Master three years ago ... it all took its toll. Before they were even a quarter of the way to Moccas, Teddy was jumpy and nervous; Simon had never seen him so unsettled.

The two of them waded through long grass, and climbed over fences. Sometimes it was quicker for Simon to carry Teddy but it was impressive just how much the fifty-centimetre tall bear could do on his own, fear or no fear. Simon's admiration was cut short by a noise.

"I'm telling you they'll see us!" said a voice in an attempted whisper.

"Shh! They won't need to *see* us, they'll *hear* us if you don't shut up!" rebuked a rather more measured but nonetheless audible hiss.

"You're just as noisy as—" the first voice tried to reply.

"SHH!" ordered a third voice.

"WHO'S DARE!" shouted Teddy, looking terrified.

There was silence.

Simon indicated to Teddy to stay where he was. Teddy's head quickly and repeatedly shook left and right to emphasise that he really didn't want to be left alone, but Simon had already moved to detect the owners of the voices emanating from the long grass.

"YOU CAN COME OUT!" shouted Teddy in an agitated voice. "WE'RE DER FRIENDLY PEOPLES!"

"No!" said someone in a terrified squeak. It was enough for Simon to locate them. He moved in, noticed something and looked down.

"Hello!" he said to the grass, with a smile. "Teddy, you need to see this." Teddy wasn't at all sure he needed to see anything, but his trust in Simon was enough that he tentatively poddled over to see for himself.

The first toy he saw was a fluffy, grey elephant, about two-thirds his own height, dirty and matted, pulling a metre-long, half-metre wide trailer piled up with motionless teddies and dogs, two pandas and a rabbit, several small, oddly-shaped plushies and a penguin. The elephant looked up at Teddy like a three-year old who'd just been caught drawing on the dining room wall. In front was a raggedy, brown lion about thirty centimetres long, trying to read a map, and between the lion and the elephant was a fat, nearly spherical penguin. They were Live toys.

"Hello! I'm Teddy!" said Teddy, beaming with happiness because they weren't Moccasins, or someone who wanted to kill him.

"You're a toy!" said the lion.

"Well, I s'pose," said Teddy, not used to being thought of as a toy. "I just ffink I'm Teddy!" he added with a roly-poly laugh.

"Shh!" said the elephant. The humans might hear you!

"It's okay," said Simon. "There's no one around. We've been checking. I can see quite a long way." Elephant didn't look very reassured.

"What are you all doin' in der fields den?" asked Teddy.

"Our owners threw us out," said the flustered penguin, raising her wings as she spoke. "It seemed like one minute we were happily playing with our owners, and the next they went all scared, stuffed us into bin bags, and threw us out of the house — same thing happened to all three of us!"

"Oh dear!" said Teddy, shocked at the idea of their owners simply throwing them away. "Don't wurry, we're friends."

"Are you all from the same house?" asked Simon.

"Ellie and me are," said the lion. He paused. "I'm Lon, by the way — we escaped cos I just used my teeth on the bag and we were out. Peng is from a few doors down the road; we found her hiding in a bush. She'd pecked through the rubbish bag she was in."

"Um, are you feelin' Tired?" Teddy asked.

"Peng is but Ellie and me were well-loved, I think we'll be okay for a bit. It's these poor guys I'm worried about," Lon indicated the stack of toys on Ellie's trailer. We stole a toy trailer from someone's front garden and gathered all the toys we could find. Most were already asleep, except for the rabbit, that white teddy and one of the dogs."

Teddy looked at the trailer and saw a white paw sticking out. A teddy paw. He let out a squeak of horror.

"Simon, look! Der white paw!"

Simon knew what Teddy meant. "May I?" he asked, indicating the pile of toys. Lon nodded and Simon gently lifted the smaller toys off the owner of the white paw. He soon revealed a white teddy, covered in slime and dirt, with her leg ripped open. She was totally still. Teddy gasped.

"Dat's her. She's a mess, but dat's definitely her!"

"We found her, just about walking — well, more hopping really — angry and shocked and Tired. Mostly angry though. Apparently, she'd been thrown out a bedroom window to the family dog below. Escaped when the dog got bored. She fell Asleep a few minutes after we found her. Do you *know* her?"

"Mmm," said Teddy, paw over his mouth, nodding slowly.

"Oh dear. Close to her?"

"No. No. Not really. Not now."

"Oh, that's okay then, cos she was a bit rude to us, to be honest. We almost told her to get lost, but look at her; we hadn't got the heart."

"Um, I ffink, actchully, it's Lady Teddy dat hasn't got a heart," said Teddy playing with the tips of the grass stalks.

Ellie and Lon looked at each other and realised they were missing something.

"Teddy," began Simon, thinking this might be a good time to talk about something else. "Don't we need to help these good toys here with some hugs and appreciation, to keep them going?"

"Ah, yes; dat's right. We should definitely give dem der cuddles and love and ffings, to help dem stay Awake ... but maybees we can help dem learn to care for each uvver, like der Dolls can do now?" Simon indicated to Teddy to go ahead, while Simon picked up Peng and hugged her, and brushed bits off her, and told her everything was going to be alright.

Teddy spent a minute or two explaining how, with practice, they'd find love didn't just flow from, or to, humans; they could learn to let it flow through them to each other.

Simon suggested they could start by listing the things they liked about each other, and hugging. After some practice, the refugees said they could feel something in them, almost like their owners' love, although not as strong yet. Teddy jumped up and down on his feet paws in celebration and waved his arms. He held his new friends, and Ellie burst into tears because she still missed her owner; nevertheless, Simon and Teddy's warmth and concern had helped, and Peng in particular felt much better and less Tired.

"I ffink dat you 'toys' need to help each uvver now, like dis, until you reach Wales. Maybees if you see uvver toys you can show dem how to care for each uvver too?"

"This really will work?" asked Lon. Teddy nodded. "Excellent. We'll definitely pass that on … though I don't think we'll ever be able to care for that Lady Teddy of yours. Do *you* want to do it?"

Teddy winced. "Um, she's not my Lady Teddy. She never really was." He thought about their question, and looked pained. "So, no, I don't ffink I *can* love her, actchully."

"Hm. Okay, well we should leave her as she is then. As far as I'm concerned she can stay on the trolly.

Teddy's head dropped a little, but he couldn't disagree. Lon continued.

"We'll try hugging the others as we go, but I really want to keep moving, we need to find somewhere safe by the time it gets dark, and this ground isn't easy going. Still, we can't exactly wander along the roads."

Simon thought it best to change the conversation while he placed the Sleeping toys back on top of Lady Teddy.

"Um, where are you all going?" he asked Peng, who was tugging Simon's trouser leg for another hug. He picked her up. Lon answered.

"We've heard of a character called 'Ramgar' who's supposed to be helping Live toys. Some say he's a Giant Live sheep, others that he's a human who has a huge house and toys can roam free and run around, and others say he's a myth and we're not going to find anyone."

"Oh, no, he's not a myth," said Simon. "Teddy's met him."

The toys turned to look at Teddy with awe.

"It's true," said Teddy. "He's an old ram and I saw him about ffree years ago. He helped me."

"A real, ordinary ram?" asked Lon, surprised.

"Um, not dat ordinary, cos he looks *really* old, and is *really* wise, but he's just a ram I ffink."

"Weird."

"No, he's nice actchully!" said Teddy, with a big smile. "He's in some trees on der uvver side of der Bredwardine bridge, but you mustn't cross der bridge at night cos der nasty troll will get you. He attacked me and I fell Asleep and nearly died!" Lon, Peng and Ellie gasped. Then Ellie frowned and tipped her head, and spoke.

"But ... er ... we've been told he's in Llandegley."

"Really?" said Simon. "When did you hear that?"

"Yesterday, we got talking to a crow. She tried pecking us to begin with, but she turned out to be quite friendly, after the initial misunderstanding. Said she'd been talking to some sheep about it, near Kington."

Simon looked at Teddy. "I suppose he might go back to Llandegley. Makes sense."

"Yes," agreed Teddy. "At least der Yorebear hasn't killed him."

"Oh!" said Peng, with a flap of her wings. "You know of the Yorebear too?"

"We do," said Simon. "He tried to kill Teddy. How do you know of him?"

"The crow mentioned him too; said that that was one of the reasons Ramgar had gone to Llandegley."

Teddy looked confused. "But why's he gone dare, where it's reeeeally dangerous? How can he survive against der Yorebear?"

"I'm beginning to think we should find out, after we've been to Moccas," said Simon.

"Poopies," swore Teddy. "I ffort you might say dat."

"You're going to *Moccas*, Teddy?" asked Ellie with an incredulous tone. "I mean the place is full of humans that will want to kill you or throw you away. All human villages are like that!"

"No, it's okay, we're not going as far as Moccas human village. We're going to see the Moccasins."

"Oh no! Not the Moccasins! We only just escaped them. They're *mad*!"

"I know. Day are totally mad, wiv der extra mad on top!" agreed Teddy.

"But we still have to go," added Simon with a shrug.

"Well, good luck!" said Lon. He looked at the others. "I suppose we should get going too," said Lon.

So they hugged one last time, with a special hug for Simon from Peng, and Simon and Teddy left Lon, Peng and Ellie, and the cart of sleeping toys, and continued toward Moccas wood.

::

On their walk to Moccas, Teddy learned something about map reading; he learned it was always going to be too hard for him to understand. To him, for a thing to be real it needed to be solid, touch-able, physical. But a map was just a piece of paper; its lines and borders were just ideas, and Teddy wasn't too sure that borders, in particular, were a very good idea since usually one group of people had killed another group of people over where the line should be drawn. It seemed, to Teddy at least, very silly and rather sad.

His pondering was interrupted by the sound he'd been dreading. "Mee, mee, meeee!" It was the Moccasins.

"Here day come, Simon!"

"I can see them Teddy, over there!" said Simon. "And over there, and ... oh my goodness! They're all around us!"

"Hmmm, day're quite clever like dat, actchuly," mused Teddy. A Moccasin flapped up to them.

"Stay still! No moving! What you want? Tell! Tell now!"

"I'm a human and this is Teddy," said Simon, flatly. "Your group have met him before. We want to meet ... oh gosh, 'Take us to your leader'," he added, almost embarrassed.

"Who is 'Teddy'? Not heard of him."

"I was here ffree years ago," reminded Teddy. "You called me der 'HUFF'. Do you remember?"

"Oh! HUFF! Oh! *Generations* ago! Heard tell of HUFF! And you bring a human! All true?! Danger! Danger!"

Teddy looked at Simon as if to highlight the craziness of these creatures.

"Will you take us to … whoever is der leader den?" asked Teddy.

"Of course! Have no choice! We are all around you! You MUST come! Come with us now!"

"Oh, no," said Simon dryly. "You've captured us. Oh woe." He glanced back at Teddy, whose worried eyes suggesting that it might not be a good idea to take them so lightly. Simon cleared his throat and looked a little more serious.

The Moccasins escorted Teddy and Simon to the edge of the wood, where a brown Moccasin was waiting.

"Why you want our leaders? Who you think you are? Can't demand things!"

"We've come to talk about your plans for The Dolls," said Simon.

"Dolls? You want to talk about Dolls?"

"Yes please," he said, as politely as possible, given that he was essentially talking to a slipper.

"And yet you human? And HUFF returns? You think me stupid?"

"No, not at all!" said Simon, lying, but with a tone of genuine concern creeping into his voice at last.

"Yes you do. Stupid. Can tell. Stone them!"

And before Teddy and Simon could object, Moccasins all around rolled out palm-sized sharp stones from within themselves, and flick-hurled them from their heels at the shocked teddy bear and human. Many of the stones found their mark, and in seconds Simon was quite badly cut in several places. Teddy fared better, with most stones simply bouncing off him; he ran to Simon to protect him, clambering onto his back, and they ran into the wood to gain some shelter from the trees, and to push on towards the centre of the wood where they hoped to find the Moccasin's leader.

While Simon ran, the Moccasins converged on them from the fields and trees, anticipating their path, and continually flicking stones at them. Teddy clung on, deflecting many of the stones from behind them, but Simon took several stones in the face. He dodged and jumped over Moccasins and roots, and avoided tree trunks and bushes, all with the goal of reaching a glade that he could see deeper into the wood. At the time it seemed to be a sensible thing to do, in the hope that they could reason with the Moccasin's leader.

Simon was almost into the glade when he was tripped by several Moccasins pulling a bramble tight across his path. It barbed into his shins, wrapped his legs, and he and Teddy tumbled to the ground to be surrounded by Moccasins. They had found the main Moccasin camp and each member of that camp was preparing new stones to fire at them.

"Stop!" called a voice. "Let's see what they want. Haven't attacked us. We've attacked them. They not attacked us. Why? See what they want." Simon and Teddy stood up again, checking themselves for damage. Simon had multiple cuts and slashes, and nasty bramble scratches on his legs, Teddy had fared much better except for one cut on his snout, and a slight puncture mark on his bottom, through both of which Simon could see a little stuffing.

"We want to talk to your leader please," panted Simon, taking them absolutely seriously at last.

"So talk," said the voice, who now showed himself to be a grey Moccasin. "I am Major Grey. What you want?"

"We want to know if you had anything to do with the death of The Dolls' mother. Please."

"Ah! Snooty dolls suffer! Not nice. Want to kill us."

"No day really don't!" said Teddy, incredulous. "Who told you dat?"

"Doesn't matter!" said Grey, looking a little shifty. "None of your business!"

"GREY!" called a voice from the centre of the glade behind the Grey Moccasin. "BRING THEM HERE!"

Grey looked embarrassed.

"Yes, sir." He looked around, snapped orders at the nearest Moccasins to surround Simon and Teddy and lead on. They were marched to the centre of the glade, where a small figure was standing, waiting.

"The Servant Master," said Grey, grandly.

"Thank you, you can leave us now," said the Servant Master.

"Leave you? No! Can't! Too dangerous," objected Grey.

"Not at all. This teddy saved my life once, I don't think he'll harm me now, and the human wouldn't like you to stone him again would he?" They all turned to Simon, waiting for his response. Simon shook his head. "So, go. I'll call you if I need you."

The Moccasins flapped away, and they were left alone with the Servant Master.

"So you heard we killed Mother then?" strutted the Servant Master. And yet something was odd about his expression.

"It *was* you!" gasped Teddy.

"It certainly was! For years, I've been trying to take those dolls down a peg or two. Now it seems I've managed to knock them to the ground completely, with their feet in the air! Ha har!" His words and tone were delighted but his face was pained. Teddy didn't notice.

"You baddie!" he exclaimed. "Dat was a lady and you killed her, and you did it just to hurt der Dolls!"

"Yes I did!" boasted the Servant Master, loudly ... and he whispered, "We're being listened to."

"Huh?" said Teddy.

"Don't you have *any* remorse?!" shouted Simon, before

whispering, "Okay." Teddy looked around, befuddled.

"None!" he retorted with apparent delight, followed by a quiet aside, "… except every night when I close my eyes."

Teddy was still looking confused. The Servant Master continued.

"Let me tell you a secret," he said out loud, beckoning them to him as if to reveal a great evil. He whispered again, with a smile that was in conflict with the words he actually said. "They're here. Three of them. They're in control. They are around us. No Teddy, don't look; look at me. When I last saw, Teddy, I thought you had come from Llandegley to destabilise me — well, I was wrong; it was the Yorebear, via Mole, who was sabotaging my plans. And now I am more of a slave than I ever was at The Dolls. There's nothing I can do about it. Okay, pretend to look shocked."

He stood back and laughed out loud, pretending to mock them. Simon pretended to look appalled.

"I'll tell you something else! Come here!" and he beckoned to them again.

"I want to apologise. You saved my life, Teddy, and everything you said was right and true, but I was too paranoid to believe it."

"Ffank you! Dat's okay," smiled Teddy. Simon screwed up his eyes for a moment at Teddy's inability to play along with the deception. The Servant Master sighed, but continued.

"Despite all that, I pride myself on being a good strategist. This is how I see things. There is someone here spying on us right now so you and I both need protection, Teddy … and your human. Now, if I give you this …" he picked up a stone from the ground in both his tiny hands and proffered it to Teddy, "… a Darkgate stone; will you protect us all? I believe you can use it to create a shield?"

"Oh, wow! Ffank you!" Teddy took the stone in his paw and felt a sizzle of power. It wasn't anywhere near as large as the rush he'd felt at the Darkgate three years ago in Llandegley, but it had the same quality. "I'll *try* to protect you but I'm not dat good wiv deez ffings."

The Servant Master dropped the pretence, and spoke normally.

"We don't have long, so I hope you're better than you think, they'll have gone to get an archer. Try it now."

"I'm ffinking about being protected; is anyffing happenin'?"

"Not really … oh wait! A leaf just bounced off … well, nothing! Maybe whatever you're doing is see-through."

Suddenly there was a voice as a Hordesman stepped out from behind the tree he'd been using as cover.

"Let's test it properly shall we?" he said, levelling his crossbow at them and firing a Darkgate bolt at the Servant Master's head.

A split-second after he'd fired, the crossbow bolt erupted into flames against a semi-sphere of protection that Teddy had indeed made with the Darkgate stone. For a moment a searing wave of heat hit them, then Teddy grasped the stone tighter and his fear and shock signalled to the stone what they needed; their protective shell hardened, and the heat subsided. It was lucky that Teddy's reaction had the effect it did because the Hordesman hadn't thought about the return shockwave from the explosion against Teddy's bubble of protection. It threw him back against his hiding tree with such force that one of his crossbow bolts detonated, causing a chain reaction that set off the other ten or so that were in his quiver. The Hordesman instantly disappeared in a sea of heat and light that spread in a blink for hundreds of metres in all directions.

No sane person would want to stand nearer than a mile from the release of power from a dozen Darkgate stones, much less a mere twenty metres, but Teddy, Simon and the Servant Master did just that, and the protection of the semi-sphere held well enough, keeping the internal temperature hot but non-lethal. However, the force of the explosion was so immense that it became clear they weren't in a semi-sphere at all but a complete sphere, half above the ground and half below. The entire semi-sphere of earth and leaves and roots below their feet was momentarily wrenched up from the rest of the ground by the force of the explosion and dumped back down again. Not that the trees would ever need those roots again since every single thing had been vaporised for two hundred metres in all directions; there was nothing but bare, black earth, and beyond that a vast ring of fire and destruction in a circle all around them.

The most shocking thing was that the Moccasin camp was gone. It simply didn't exist any more. It wasn't that there were fallen trees under which some might be rescued; the trees had been obliterated and the Moccasin camp along with them. Just bare, steaming funeral earth all around.

"Woah," said the Servant Master. "Thank you."

"Oh my goodness, der Moccasins are gone!"

"Some must be … um …." the Servant Master stopped talking and just looked, he blinked repeatedly, filling with emotion. "I don't understand it," he said, "I thought I hated those stupid pieces of footwear!" He turned away.

"There's a problem," Simon began. "How do we escape a forest that's on fire in all directions around us as far as the eye can see? I mean, we could just wait here on this black, burned, circle bit until the fire services arrive, but I don't really fancy explaining things to them."

They were without a solution for several seconds until Teddy had an idea.

"Do you ffink we can be like der hamsters?"

"Huh?" said Simon confused, before understanding what Teddy meant. "Oh! Yes, I like it!" he agreed. "But you'll need to try to make the sphere appear above ground. Can you do that?"

"I ffink I can try."

So Teddy experimented. He thought about the sphere becoming smaller and smaller until they felt a tickling, snagging sensation around their toes and feet, as the sphere shrunk too small, followed by an intense burning because their feet were now outside its protection. Teddy concentrated and made the sphere slightly bigger and they tried to roll it. There was still some dirt in the bottom of the sphere but Simon's weight was enough to roll it. Teddy added a little extra to their forward motion, and Simon picked up the Servant Master and lowered him carefully into his shirt pocket.

They rolled the sphere, slowly at first, testing it to make sure it remained secure and didn't leave parts of anyone's body behind, then they started to move at walking pace towards the largest gap between the burning trees. There was a very slight increase in temperature as they approached the fire, but it was bearable. Soon they were inside the fire, surrounded by it and rolling over burning branches. The temperature inside the sphere was gradually increasing.

It was hard to see the edge of the forest through the smoke and flames, plus the need to turn left and right to avoid trees meant they weren't sure they were still heading in the right direction, but about five minutes later the Servant Master saw the outer edge of the fire ring. Another minute later and they were rolling over the burning grass of the field.

It was painfully hot inside the sphere now, and Simon suggested that the Darkgate stone might be running out of power. Since they were nearly off the burnt grass and into the open field, they decided to run the last few metres: the air inside the sphere was almost too hot to breathe. Simon picked Teddy up, so his feet wouldn't catch fire, and Teddy let the sphere dissipate. A wave of smoke collapsed in on them and the heat was only slightly less intense, even here. They realised they might have made a mistake. Simon ran with his last breath of smoke-free air and made it beyond the edge of the flames and smouldering grass, running, running until he had to take a gasp. It was clean enough and cool enough and he breathed and breathed. They lay on the warm grass and surveyed the disaster before them. The remaining Moccasins were flapping around in a mad panic, but there was nothing to be done; the Moccasins world was ruined.

::

The Servant Master was no longer a ruler, he was just a small, damaged, pug-nosed plastic toy, with a wisp of white hair, chewed on the outside by a dog, and broken inside by The Dolls, Arthdu and lost Moccasins. It was all over. He had nothing.

Simon still carried him, as they walked back towards The Dolls, not because he wouldn't have walked fast enough — true though that was — but because it seemed unlikely he would have walked anywhere. He would probably have stood still, surrounded by the sound of the swaying grass, dazed and without purpose; he would probably have stayed there a very long time. Teddy looked up at him, sitting in Simon's shirt pocket, staring into space.

"What are you goin' to do?" Teddy asked.

The Servant Master didn't react at all for a moment. Then blinked and gave a sharp shake of his head.

"Sorry?" he asked, looking down at Teddy.

"Now dat der Moccasins are, you know, pretty much gone — what are you going to do."

"I don't know, Teddy," he said quietly and plainly. Teddy glanced at Simon, who raised his eyebrows and shrugged. Teddy continued.

"You could come wiv us I ffink? … couldn't he, Simon?"

Simon puffed out and thought. "I suppose so, I mean you did save our lives, so whatever else you've done, we owe you. But could you tell us what happened to The Dolls' Mother, please?"

The Servant Master winced and closed his eyes. After a breath, he opened them again, turned around in Simon's pocket and looked up at him.

"If you think it will help," he said weakly.

"Anything you can say could be valuable. This is becoming really serious."

"It's worse than serious. It's war," he said, a flicker of intensity returning to his eyes. "Don't make the mistake of thinking it's anything else. It's always been war for Arthdu. He wants Briton back. All of it."

"What? The whole of Britain?"

"No, *Briton*, as it was. He was born while the Saxons were invading. While he slept the Angles, Norse, Normans and a number of others attacked. His people were pushed back into what is now Wales. He wants Briton back, and he wants to make it great, and he wants to lead it."

"Seriously? He really thinks he can do that?"

"Seriously. He has a plan. Killing Mother was a small part of that plan. I mean, you know The Dolls are not my favourite creatures, and we all know Mother wasn't a very pleasant person, but I would never have killed a human. It's not their battle. I wanted to belittle The Dolls, to humiliate them, that's all. Maybe to make them feel what I had felt. I was angry with them ... okay, I hated them. But to kill their Mother ..."

"Why did Arthdu want to do it."

"If he'd just killed The Dolls then those who serve them might still have risen up to fight for their memory. However, by killing Mother and kicking The Dolls out of their house, he diminished them. He made people question whether they were worth following — or at least that's what he thought would happen, because that's how he himself thinks. It hasn't worked. People feel sorry for them, angry for them. Even *I* feel sorry for them. Guilty, actually. And I could have told him this would happen, if he'd asked me. He didn't, of course. He just used me as a figurehead. Everywhere are figureheads, except The Dolls, the Dwarves and Ramgar. That's why he had to deal with them all before he begins his plans. Ramgar's run off, so I hear; The Dolls have been massively weakened, and the

Dwarves can't even come up out of the ground."

"What? What's happened?!" asked Simon, concerned.

"They're under siege. I don't know the details, but the last Arthdu messenger I spoke to said Dwarves are being kept underground in several places — not just the Dwarves who you know in Dunan — I imagine there are several Hordesmen in their wood."

"We've got to do something!" said Teddy.

The Servant Master sighed. "What *can* we do? Do you want to take on the Horde? I mean you, Teddy, might have a chance because you seem to be amazingly able to walk through *anything*, but Simon and I would be dead in seconds." He shrugged. "Don't get me wrong, I have no quarrel with the Dwarves; they keep themselves to themselves, and I've never had any trouble with them, but seriously, what can we do?"

Simon and Teddy thought for a few seconds, racking their brains.

"I see what you mean," said Simon. They walked in silence, then Simon spoke again. "Do you know where Ramgar went?"

"I don't know anything for sure, but I'd guess he's gone to Llandegley."

"Good. That's what we've heard too," said Simon, nodding. "But why would he go *there* of all places?"

"Because he's a direct kind of character. He'll want to confront Arthdu; he'll want to comfort The Flock in Llandegley, and most of all, he'll want to show the followers of The Way that he's not afraid."

"But Arthdu will *kill* him!"

"Maybe not. I've heard rumours about Ramgar from Hordesmen and blacksheep alike, and the feeling I get is that he's stronger than he looks. Then again, Arthdu has an entire Darkgate at his disposal so I'm not sure how Ramgar intends to beat that."

"So we have a choice: either we go to help the Dwarves and risk death there —" began Simon.

"Near-*certain* death, I'd say," the Servant Master interrupted.

"— Or we try to help Ramgar and stop Arthdu."

"Like I said, this is war. You need to treat this like a war. You need to *fight* this like a war."

"So you think we should go to Llandegley and try to stop Arthdu?"

"I do. But first I need to go somewhere far more terrifying."

"Where's that?"

"The Dolls."

"Blimies, you're brave!" said Teddy.

"Yes. I owe them. And I have to talk to them."

"What do you want to say?"

"I want to tell them what I did, and why Mother is dead, and how it was done. And I need to tell them something else."

"Tell us first," said Simon. "I'm not having you upsetting The Dolls for no good reason."

"Hm," thought the Servant Master. "I don't want to make things worse either. Okay."

So he told Simon and Teddy how, three years ago after Teddy's intervention, he'd left Moccas wood and travelled up and down the Golden Valley for months looking for an opportunity.

He'd bumped into Mole again, but soon realised that it was no happy coincidence; Mole had been sent to find him, and he had no choice; he was going to take over again at Moccas because it was Arthdu's will. Arthdu's existing method of controlling the Moccasins with drugs and fear wasn't working. It kept killing them and turning them into vegetables, so Arthdu needed someone he could 'trust'. Someone with a brain. Someone Arthdu could really use.

To begin with, it wasn't too bad. The Servant Master had kept the Moccasins under control but he let them live their lives how they wanted, mostly. He was frustrated, however, because he wasn't allowed to execute any plans of his own. There was no pretence this time. No 'accidental' failure of his plans, engineered by Arthdu's agents. It was all perfectly up-front: 'Do what you're told, and nothing else, or you die'. So he was a puppet, and he hated it.

One Thursday, the order came through to kill Mother. Arthdu would send a special Hordesman, trained in herbal poisons, to do the job — but the Servant Master had to ensure his safe passage and give him on-the-ground intelligence, especially about The Dolls' manor house and garden. Every moment he wished he had the strength to rebel, but each small step towards the final goal seemed acceptable in itself. He'd found himself hoping Teddy would turn up again. But Teddy didn't come; he was just a teddy, things happened to him, that was all — he didn't go walking through the world helping people, and he wasn't going to come to The Servant Master's rescue. So all the Servant Master had had left was the hope that he would die before Mother was killed.

"That's what I want to tell them, and I want to tell them something else too. One last thing. I promise you it will not hurt them. In fact, I think it will mean nothing to them at all; nevertheless, I need to tell them myself."

Simon took the Servant Master out of his shirt pocket, held him in his cupped hand, and looked straight into his eyes. Then, sadly, Simon stroked the Servant Master's shock of white hair with his thumb.

::

As they approached The Dolls' land, the Servant Master became increasingly pensive, and eventually outright scared.

As they stepped over the fence into the Dolls land, a servant was waiting to meet them. He bowed with his usual calm demeanour ... then gawped at the sight of the Servant Master in Simon's shirt pocket. The Dolls' servant was unable to articulate his feelings: the first emotions on his face were those of shock and disbelief, followed in quick succession by flushing anger and hatred. He spoke:

"With the utmost respect, sirs, what the HELL is THAT doing

here!" and he pointed at the Servant Master his finger quivering.

"It's okay," said Simon, soothingly. "He is ... our prisoner ... although I should add he helped to save our lives."

The servant breathed noisily and fast, his nostrils flared, trying to control himself.

"I beg your pardon, sir, for my easily perceived, distasteful reaction, but it is my understanding that he is responsible not just for the misery in Moccas these past few years, but also for the dire straits in which my mistresses, my colleagues and I now find ourselves."

"You're partly right. But despite all that, despite everything he's done, we still need to take him to see The Dolls. He has something to say to them."

"Much as I would like to honour your wishes, sir, I cannot bring this ... *thing* ... anywhere near my mistresses."

"Hm. What is your name?"

"Dee, sir."

"Well, Dee, I completely understand your point of view, so can you instead please go with Teddy to tell your mistresses that *I* would nevertheless like them to meet ..." Simon realised that he couldn't continue to call this little creature the 'Servant Master' — he looked at him, raising his eyebrows in a question, to ask for his real name.

"Ess," he answered, returning himself to his old role. Simon continued.

"Ess needs to talk to The Dolls, I'm afraid. He has something important to say."

Dee took a deep breath, nodded brusquely and looked at Teddy to lead on. They walked towards the gazebo.

To begin with, The Dolls were immensely relieved to see Teddy was safe. They asked after Simon and were gratified that he too was well.

"We also got der Serv— der servant called Ess with us,"

bumbled Teddy.

Agnes look puzzled, her mouth dropped open; she twice tried to speak but failed. Finally, she succeeded.

"WHAT?!" she spat.

"Yeah, um. Didn't ffink you'd be very happy, cos he kind of helped to kill Muvver and ffings, but he saved our lives and he wants to tell you sumffing."

"Oh *DOES* he indeed!" snapped Agnes, with razor-sharp sarcasm. She spoke but it was not her usual voice. It trembled with revulsion. "Teddy, this is the first time in my life that I have really considered killing someone. It sickens me that he has this effect on me. *He* sickens me, full stop. Whatever he wants to say, it won't bring Mother back."

"No, it won't, dat's true. But I ffink you should see him. I ffink it might help you. I ffink it's helped me, actchully."

This made an impression on Agnes; she trusted Teddy's opinions. He was not the most intelligent being in the universe, but he could often see right through a complex issue to the simple thing that should be done.

"Do you promise me that you yourself will defend us if he turns violent?"

"I do," said Teddy, still holding the Darkgate stone Ess had given him, although he noticed that it was a little browner than it had been. He wondered exactly what Ess could do to attack The Dolls. He wondered what he would, in fact, do to defend them; he knew he wouldn't — couldn't — kill Ess.

It took ten minutes to negotiate an acceptable method of presenting Ess to The Dolls, but eventually The Dolls, Teddy and Simon agreed to tie Ess up, Simon would carry him and hold on to him at all times, and Teddy would stand guard with his Darkgate stone. So they brought Ess into the gazebo, and Agnes looked at him with pure hatred; it didn't suit her at all.

"So, Ess," she hissed. "What the HELL do you want?" Teddy

had never heard her talk like that before. Several of the other Dolls were unable to look up.

"Mistress," he began, but was immediately cut off.

"DON'T YOU DARE CALL ME 'MISTRESS'," Agnes bellowed. "You are NOTHING to do with me!"

"I beg your pardon. Please, how may I address you?" Agnes was clearly surprised by his genuine subservience.

"Just say what you have to say, and get out."

"Very well. Mother is dead because I was weak. I didn't fight for what I knew I should do. I compromised on what I really wanted. As a result, I have decided to go from this place, I will travel to Llandegley, and I will find Arthdu. I will either find a means to kill him, or I will die. Most likely the latter. I give you all my life. It's all I have." And he bowed his head low as Simon held him.

There was absolute silence. No one moved, not a sound of breathing; nothing. In the distance a crow cried out.

"Very well. Go," said Agnes, with a slightly less violent tone. "Die well ... or bring us victory. Prove your words to us; prove that's really what you want to do." She looked up at Simon. "Take him away now, please. We've heard enough."

::

After Simon had removed Ess from the gazebo, Teddy talked to The Dolls about the things Ess had revealed on the way back from Moccas, and about travelling to Llandegley. Strategically, it seemed sensible to search for the answers there, and if Simon, Teddy and Ess could help Ramgar that would strengthen their joint position; emotionally, they were very disturbed by what Teddy and Simon planned to do, particularly since Ess would be with them; they still didn't trust him.

One thing was clear: if Arthdu were not challenged now, things would soon become worse for everyone, especially for the humans in England. So it was agreed that the mission was to locate Ramgar, to hear his advice and to find out what he knew. Whether they could find Ramgar or not, Simon and Ess would try to find some sort of distraction that would draw Arthdu and the Horde away from the Darkgate; anything that would give Teddy enough time to reach it and place his paw on it, in the hope that it would put Arthdu to sleep again. If that didn't work, maybe Arthdu had been foolish enough to leave the key in place at the top of the Darkgate, so Teddy could simply turn it off — but none of them really believed Arthdu was that stupid. Nobody was happy about the mission, but nobody could think of a better plan and, given all the things that Arthdu was doing, they were out of time.

So Simon, Teddy and Ess left The Dolls. They crept carefully back up the hill, through the wood, and over the field to the derelict house, then walked around the back and found their beaten up, scraped car exactly where they'd left it.

Simon started the car and they rolled over the stones and drove off, hoping they'd make it to Llandegley without the police stopping them. For most of the journey, they travelled in silence, gazing out at the trees and fields, feeling the rush of the high-speed air that flapped the loose contents of the car, lost in thought.

After they'd been travelling for ten minutes, The Dolls phoned to say Rufus was back. He'd returned from the Dwarves who were indeed under siege, just as Ess had said, and one of The Hordesmen had shot at Rufus. The explosion was so close that it had singed one of his paws. He'd retreated, bounding off faster than The Hordesmen could run. For an hour he had investigated the possibility of approaching again from another direction, but it was too well guarded — he was not going to make contact with the Dwarves.

So he left, and it was on the journey home that his luck ran out. As he was travelling through Moccas village, he took a shortcut and surprised a human who was tending his allotment. The man was terrified, slashing at Rufus with a garden fork. One prong cut Rufus' right back leg wide open, so he was leaking stuffing, and another snagged on his right ear and pulled it loose. He yelped and ran into the nearest bushes, so the man couldn't follow.

After that, Rufus had been careful to avoid humans and human settlements so, combined with the pain of his leg wound, the rest of the journey was slow and indirect. He limped and tried not to move his leg, to save all the stuffing he could. He found a piece of material and managed to make a bandage, which allowed him to move a little faster — it was still slow going but eventually he made it home. He and The Dolls had learned a lesson: it was too dangerous for him to go out and about while England was terrified of Live toys.

Agnes made Simon promise to phone Joanne, for her to ask if Emily could mend Rufus. So, as soon as The Dolls hung up, Simon asked Teddy to phone Joanne's number. She reacted weirdly to the call, ringing off saying she had no credit left when Simon knew she was on a contract phone. A few minutes later she phoned from a phone box and again wanted to be brief — although, this time, Simon managed to tell her about the need to fix Rufus. That was all Joanne would let him say because she 'had to go', but promised to phone properly in a while.

Eventually, she phoned, almost an hour later, from a totally new phone she'd just bought, for a proper chat. She explained why she'd rung off, and had phoned from a phone box, and she shocked him when she recounted the things that had happened to her and the boys since they'd last spoken. She explained it had all begun back at Arthgwyn's Darkgate.

- CHAPTER 7 -

Home is Where the Horde Is

At last, a small group of people were bouncing and rolling their way up a Welsh road in Gwion's burgundy 1952 Morris Minor, away from Aberystwyth, up into the hills on the main road east. The only hitch had been locating car seats for the boys; in the end they bought two new appropriately sized seats from Halfords, fitted them (with some inventiveness) to the old car, and set off for the pub in Dŵrgoch.

After what had happened at Gaufron farm and Carys' house, Joanne was not going to walk blithely into her home with her children, so Gwion parked opposite the Llew Du Inn in Dŵrgoch, from where he and Gundy would make their way to the house. Joanne had agreed to drive the car the remaining mile or so once he'd assessed the situation.

Gwion parked the car facing forwards for Joanne's sake, 'to make it easier to get out' — whether he anticipated an emergency or otherwise he wouldn't elaborate. He locked the car and gave Joanne the keys. Then they all carefully crossed the road to the pub door, where Gwion doffed his imaginary hat. Then he and Gundy set off through the woods to the left of the pub, so they could emerge in secret behind Joanne and Simon's cottage. Joanne watched them go, then she and the boys entered the pub and settled themselves inside at a window table, waiting for Gwion's call.

After a while, Gundy finally had to admit her legs were too short to keep up with Gwion, and the dense wood was too much of an obstacle course, so Gwion carried her, hugging her under one arm as he walked, like an eccentric, tweedy, lost boy.

Joanne waited, absentmindedly rotating her phone on the table while gazing out of the window. Playing under the table, Bertie pretended it was a house and mumbled to imaginary guests, while Oli, who had fallen asleep on the journey, made rhythmic baby sleep sounds in his carry seat. Joanne noticed what she was doing to the phone, and had an idea. She picked it up and dialled Simon to tell him their schedule — 1:15pm, check house; 2:15pm, get book from Llangurig; 2:30pm, read book to Arthgwyn over the phone and discuss; 4:30pm, meet Emily in Hereford; 5:47pm, train to Somerset — but Simon was out of range so she had to say it all to his answerphone.

Twenty-five minutes later, Joanne's phone buzzed a few centimetres sideways across the pub table. It was Gwion. She picked up the phone and pressed to accept the call.

"Hello?"

"Hello, Joanne, Gwion here. You'll be glad to know all is well. We've checked the garden and have just had a good look inside too. There's no one here. Gundy did a search using the stone and there's nothing of Darkgate origin nearby, so there's no one with one of those crossbow bomb things around, and I physically searched the garden too. Can you bring my car up to the house now?"

"Sure, will do. Thank you Gwion, I really appreciate this. See you in a minute."

"See you in a minute," agreed Gwion. Joanne pressed to end the call and tossed the phone into her bag.

"Okay boys, let's go home and get those things we need!"

After the inevitable ritual of the boys and their car seats, Joanne settled herself in the drivers seat, started Gwion's old car, and gingerly pulled out of the pub car park, and a minute later, Joanne was leading an unwilling Bertie toward the back door, sullen because he'd had to leave his 'house' back in the pub — his mummy was oblivious to his mood; she was still half-terrified that

Gwion and Gundy might have missed some hidden threat ... yet they reached the back door safely, which had been left open for them, and Joanne smiled at the sight of the familiar things inside.

As she neared the lounge's open door she caught sight of Gwion. There was something odd in his expression: his face was set and he was staring at a wall. But there was nothing to warn Joanne to stop walking, until Gwion caught sight of her and gasped. It was too late, her next step took her into the lounge, still carrying Oli on her hip, held safe by her left arm, with Bertie grumpily stomping behind her.

As she did so, she caught a glance of the Hordesman from Carys' house pressing himself flat against the wall, a stone in one hand and his foot on one of Joanne's larger handbags. He let the stone fall and, in a single, violent movement, his arm darted out and grasped Joanne firmly by the throat, wrenching her towards him. Oli's weight meant her natural counter-action was off-balance; she had no time to steady herself so both she and Oli started to drop. But the Hordesman was taking no chances: he sunk down on his haunches and continued to pull her towards his sneering face, her scream garbled by his grip. She had no chance of fighting back properly with her one free hand and his face showed delight at her misfortune. When she was diagonal, he loosed his grip and let gravity do the rest. She couldn't stop herself from tumbling but she was not going to crush her child; in the final falling moments she contorted herself so that Oli fell on top of her, and she hit the ground on her right hand side, her back to the Hordesman. Almost immediately, Oli started screaming. Joanne twisted to the left in time to see the crouching Hordesman draw his arm back, ready to punch Joanne around the head with the fist of his viciously spiked metal glove.

"No!" shouted a little voice. It was Bertie. "You are naughty!" He set his bottom lip and, without thinking, thrust out his hands and fired a blast of light from each hand into the Hordesman's mutated face. The attacker immediately fell to his knees, arched his back and covered his face with the palms of his gloved hands, screaming in agony. Gwion saw his chance and rushed over to slam the Hordesman's head hard into the wall: once, twice, three times. The man slumped into a heap by the skirting board. Gwion had moved faster, and acted more powerfully than Joanne had expected for someone of his age. Then again, she had no idea how old he was.

Using a pair of Bertie's trousers, from some washing left folded on the sofa, Gwion quickly tied the man's wrists. Taking no chances, he tied the Hordesman's ankles in a similar manner with a Thomas the Tank Engine long-sleeved top. Once he'd vaguely secured him, Gwion knelt down and listened to the creature's heart: he was alive.

Joanne sat up, rubbed her throat and hugged Bertie and Oli, both bawling from the shock. Even with all the noise one thing was clear: there was an attacker lying unconscious on the floor of her lounge and they had to get rid of him somehow. Moreover, he was definitely the Hordesman from Carys' house; she recognised his odd mutations.

"Joanne," said Gwion, above the screaming din, "We need to bind him with something better than clothes. Do you have anything?"

"I can't think of anythin— ah! Garden twine."

She picked Oli up and ushered Bertie out of the room, hoping she could remember where it was. Gwion watched the prisoner nervously, but he showed no signs of waking up. Joanne returned as quickly as the boys would allow, and peered around the doorframe. Once she saw all was safe, she bustled over to Gwion and gave him the roll of twine. He knelt down and tied the Hordesman's wrists and ankles properly, linking them together with a single, continuous, tightly-pulled piece of twine. Then he took out a pocket knife and severed the rest of the roll from the Hordesman.

With a gasp, Gwion remembered that Gundy had been zipped

into Joanne's big handbag, he threw his hands in the air in annoyance at himself for forgetting, and rushed over to let her out. Gundy was livid. Not with Gwion but with all that had happened, and with herself. She ran over towards the man, picked up her Darkgate stone from the floor, and kicked him in the face with her soft feet, trying to harm him as much as possible but failing dismally. But it was Joanne who spoke next.

"This is *exactly* what I was trying to avoid! In fact it's worse: now Bertie can injure people! Their lives are being messed up, and it's my fault!"

Gwion gently disagreed. "There are many children around the world who face worse danger each day of their lives, and they can't defend themselves. Maybe not the same sort of danger, but danger all the same. The point is how we and they *react* to the danger. Yes, they are upset, but Bertie here was amazing. I failed to act properly, but I think your boy acted very bravely and just saved his mother's life; maybe all of us."

"I know, I know," agreed Joanne. She hugged Bertie to her again as she spoke. "But this was my fault. I brought them here."

"No, it was my fault. Your home should have been safe; I didn't check properly. I assumed the same sort of attack that Teddy found at the farm, and you experienced at Carys' house, but this fellow was clever, he went for a stealthy approach. He was hiding in the cupboard there, and he burst out about five minutes after I phoned you: he took us completely by surprise."

"I don't think he had much choice," said Joanne. "Gundy destroyed his crossbow back in town."

"Oh! It's the same chap is it? So, he *had* to be more stealthy. Hm. He probably got in to the cupboard when he heard me open the back door. In any case, I don't think he was waiting here to kill us, I think he was trying to gather information about what we're planning. If you've already met him then that explains what he did when he burst out — as soon as he saw Gundy he attacked *her*, not me, and grabbed The Darkgate stone from her; he threatened to blow us all up unless we did what he said. I was confused because I couldn't see how a hordesman could use a Darkgate stone like that, and I made the mistake of trying to *think* my way out of things rather than rushing at him. Before I could come up with a plan, Gundy was in the handbag and, almost immediately afterwards, you were walking in through the lounge door."

Joanne didn't say anything, she just looked at the scorched, hog-tied Hordesman lying on the lounge floor, dangerously near to her two children. Gundy saw the horror of it too, anger rose up in her, and it bubbled over.

"Get him out of here, Gwion!" she ordered.

Joanne looked at her, astounded. But Gwion obeyed, as if taking orders from her was as normal as making a cup of tea. He looped his arms under the Hordesman's armpits and started to tug him up. The assailant was either a very short human or a very large dwarf, or perhaps some other creature that Arthdu had found somewhere. His face was quite badly scalded. Gwion struggled to pull him up high enough, and dragged him backwards through the house to the side door.

Gundy was still incandescently angry, mostly with herself. "My Bertie could have been hurt. I should have *stopped* him, it's my fault," she snapped at herself.

"That's not what Gwion just said," disagreed Joanne. "Once the Hordesman had got your stone, there was nothing you could do."

"I had my back to him when he burst out, I was still turning rou—"

A cry from the back door interrupted them both.

"Stay there," ordered Gundy, gripping the Darkgate stone as she rushed out of the room.

She had almost reached the back door when she saw the Hordesman, hopping through the doorway, contorted because his legs and wrists were still tied tightly together, his eyes open and mouth raging with meaningless half-words. As soon as he saw her, he leapt at her, despite being bound and unable to break his fall. He was going to crush her. She wrinkled her snout and eyes in fear and anger, raised her paw and fired before she realised what she was doing. The Hordesman disintegrated, and all except his boots, still in mid-air, turned to dust. The bolt of superheated light continued through the doorway and disappeared into the sky beyond, while the boots fell to the floor and rolled over a couple of times before coming to rest either side of Gundy. A faint smell of fried Hordesman lingered for a few moments, before the breeze from the open door diluted it to nothing.

Her eyes opened wide and she panted in shock at what she had just done.

Two small figures dropped down from above the doorway on to the back step, bouncing slightly as they landed. They stood up.

"I say! Did *you* do that?" said an odd-looking light blue toy rabbit, with fluffy white cheeks, gulping. His companion, a raggidy, tall, lady panda, looked less sanguine but nonetheless impressed. The rabbit was slightly shorter than Gundy, and the panda somewhat taller. Gundy had two new fans.

"Who are *you*?!" said Gundy as calmly as she could under the circumstances.

"Well, that's a bit of a sore point. We're Barbaz and, I have to say, we were here before Teddy and you, young lady — but Simon seems to have forgotten that."

"You're *Simon's* toys?"

"Yes, although it might be nice if he played with us now and again."

"Um. You *do* know he's 41yrs old and has a wife and two children?"

"Yes. Does that mean he can't play with us though? Hmmm? Does it?"

"Er, normally it does, yes. He doesn't play with Teddy either."

"Oh."

"You seem to know me," said Gundy, changing tack. "Who are *you* though?"

"Apologies, ma'am. I'm General Bunge," said the threadbare rabbit, "and this is Colonel Pwaa," he added, indicating the panda with scuffed eyes and messy light grey and black fur. It was likely that the grey had once been white a few decades earlier.

"Good afternoon, ma'am," she added, with a salute.

"So, what happened?" asked Gundy, indicating the still-steaming boots, with an appalled look on her face.

"Well, um, I think you killed him," offered Bunge, rather matter-of-factly.

A look of pain crossed Gundy's face, "I know that; I meant what happened *before* that. The last I saw was Gwion dragging him out of the house, unconscious, but when I got to the back door he was trying to hop back in, half-awake, lunging at me."

"Well, we heard him breaking in, so we were waiting for him to come out — admittedly it took us a while to get into position, but we are not as well trained as when we were fighting every day — anyhow, the two of them left the property, and we had to make an executive decision which one to hit with our rock, so we chose the one who seemed most dangerous; the one who wasn't tied up. We rolled it off the roof and stunned him. He staggered off and collapsed, while the other one opened his eyes and hopped back into the house. I think he was just pretending to be unconscious; the enemy has no honour! We saw your blast of light and we dropped down to finish the attack, if needed. I mean, we're soldiers, that's what we do."

"You're soldiers?"

"Of course. We protect Simon and his brother from … well, anything and everything really."

"Simon's brother? You really are Simon's toys from when he was little! Did you look after him? Like I look after Bertie?"

"Absolutely, and we still *are* his toys: that doesn't change just because he's got a bit taller, you know."

"Well, um, we can talk about that later. More importantly, what happened to Gwion after you dropped a stone on him?"

They didn't need to answer because Gwion appeared behind them holding his head. Before there could be any more misunderstandings, Gundy raised her paw to stop Gwion saying or doing anything.

"They're friends, Gwion. They're Simon's old toys; they were trying to protect him."

"Well, they didn't have to do *this* to me," he complained, indicating the bloody mark on his head where he had been hit.

"Sorry," said Bunge. "We didn't know you were with Gundy. Thought you were a baddie."

Gwion grunted an attempt at, "It's okay," which was unconvincing at best.

Bunge continued. "When we heard what was going on this morning, we thought you might need some professional help, so we escaped from our drawer and executed our defence plan. Um, you'll find another rather big rock in the guttering over the front porch too. Better be careful. Took us ages to pull them up above the doors with ropes and things. Good thing we did though!" Gwion's brain was struggling to decide which of the two meanings of 'impressed' was more appropriate to describe himself at this point in the conversation.

Joanne gingerly peered around the doorframe to see what was happening.

"Where's the Hordesman?" she asked. "And who are you two?"

"They're Simon's toys," said Gundy quietly. "And I killed the Hordesman by mistake," she admitted, looking at the floor.

"You *killed* him?!" exclaimed Joanne. "How?" Gundy looked up and proffered the Darkgate stone.

"It was a mistake. He was falling on top of me — well,

jumping on top of me really — and I put my paw out in defence and the stone must have felt my fear, so it ..." she trailed off.

Joanne breathed out in realisation of what Gundy had done.

"She's amazing isn't she!" said Bunge excitedly. Joanne felt the ridiculousness of the moment and an hysterical laugh squeaked out .

"I don't know what to say, Gundy, but ..."

"I know. I've killed someone. I never meant to ... I wouldn't ... I mean ..."

"I ... I don't believe you did it on purpose, Gundy," Joanne sighed, before her concern bubbled up again. "Oh, I *hate* all this! My son can wound people; Gundy's *killed* someone, what about Oli and me? What are we going to do next? Eh?"

"We should leave, Joanne," said Gwion calmly. "I think, the sooner you reach your parents, the better."

Joanne nodded once. She glanced at Gwion and something in her altered.

"You think I'm running away, don't you?" she snapped.

Gwion was taken aback.

"No, Ma'am, of course not."

"You do. I can see it in your expression. But that's not why I'm leaving. I'm leaving because these two boys haven't asked for this; they've made no choice to be here, and it's my job to keep them safe. I will not allow a repeat of the things that have happened to them today. I will *not* fail to protect them again!" Joanne was fully shouting, something she rarely did.

Gwion agreed. "Yes, ma'am." There was a crisp silence before Gwion spoke again. "So will you take Gundy?"

"I would like to," said Joanne. She turned to Gundy. "I know what you said before, Gundy, about staying with Gwion once we get to Hereford, but after this I think we need your protection. Do you agree,?"

Gundy sighed. "I'm beginning to hate this stone, and I want to help my Teddy, but this sort of thing is a more immediate danger to my Bertie ... Oh! I don't know *what* to do!"

"Excuse me Miss," proffered Gwion, "Much as I would enjoy your company, I believe only you can properly protect Joanne and the children, given what we've just seen, if you should come across any others from the Horde."

Gundy nodded, silently.

"Thank you, Gwion," said Joanne, politely.

"We do have two more jobs to do," reminded Gwion. "We need to retrieve Robertson's book and we need to meet Emily. Miss Gundy, could you help me retrieve the book, if we first make sure Joanne and the boys are safe?"

She looked at Joanne, who nodded. "Yes," said Gundy.

::

Before they left they spent a few minutes talking with Bunge and Pwaa. Both had found they were more Awake than they had been in years, and yet it was nothing to do with Simon spending more time with them. It was as if there was something electric in the air. Gundy assured them that Simon would never have neglected them on purpose, and that they would all be together again when everyone was home once more, but she realised that no one knew when, or how, that could ever happen.

Gundy asked Gwion to use a chisel to split off two small chippings from her Darkgate stone. She had showed Bunge and Pwaa how to use them, but for some reason they found they didn't have the same power as Gundy. They could burn or scorch surfaces, much as Bertie had done, but nothing else. Gundy thought it might be something to do with the size of the chippings, but Gwion said his research had shown that the size of the chippings only limited how *long* their power would work, not how intensely.

"Um, you're special, Miss Gundy. You're a bear. You may have realised, The Darkgate responds well to bear-like beings. That's why I asked you to open the Darkgate this morning; The Darkgate would see you as the leader of your group."

Gundy's mouth dropped open. Gwion cleared his throat and continued.

"But this isn't the time to discuss these things. Bunge and Pwaa will be able to use these chippings a few times before they run out of power. I don't think many people will stay still long enough to be burned several times."

"What about Hordesmen with crossbows?" asked Gundy.

Gwion looked guilty, "I'm sure the Barbaz will be fine."

"We've faced terrible odds before, and prevailed," stated Bunge bravely, as if no one would challenge this apparently insane assertion. Gundy sighed and shook her head.

All the while, Joanne had been packing the things they needed. When she'd finished, they were ready to depart. Bunge and Pwaa hugged each of them and watched them leave from the wall outside the backdoor, while Joanne smiled sadly back at them and waved. The house was in slightly mad paws, but at least it was being protected to some extent.

Before long, the strange car-full of travellers were once again being gently bobbed along on the springy 1950s suspension of Gwion's car. Bertie was screaming about leaving a toy behind in his bedroom but Joanne reminded him that he had packed many other favourites, and he could play with them at Grandma and Grandpa's house. The Barbaz were looking after the house while they were gone, so the rest of his toys would be safe until they returned home. Something in the tone of Joanne's voice made Gundy wonder if she ever intended to return.

::

Twenty minutes later, Gwion's car was pulling into the car park behind the Blue Bell Inn in Llangurig village. It took a minute to unbuckle everyone from their seats and help each of them out of the car, then they wound their way down the road by the side of the pub, around the front, and stood outside the entrance.

Joanne looked nervously around the village, which was so small that, by the time they'd reached the pub's front door, they'd seen almost every building. There was no sign of anything suspicious, nor could Gundy sense anything with the stone. It was a good start.

The church was over the road, through a gate and down a path. It was decided that Joanne and the boys would wait in the pub, while Gwion and Gundy crossed the road to look for the minister. If all went well, the whole operation would take no more than fifteen minutes. If it didn't, they might hear the blast from here. Gwion gave Joanne the key to his car, just in case she needed to make a quick getaway, and she and the boys went into the pub to order some pudding to reinforce Bertie's lunch.

To avoid any strange looks from villagers, Gwion held Gundy to his chest, inside his buttoned-up jacket, and she found she could peer through the gap at the top without being too obvious. Together they crossed the road and walked up to the church gate at the top of the churchyard path. Gwion lifted the gate latch and pushed. It squeaked open, He walked through, squeaked it shut again, and looked around for signs of movement in the churchyard. Gundy twitched nervously against his chest but there was no sign of anyone else. Maybe this would be easy? A bird flew overhead and Gwion paused to look up at the sky — it was clouding over: the light grey clouds of earlier were now more a solid mid-grey; there might be rain later — then he started down the path, towards the church.

They had almost reached half-way when a man appeared, walking over the grass around the outside of the church. Gwion kept walking, since that was what a normal person would do, but the man saw Gwion and changed direction towards him. Gundy clutched Gwion's jacket pocket with one paw and readied her stone with the other.

"Hello!" shouted the man, waving.

"Hello!" Gwion shouted back, waving too, a prickle of worry in his voice.

"Can I help you? I'm the rector here," the man claimed.

Gundy gripped The Darkgate stone and concentrated. This was exactly the sort of lie that one of Arthdu's men might make up, but he didn't look like a Hordesman. Gwion turned the conversation to what they needed.

"We're, that is to say, I'm looking for something, maybe you can help me?"

The men reached each other, stopped walking and shook hands.

"Well, I'm more used to helping people find Someone ..." said the rector, pointing upwards and smiling, "... but I'll certainly do what I can. Would you like a cuppa?" Gwion nodded, a little more trusting. "Follow me then!" said the man, and he turned toward the rectory.

"Gwion," whispered Gundy. "I can't feel anything Darkgate-y, I think he's for real."

"Excellent," said Gwion gently, relaxing a little.

Five minutes later, Gwion and the rector were talking over a cup of tea.

Gwion explained Gundy's presence by saying she was the property of his grandson, and he was going to meet up with him and his mother in the pub over the road, to return her to him, which was almost entirely the truth.

"So ... what are you looking for?" asked the rector.

"A book."

"A book eh? What sort of book."

"Well, it's a rather old book written by a man called Robertson, he used to be the—" Gwion stopped talking because the rector's expression had changed from jolly, helpful-man-of-the-cloth, to shocked, slightly-scared-man, quietly calling on God for help.

"You want to see Robertson's book?" he swallowed.

"Yes, please."

"But how do you even know it exists?"

"I can't say."

"I rather like you to try please. It matters," insisted the rector.

"Oh," said Gwion, not sure how to proceed. "Well, let me think what I *can* say. Hm."

He thought, while Gundy lay motionless on the table listening to the rector's nervous breathing.

"We know about your book," continued Gwion, "because we have *another* book, written by someone called—"

"Pale?" interjected the rector.

"Yes. Pale."

"So is it all real? I mean Pale, Robertson, the Yorebear, all that happened in Llandegley? The whole lot?"

"Yes."

"And the Yorebear is *awake*?"

"Yes."

"And you've come to get the book to discover how to stop him?"

"Yes."

"Wow." The rector took a moment. "I mean, in my job I'm used to believing things deeply that others find laughable or pointless, but I never expected *this* to happen in my lifetime."

"Before we move on," said Gwion. "There's something else. Um, this is going to sound a little odd but have you ever seen a children's toy move?"

"Oh my. Oh gosh. I think I know where you're going with this," said the rector, eyeing Gundy with concern.

"Gundy, I think you can move now."

The rector took a sharp intake of breath in preparation, and Gundy sat up. He put his hand to his mouth.

"It's true! I've never seen a Live toy before," he gasped, dropping his hand to his chest. "Can it walk?"

"I can," said Gundy, slightly irked to be called 'it'. "And I can talk too. How do you do?" and she proffered her paw. The rector shook it like he was surely going to wake up soon.

In his assessment of the rector's reaction, Gwion looked more steely than Gundy had seen before.

"So, I think we are all friends here, yes?" asked Gwion. This wasn't England, so there was a chance the rector would be able to cope with a Live toy on his kitchen table. He bobbed his head once, gradually regaining composure.

Gwion smiled, but he wasn't finished.

"Rector, may I ask: how did you learn about Robertson's book?"

"Oh. Well, an odd-looking chap gave it to me soon after I started here, three or four years ago — he was kind of crinkled, and hairy; odd nose — he pretended it was just a valuable old book that I should keep safe, but he wasn't very convincing; I thought there was something more to it than that. It was almost like he expected me to disbelieve the book. I don't know why. But I've studied old manuscripts before and this book has that ring of authenticity to it. And — when you read it — the end makes it clear why he was giving it to me ..." The rector paused for a moment, Gwion waited. "Um ... you might think I'm mad, but I know the man who gave it to me was the author. Not only was there something in his eyes when he handed it over, like he was giving up a part of himself, the book itself says the writer was going to give it to me. Very self-referential. Strange."

Gundy could see Gwion's mind fill with thoughts, but his eventual response was simple.

"Well, it's all real!" he said.

The rector vaguely shook his head and smiled, like it was a relief. He shrugged.

"Then I suppose I'd better get the book for you to have a look; it's upstairs."

"Thank you, I'd very much appreciate that."

The rector stood up, smiled, and bustled out of the room. They could hear his feet clumping up the stairs, the creak of floorboards as he walked to wherever the book was kept, then silence for a minute or so.

More creaking over floorboards and clumping down stairs, and finally the door latch lifted and the rector was back in the room, waving a small leather-bound book in his right hand. He walked back to the table and put it down next to Gundy, who picked up her stone as if nervous of the book.

"There you are. Do you need to keep it? I'd rather you didn't if possible."

"I'm afraid we will, yes. It's not safe to leave it here. And we might need to read it several times. Maybe we can bring it back in a few weeks ..."

"Not safe? Why?"

"Because there are 'people' who want to stop us *ever* reading it. 'People' who work for the Yorebear."

Gundy gasped.

"People who are outside right now!" she whispered forcefully, her eyes wide with fear as she gripped the stone tightly. Gwion and the rector spun around to look out of the two kitchen windows, but could see nothing.

"They're *there*," Gundy asserted, and moved the stone around as if it were a compass. "Over by the back door," she hissed. "It's very strong."

"Is there anywhere we can spy on whoever's outside?" whispered Gwion to the rector.

"Um, yes, from the lounge, through the bush in front of the window, that way," he whispered back, pointing at the door through which he'd gone earlier. "But be careful, there's a window in the dining room, before you reach the lounge."

"I'll keep low," assured Gwion, and he padded over towards the door and left the room.

"How do you know there are people out there?" the rector

asked Gundy.

"I've been given this stone," she said, holding it in mid-air like a rough globe. "It's part of a Darkgate, it can detect when someone has something, or someone is … Darkgate-y. Hm. Gwion's better at explanations than me."

"I see," said the rector cautiously. "Robertson writes about The Darkgate … and there's someone Darkgate-y out there, right now?"

"That's right."

"Do you know they want to harm us?"

"I suppose not, but it's not likely to be anyone we know." She thought for a moment. "But then, how do they know *we're* here? Oh! What are they *doing* out there?"

The latch lifted on the kitchen door with only the gentlest 'tick', and Gwion quietly re-entered the room.

"It's a woman. She looks normal, human, but she's not one of us. I think we need to leave this good gentleman here and act as bait so she follows us."

Gundy nodded. "Is there another exit, rector?"

"Yes, out the front, but be careful because we're right on the road here; the main road through the village."

"I saw the door on the way back from the lounge," nodded Gwion. "We'll go out that way, and make enough noise to lead her towards the church. Thanks for your help and sorry about this."

"Be safe," said the rector. "Good luck, and God bless you."

Gwion nodded and quickly gave the book to Gundy, then he put her back under his jacket, and rushed for the door, leaving the rector sitting at the table, looking rather anxious.

As Gwion opened the front door a lorry thundered past, but he didn't stop for a moment. He deliberately slammed the door behind him and ran along the pavement towards the end of the house, nearest to the church. Despite his age, Gwion vaulted the garden gate and ran between the beds of rose bushes by the side of the

house until he and Gundy saw the church. Gundy looked out from
Gwion's jacket to the right and saw the woman struggling to get to
them, pushing through some trees, presumably alerted by their
noise, and their movement through the garden. She saw them and
shouted.

"HEY! STOP!"

They didn't slow down.

"Now, I suppose we'll find out whether she's friendly or not,"
said Gwion dryly.

"STOP!" she bellowed again, but there was no sign that she
was going to fire at them or harm them.

Gwion neared the church and looked over his shoulder. The
woman stood still, frustrated and resigned to Gwion's escape. Gwion
reached the church, ran out of sight behind it, and pressed himself
against the stone wall, heaving deeply. After a few seconds he
spoke.

"I'm going to find out who she is."

"What? Are you mad?" asked Gundy, incredulous.

"Not at all," he said, unbuttoning his jacket and placing
Gundy on the ground. "Keep the book safe, I'm just going to find out
what she wants, and who she is."

"Please, Gwion, no!"

"It's to protect you, ma'am. That's my job."

He rested his hand on the left side of Gundy's face, withdrew
it with a smile, then stood up and ran back around the church.

Gundy carefully crept along the wall so she could peer around
to see what was happening. By now she was considering the
possibility that she had made a mistake about what she had sensed;
perhaps this was actually no more than a parishioner wanting to
chat with the rector.

Gwion reached the lady and started to talk to her. Gundy
couldn't make out the words but it seemed to be going quite well.
The woman smiled. Gwion's hands moved in time to his words.

Suddenly Gwion exclaimed.

"But that CAN'T be true!"

The woman nodded her head with a smile, raised her hand to the old man's chest and fired. Gwion disintegrated in a roar of fire and light. Then she brushed her long, brown hair behind her ears, knelt down to quietly destroy each of his shoes in turn, and stood back up and walked off towards the pub.

::

Gundy held her paw to her mouth to stop herself from making any noise. After witnessing two deaths, she was beginning to understand what her beloved Teddy must have gone through on his journey. She had been missing him all day, but never more than right now. The birds were still cheeping, the sound of cars and lorries passed through the village, and none of it showed any respect for Gwion's death. Gundy closed her eyes and slowly breathed in and out. She needed to calm herself; she had a job to do.

It looked like the woman had left via the churchyard gate, so Gundy would have to take a different route. If the woman saw her — a small, walking teddy bear holding a black leather book and a Darkgate stone — she would be an obvious target. Focussing her thoughts on how she could return to the pub, she considered waiting until dark … but Joanne couldn't linger that long in the pub, with two children; not without raising a few village eyebrows, not to mention several inevitable three-year-old tantrums and a regularly screaming baby; besides, Joanne would be worried sick by then.

Gundy heard the sound of a girl playing nearby, and had an idea.

Next to Gundy, two trees were growing in the churchyard; she could use them to give her protection while she ran towards the sounds of the girl. There was a gap between the trees but it was worth the risk. Gundy ran hard and low, hoping the grass would give her some cover, and she reached a stone wall and lay against it. She wasn't dead yet. She looked up at the wall, gripped the book in her mouth and awkwardly mountaineered up the jagged stones, holding her own stone in her right paw. At the top, she looked around furtively for any signs of the woman. Nothing except a small girl on the other side, perhaps seven years old. She was playing behind the post office shop, drawing people with a stick in the dust and singing to herself. Gundy jumped to the ground and rolled over once, with the book still in her mouth. The girl stopped playing, looked at Gundy open-mouthed and pointed silently. Gundy grabbed the book from her mouth.

"Hello!" she said, as brightly as she could manage.

"Hello," said the girl, uncertainly.

"Can you do me a favour please?"

"Um. Okay."

"Can you pick me up and take me to the pub?"

"Oh, no, not really 'cos my mam won't let me cross the road on my own, see."

"Oh. Well, maybe just this once, if I help you."

"Can't. She's in the post office, so she'd see me, and then she'd shout, 'What the 'ell do you think you're doin' young lady,' and all that."

Gundy was becoming desperate, this was her only hope. Then she had it.

"Alright, how about this: could you tell your mum that you found me and that I belong to a little boy who's in that pub?"

"Okay, I could do that! Can't I keep you though? A talkin' teddy is *really* cool!"

"No, sorry, I belong to my little boy."

"Oh," sighed the girl.

So she picked Gundy up, put her under her arm, and took her into the post office.

To Gundy's horror the woman who had killed Gwion was at the counter, questioning the post mistress.

"... So, he's been rector here for three or four years you say?"

"Yes, that's right. Nice man, friendly. English, but nice, see? Ooh, that didn't sound good, sorry! But he's not like some of them who just sit and drink tea in their big houses, he's nice. Helps out. Seems to care, like."

"Lovely. Have you ever heard him tell any stories about a small black book? ..."

The girl tugged on her mother's sleeve to get her attention.

"CAN WE TAKE THIS TALKING TEDDY BACK TO THE LITTLE BOY WHO DROPPED HER?" asked the girl loudly.

Gundy winced and hoped the murderous woman hadn't heard, trying not to move a millimetre as the mother gave her daughter some attention.

"Oh, did you see the little boy drop her?" The girl bit her lip and nodded. "Oh, dear. Where did he go?"

"HE'S IN THE PUB," the girl announced, loud enough for the whole shop to hear.

"Really?" said the mother, disapprovingly. "Well, s'pose it won't take long. Wait a minute though, I need to buy my things."

The girl smiled and hugged Gundy to her chest, helpfully concealing all signs of the black book and Darkgate stone.

The mother edged towards the till, where Gwion's killer was standing, still asking questions. The post mistress saw her chance.

"Well, I'm sorry my dear, I have to serve this lady now."

"Oh, very well," snapped Gwion's murderer, she turned on her heel and walked crisply towards the door.

"Sorry," apologised the little girl's mother, as the annoyed woman walked by, almost brushing into Gundy.

The murderer stopped and turned to the mother. It was as if she'd sensed something. But the girl's mother was not someone to put up with odd women.

"I said 'sorry'! No need to look like *that* you know!"

"Pah!" said the woman grumpily, and she stomped out of the post office.

Five minutes later, a very relieved Gundy had been delivered to the pub, back in Bertie's arms, feeling loved but having to tell Joanne the dreadful news about Gwion, using the longest words she knew, so Bertie couldn't understand.

Gundy had just had time to explain what had happened, when the door to the bar opened and Gwion's killer walked in. She calmly walked over and sat down next to Bertie. The atmosphere froze.

"Hello, I'm Rhiannon, and you have something I want. Don't be afraid. I'm probably not going to harm you, and I must say I was very impressed with this teddy here," she said, indicating Gundy. "A nice manoeuvre in the post office. There was nothing I could do except leave, and watch you being carried here. Hm. So, actually not so smart after all eh?"

Gundy wrinkled her snout into a sneer.

"What do you want?" asked Joanne icily.

"The book, and hostages. Oh! I seem to have both!" She put out her hand to receive the book. Joanne had no choice and, after a pause, handed it over with a 'tut'. The woman slipped it into her bag.

"Thank you. Very civilised. Now, lets go to my car shall we?"

"No. First, who are you?" demanded Joanne.

"No? Really? Do you want to try 'no' while I'm sitting next to your cute little boy here?" Rhiannon said calmly, looking down at Bertie with a disarming smile.

"Pretty, sparkly lady!" said Bertie, pointing at her and giggling.

"Adorable!" said Rhiannon. "For now at least. Let's go."

Grimly, Joanne stood up and started to gather up Oli and the boys' belongings.

"Shall I carry your little boy for you?" asked Rhiannon. "You seem to have your hands full. In fact, you know, I'm sure that's a good idea."

She clearly relished the power she had over them. Joanne had no choice so she quickly rammed all her things into Oli's baby bag, lifted the strap over her head, picked up Oli and Gundy and left the pub. Rhiannon strode ahead, carrying Bertie, and Joanne had to hurry around the side of the building to keep up.

Rhiannon's car was parked around the back, a few metres from where Gwion had parked. The lights flashed as she unlocked it from her key fob while walking, and she opened the passenger back door to deposit Bertie onto the seat.

"No car seat!" said Bertie.

"Never mind, you're a big boy aren't you?"

"Want my car seat! Can't see out d'window."

"That's the least of your worries, dear," she countered, and slammed the door before he could answer back.

"Can anyone see us, Joanne?" asked Gundy grimly.

Joanne looked around, then realised what Gundy was thinking.

"*Wait*! No, you can't!" she whispered. "You can't do *that*, and it's not safe."

"Nor is shutting ourselves in that car. Quickly, please, look around."

Joanne scanned for people, her heartbeat accelerating.

"Can't see anyone." Her mouth was dry.

Gundy held the Darkgate stone firmly.

"Go around to Rhiannon's side of the car, as if you're going to put Oli in the back."

Joanne did so, attracting Rhiannon's attention in the process. Joanne hid Oli's face.

"What are you doing? Oh, the other child, of cour—"

Gundy fired with all the anger and fear she had within her. Rhiannon disappeared in a searing flash and her shoulder bag fell to the ground, scorched on one side but still complete. The blast was so powerful that it passed through Rhiannon and destroyed part of a retaining wall at the back of pub. The brick fragments fell to the ground and rested.

"We just *killed* someone!" Joanne hissed to Gundy. "And we've nearly blown up a pub!" She felt sick.

But Gundy calmly remembered what Rhiannon had done after she'd killed Gwion and she pointed her paw to the ground and let rip calmer blasts to remove all signs of Rhiannon's knee-high, brown leather boots with only a little blackening of the dirt.

"Quickly, Joanne; cover the burn marks on the ground." Joanne rubbed the gravel with her foot and covered them up. "It was a lightning strike, okay?" Gundy suggested. Joanne agreed, and a few seconds later the pub's back door opened and the concerned owner ran out.

"What was *that*?!"

"I think it must have been lightning! It was so quick!" said Joanne looking genuinely flustered and shocked.

"Oh no! Are you okay?"

"I think so."

"What about your car?"

"Huh? Oh my car! Um, not sure." She had a quick look around Rhiannon's car and there was nothing obvious to report.

"No, I think it's all okay, but your wall's not looking so good."

"Wall? Oh! Oh crap! What a mess."

"Is it serious?" Joanne asked.

"Hm. Just annoying really, I s'pose; it's a retaining wall for the car park. But where did the lightning come from?"

"I've no idea, it was so frightening!" And as if on cue, Oli started crying.

"Oh, sorry, of course, you'll want to look after your boy. Wait there a moment though, I'm just going to call the fire station to see if we need to do anything."

"Okay," said Joanne, feeling guilty that she had no intention whatsoever of waiting.

As soon as the owner had gone back inside, Joanne grabbed

the strap to Rhiannon's bag and hoisted it onto her free shoulder, now carrying two bags, then she rushed around to the other side of the car to retrieve Bertie.

She raced him, hand-in-hand, across the car park, while carrying Oli with the other arm, to Gwion's car, and secured them both in their seats (with much crying because Bertie's soft, green dinosaur, 'Gordon,' had fallen on the floor of the car, out of reach). Gundy climbed up into the car, tossed Gordon onto Bertie's lap, and joined the still-floppy Mundy between the boys, while Joanne went around the car slamming the rear doors. She rushed around to the driver's door, tugged it open, threw both bags across to the passenger seat and jumped into the driver's seat. The engine roared, the wheels spun on pebbles, and they sped out of the car park.

"What happened to d'sparkly lady?" asked Bertie.

"She had to go," said his mummy.

- CHAPTER 8 -

Disintegration

Joanne drove down the side of the pub to the main road, indicated left towards Hereford, and stopped. She looked right, towards Arthgwyn, unaware in Aberystwyth, and kept looking. The indicator ticked and tocked; outside the left-hand light flashed on and off, but the car remained where it was. Arthgwyn would need to be told in person, wouldn't she?

In her rear-view mirror, a car appeared over the hill behind them and Joanne had to decide. She engaged the gears and turned left.

Joanne had no idea how to deliver the news of Gwion's death over the phone: all she could see in her mind was Gundy killing Rhiannon, and all she felt in her heart was the fear that Bertie could use the power of the Darkgate to damage people ... and even little Oli's hands had glowed when he was worried in Carys' house. It was madness, but this felt like a battle ... yet all around them, people were going about their daily lives, completely unaware.

Joanne was mumbling her thoughts out loud to herself when she realised Gundy was very quiet. More precisely, she realised the boys were very noisy and Gundy wasn't helping to settle them.

"Gundy? Are you okay?"

In between the howling and shrieks of the boys it became clear that the utterly silent Gundy was not okay at all.

A minute later Joanne parked the car, in the first lay-by she found, to comfort all three on the back seat. Oli needed a feed, and Bertie needed some hugs and attention, but Gundy was blank. She stared forwards at nothing, and Joanne couldn't find a way to break her dark reverie.

After a few minutes of feeding, Oli had had enough and, after a few more minutes, he was fast asleep; Bertie cuddled up to his mummy and they looked at a book together, before he too went quiet and struggled to keep his eyes open — eventually, it was just Gundy who needed attention. Joanne reached out to stroke her head, but Gundy sharply moved it out of reach.

"No! I killed someone, Joanne," she said, with frosty calm. "In cold blood. How could I do that?"

"You were defending the boys," said Joanne, slightly unconvincingly.

"I was. But does that make it right? Is it *ever* right to kill someone? I mean I know I also killed the Hordesman at home, but that was an accident, I just reacted, there was no intent. But this was different, I planned it."

Joanne was silent. She couldn't think of anything helpful to say.

"So, you think I'm a murderer?" asked Gundy.

"No ..." said Joanne with a tone that suggested she was looking for a set of words that she couldn't quite find. "That doesn't seem to describe what you did. Not properly. It's like we're at war now. You acted as ... a soldier, I suppose."

"Does *that* make it right? Does even a soldier have the right to kill someone? To take their life? To break the hearts of those that knew that someone?"

"I really don't know. I'm not a philosopher, Gundy, but if people didn't fight, wouldn't the world's worst rise to the top and take over? In a world with no fighting, those who chose to do whatever it takes, including murder, would always win, wouldn't they? If there was no threat to them, what could stop them? Maybe there's another way, but I can't think what it is ..."

"Do you really think we're at war?" asked Gundy.

"I didn't. Back at Arthgwyn's I thought she was exaggerating ... now I'm not sure. When Arthgwyn talked about Simon being 'at the front line' I took it as a metaphor; scary but not real. But maybe she was right? Maybe that's what's making me so afraid? The fear that a force out there is threatening my family, and tearing it apart? Simon's not here because he's off 'fighting', and we're having to make do, evacuated from our home because of the danger there. Maybe that's *exactly* like being at war?"

"Maybe," Gundy shrugged, unable to fully engage. "Do you think *Rhiannon* thought she was at war though? And if she did, do you think she'd say it was 'fair' that I killed her?"

"Hm. What we *do* know is that she was going to take us hostage, and threaten us, and probably hurt the boys and you and me, and maybe kill one or more of us. And I'm pretty sure she didn't care whether *that* was fair or not."

"True," Gundy sighed. "But I still killed someone in cold blood, and I don't know how to cope with it."

"You did it out of love for the boys, Gundy. You've got to hold on to that."

Joanne paused, not wanting to over-simplify things.

"But, if you have done wrong then I suppose you'll have to deal with it. I'm not trying to dismiss this as nothing, I know what you did is a big thing, but I also hope it's not so big that it crushes you … I don't know what else to say."

By now Bertie had also fallen deeply asleep. It seemed strange that someone could happily ascend into dreams during the conversation they'd just had.

With a start, Joanne remembered she had to phone Arthgwyn. She picked up the phone, puffed out in preparation, and dialled the number.

::

Joanne hadn't expected Arthgwyn to weep so loudly. But it all poured out. She'd never felt able to tell Gwion that she loved him. He'd started off as a servant but become so much more. They'd been together for over one hundred and twenty years, and how could she *not* love him after all that time? His love had healed the heartbreak that had shattered her as a young girl of seventeen, which she'd nursed, almost alone, for a very, very long time. But now her Gwion was gone. She knew she shouldn't act in anger but she wanted to kill the person who was *really* responsible, the person who had sent Rhiannon, but she wasn't sure who it was.

"Could it be Arthdu?" asked Joanne.

"It could be, but in all of the last fifteen hundred years I have never heard of Arthdu allowing a woman into his Horde — probably something to do with me — but it seems he's changing his approach for some reason, if this 'Rhiannon' was working for him."

"It's possible though?"

"Yes, and it makes sense. He needs someone a bit more up-to-date. His Hordesmen are something of a blunt instrument, and one of the reasons Gwion and I are … were … able to stay ahead of him is because we adopt useful new technology. Computers, phones, various modifications that Gwion had made and was working on. However, the last 'new' thing Arthdu introduced was the crossbow, although I suppose their exploding Darkgate tips are new. Still, it might make sense if she was working for him; perhaps he's realised he's got to start embracing the new. It seems he must be using phones too, if The Hordesmen are able to communicate with Arthdu. It's worrying though. We've just lost dear, wonderful Gwion and, although Arthdu's lost Rhiannon, what if he has others with similar skills?" Arthgwyn mulled it over.

"What will you do now?" asked Joanne.

"I'm not sure. I suppose I've become exclusively reliant on Gwion. Obviously I knew he was going to die one day, but I thought I had time. I didn't want to …" she trailed off in order to regain her poise.

"I didn't *want* to find someone else because I loved him."

Arthgwyn paused again to control herself, this time for ten seconds or so, and Joanne let her take the time she needed

"I don't want vengeance, you know, I just want to stop this from happening again." She sighed. "Actually, I *do* want vengeance, but over the years I've seen that it's a pointless path and I'm *better* than that. I've been through this before you know, sort of. All the men I've been with, have ended up aged to death or killed. I swore I'd never be with someone again — I warned Gwion, but damn him he wouldn't take no for an answer! He just waited and wore me down! In all my life there was never anyone like him. I'd like to believe he knew I lo—" She couldn't say it. Arthgwyn went quiet and Joanne knew tears were welling again. "He called me 'Gwyn', Joanne. Just 'Gwyn'. To him I wasn't a bear-woman anymore, just white and pure." And she wept again, tears of pure want, swelling and dripping from her.

"I think," she said between sobs. "I need some time alone now."

"Of course," said Joanne. "But please phone again, soon. I'm here to help. In fact, I think I'm going to leave the boys at my mum and dad's and drive back tomorrow to be with you."

"No, no! Don't do that! You're very kind, but your boys need you. It's okay, I'm a big girl. But, yes, I'd like to phone later; thanks, I appreciate the offer."

They said their goodbyes and rang off.

With two sleepy boys, and a war-damaged bear, Joanne set off again for Hereford.

::

On the passenger seat, Joanne's phone rang. She glanced at it and it said 'Simon', but there was another noise, *another* ringing, and it was coming from Rhiannon's bag.

For a moment she was confused, she indicated to Gundy to investigate, which was easy because there was hardly anything in the bag. It was Rhiannon's phone and Gundy showed the display to Joanne; it read, "Joanne". It took a moment for the implication to register: her phone had been hacked.

She picked her own phone from the passenger seat and answered it.

"Hello!" said Simon, glad to hear from Joanne. "We're with the —"

"Never mind that, Simon," said Joanne gruffly, interrupting him in case he said anything important. "I'm running out of credit; I'll phone you from a phone box."

"Oh, ok—" said Simon before Joanne cut him off.

"Oh. My. Goodness," said Gundy.

"We need a garage with a public phone," said Joanne. "There's one in a mile or so."

A minute later, Joanne pulled up on the garage forecourt and checked the change in her purse as she walked towards the building. She found the payphone inside and called Simon.

"Sorry, Simon I've got to—"

"Very quickly, we need you to help Rufus!" said Simon before going on to explain briefly what had happened to him.

"Okay," said Joanne. "Have to go, not much time. I'll phone you in a bit properly," and again she cut Simon off. She returned to the car quickly, to find out if Rhiannon's phone had rung.

"Nothing," said Gundy. "Looks like it's just your phone. If they'd hacked his phone too then I expected it to ring and say 'Simon' on the display."

"Me too," agreed Joanne. "Actually, whose names are in the phone?"

Gundy checked the address book; it was almost empty. It only had entries for "A", "Joanne", "Tia" and "Westie". She copied the numbers onto a piece of paper in her wobbly, big writing.

Joanne was thinking.

"They sell cheap phones in there," she said, pointing to the garage service station. "I'm going to buy one."

She returned to the forecourt shop and found a phone that had a speaker, so she could talk while driving, bought the phone and a SIM card, and put it in the phone as she walked back to the car, then handed it to Gundy.

"Try it. Phone Arthgwyn to give her the new number. Rhiannon's phone shouldn't ring, unless they're doing something *really* spooky. Right, let's go." Joanne started the engine and they trundled up to the road, she looked left and right and drove off.

Using a pen to poke the buttons, Gundy phoned Arthgwyn. She explained what had happened to Joanne's phone, and gave Arthgwyn the new number.

Arthgwyn was feeling a bit brighter, so Joanne thought she would ask about the boys and their abilities.

"I know this isn't the best time to ask this, but I'm concerned: Bertie burned a Hordesman really badly with Darkgate power, I think. And he said Rhiannon was 'sparkly' and I'm wondering if that's because she contains concentrations of picocells, since Gundy could clearly detect her with her Darkgate stone. And, back at Carys' house, Oli's hands glowed just before we were attacked. What's happening to my boys?! You said the Darkgate was safe, are they okay?"

"Oh gosh. Well, the Darkgate *is* safe, for me, yes. It's the source of my power, as you've seen, and I've been living in it for fifteen hundred years. It's safe for you — at least for a few months. But for your children ... I'm not sure anymore. I'm quite shocked that Oli and Bertie seem to have picked up some of its power so quickly. It means it was trying to change them to be like me." Arthgwyn gasped. "Oh no! I've just realised. Oh Joanne, I'm so sorry. I think I can guess what's happening!"

Fear, then anger, filled Joanne's voice.

"But you said IT WAS SAFE!" she shouted at the phone that Gundy had placed on the passenger seat.

"I know, I know. It's because they're children! I didn't think. It sees them as unfinished, it can change them more easily. I'm so sorry. I didn't think about it, I've been old for so long the idea of being young just … just … I've forgotten what it's like!" Arthgwyn began to cry again. It was all too much. Joanne closed her eyes and breathed in and out several times. She regained composure, and spoke."

"I'm sorry, but I need to know: can you stop it?"

Arthgwyn didn't or couldn't respond.

"Can you *undo* it?" Joanne insisted gently.

"I can try," Arthgwyn said, her voice cracking. "I might be able to, but I can't guarantee anything."

"Do your best," said Joanne, remaining calm. "We'll come to see you as soon as we return to Aber."

"I'll do all I can to help," Arthgwyn promised.

Gundy interrupted them. Using Joanne's old phone, Gundy had been checking the news. It was buzzing with stories about Live toys. It seemed to be all people could talk about, even in Wales. However, whereas in England people viewed Live toys with varying degrees of mistrust, fear and terror, in Wales it was more about mocking the hysterical reaction of the English. Even the reporters jokingly suggested the English should move out if they were so scared, and good Welsh people would take their houses.

"It's looking more and more serious in England," said Gundy. "And it looks like the Welsh could soon start moving into England."

"You mean *invade* England?!" said Joanne.

"Looking at some of the things being said here, it won't take long for today's jokes and half-serious comments to become tomorrow's cold intentions," agreed Arthgwyn.

"Arthgwyn," said Joanne. "We need to read Robertson's book. We need its help before this gets out of control. Can you stay on the line and help?"

Arthgwyn agreed, so Gundy picked up the book, and started to read…

On Arthdu and The Darkgate

A.D. 1743, June 14th

Herein are the thoughts of William Robertson. I am a man broken
by circumstance and time, writing in the hope that, should men
follow my path, they will have success where I have, as yet, failed.
As I write, it is the year of our Lord 1743. You will think me
consumed by madness but I have, in all truth, been alive for some
one hundred and fifty-nine years, and I show no sign of death nor
frailty, nor have I done so for many a decade. So help me, I swear
this is the truth.

Though my current state would seem set to continue for many
a year, I intend the reader to hear such tales of my life that, when I
finally shuffle off this mortal coil, it might arouse a state of mind in
him that he should take up my cause and march forward, in my
place, to realise my dearest hope: that I should inspire such a man
with courage to face the darkness, and that he may prevail.

I begin with the details of my birth. For me to state, in all
seriousness, that I was born in the year of our Lord 1584 will
undoubtedly arouse such a disbelief in you that you may think I
have a fever of the mind. Nevertheless, I am of sound mind and
body. I wish I were not. I wish, from the depths of my soul, that the
ground would take my body; that it would decay, and I may at last
lie in peace with all those I have known and lost over the years.

I was born the youngest of but three children, for my mother
died as I was born, and my father was a man much broken and
preoccupied with her death, and as such did not remarry. I was
fortunate enough to have access to some minor finery in life; a nurse
tended to my brothers and I, and we grew and made good.

By my seventeenth birthday, I undertook a promise to myself
that I should serve my community; not in the manner of a parson,

but as a leader who would listen. And that I did, gradually growing into such a role by hard work and travail, until I met Pale.

A.D. 1743, June 16th

Pale was our salvation, but my undoing. He came unto me one night, a strange disfigured man, telling tales that were stranger still. He told of a means to remove the Yorebear from his place of dominion over our village, and our region. What else could I have done, but help him? He knew what manner of man I was; he knew I would aid him. I do not, however, believe he had foreknowledge of the man I would become once he was asleep and cold, yet not dead.

He showed me how to defeat the Yorebear — it matters not how we did achieve this feat, for it will not work again, as shall become clear, dear reader — and yet, for a time, we did defeat him. Pale believed the Yorebear would fall and never rise, sleeping in death, or a state so similar as to be indistinguishable, with those who served him, a band of vagabonds known as The Horde. It was to my surprise that Pale belonged to The Horde, for he was a thoughtful man, and he fell also on the day that I placed the Darkgate key that we had constructed into the head of the Darkgate.

This was the moment of my loss, my crossing-over into a state of purgatory, for at that moment not only did the Yorebear, and all in The Horde, fall to the ground and lose their senses, and become as though dead, so also did I become something other than I had been to that point. My hands and arms burned, I felt the sensation of a strong power rush through me such as a torrent of hot water. My mind filled with visions of blackness and sharp points of light, as if many stars filled my head, and I became changed.

The feelings did pass and I regained my senses and disposition. I attended to my thoughts for the remainder of the day and decided to rejoin my duties, but I was constrained not to leave the Darkgate. I felt a strange compulsion to remain until something had been completed, and thoughts appeared in my mind that made it clear what must be done. I was to pull each man — if 'man' is a fair and honest description of the Hordesman and the Yorebear — from the field in which they fell, deep into The Darkgate itself, for there was now a hole, a door if you will, in the side of the Darkgate where there had been none, then down into the ground beneath. Yet, I found it not surprising, it seemed to me to be the natural way of things, and to be expected.

I undertook my task for several hours until mid-morn and at last it was complete. Without a thought, I raised my hand towards the door, and the hole of the door became as stone! Only then did I feel a release in my mind and a freedom to retire to the village from whence I had come. Yet all was not well.

On return to my dwelling, I greeted my wife but she regarded me almost as a stranger, saying I did glow, and she was much afraid of that which I had become. My children likewise felt fear and would not come near unto me. By the end of that day many men of the village had told me that I should leave and not come back, for I was frightful to them and not the man they had known for many years. When I refused, men took up arms to attack me and, as I raised my hand, they could not strike me, hitting instead hard air in front of me. I was thus accused of sorcery and dark practices and caused great confusion to myself and my village. I left in haste and returned to The Darkgate, where I knew I would find shelter and protection.

And so The Darkgate became my home. I expected to live my life in quietness and stealth, and then to die. But I did not. I did not age, or grow ill or weary. I felt no need for food or drink. My body grew hair on the palms of my hands, and on my face and body in places not normal for a man; even my nose changed its appearance. For many a year I was troubled of soul, I lived in darkness and despair and wished to die, but I could not. And my only companions were the sleeping Yorebear and his Horde who have made not a sound nor a movement in one hundred and fifty-nine years.

At last, I have embraced what I have become and begun to learn of my new nature. I have discovered life, of a sort, in communication with The Darkgate, in its sense and discernment of my existence, and its willingness to commune with me in a way I cannot describe. It is not of speech, nor of hearing, nor of apprehension by any daily sense. I feel its thoughts in my mind, directly, without need for intermediary or interpretation.

My disposition has improved greatly. While still not as the man I was, I am not alone, and it is my belief that The Darkgate is gratified also. While my use of the key has greatly restrained its faculties and abilities, we may communicate and have much to share. What I have learned, and am learning, will form the rest of these notes.

A.D. 1743, August 23rd

The first lesson I have learned is that I am the Guardian of the Darkgate while it is inactive. It is my belief that the 'key' I used was in fact a conduit for the Darkgate's power, and that I am become an element of the Darkgate in living form. While I live, the Darkgate may be returned to operation. I would willingly die, and end the Yorebear's existence, and yet I cannot die because its power in me keeps me alive. These thoughts did not please me, and yet they explained my existence and so were valuable unto me.

From this I moved in my mind to as yet unopened rooms of knowledge within. I learned to make clear my wishes and desires to The Darkgate, and I apprehended its manner of existence, such as it is. At first, I feared that its nature may be despicable, and that I might have need to find a way to destroy myself somehow, to sever my link and disarm it forever, but it is neither good nor bad.

I have come to learn that The Darkgate wishes me to be more like an imprint that it contains. 'Tis an imprint of a being, not human, and indeed it has changed me to an approximation of that image — but it has failed. Its purpose is not to imprint that image upon the world, but to change some of us that we may lead a change of society and the interaction of one man with another. However, The Darkgate is aware of the lack of success it has had with the Yorebear, for the Yorebear has learned to control The Darkgate and use it for his own ends. It will help all who challenge the Yorebear, while it can, and yet acknowledges that the time may come when the Yorebear will gain such complete control that The Darkgate will be entirely his servant. At that point, he will be able to stamp upon the affairs of man, at least within the shires nearby here, whatsoever image may delight his dark soul. Upon learning this, I made it my duty to find a way to stop such an event from ever occurring; it is my hope that you may play a part in achieving this end since, if you are reading this, it is entirely possible that I have, somehow, finally found rest in the ground.

I intend, over the next few years, to methodically test various forms of interaction with The Darkgate to find a path that would, when taken, lead to the destruction of the Yorebear.

A.D. 1789, January 19th

In the last several years since I wrote in this book, my life has taken many turns. On many a day I have felt a near-tangible grasp of the knowledge we require, yet on others deep despair has again returned and I have lain for night and day without sleeping or moving, nor eating, nor drinking, since these actions are no longer needed, and remind me of all that I have lost. Still I have made some progress, and I shall now tell of that.

I have developed, and to some degree tested, a technique I call "The Pearls of Stone", which may divide control of The Darkgate such that it cannot be entirely ruled by one man. In this manner, another man, or men, must place sufficient numbers of Darkgate stones at locations, regularly spaced at one or two league intervals, in such an arrangement as two horses may walk from The Darkgate in two opposite directions. I have furthermore discovered that, by placing them in the compass line west north west to east south east, both sides of The Darkgate, the effect is at its strongest. The nature of that effect is to make the Darkgate but one link in a chain, albeit the largest link but, notwithstanding, less influential. It is my theory that the energy from The Darkgate, whatever its nature, does move and spread, as water, into the more distant stones, whence they can be set up in opposition to the Yorebear controlling The Darkgate.

A.D. 1815, July 25th

The recent events in Belgium by the forces of The Duke of Wellington against Napoleon have reminded me again of the pointlessness of war. The boundaries on the map move and float around, at great cost to life, and yet life and society seems to advance and shrink almost independently of it all. I am beginning to fear that my efforts are equally ill-fated and without point. I have not in the last twenty-six years found even one single other strategy with which to defeat or inconvenience the Yorebear, and I am greatly afraid that on the day that he awakens my single plan (above) may be easily defeated by his agents, by some knowledge as yet unknown to me, or indeed by his own force of will upon The Darkgate. Yet, I do not give up hope, if executed with speed and stealth my plan may lead to success.

On a more vain note, I have discovered how to affect my appearance! I may now remove, for a number of weeks, my facial hair; I may also shed the hair on the palms of my hands and feet, and joy-of-joys return my snout to a nose! Hoorah! Last week, I took a risk and walked into the village and was treated much as any other man. It was a revelation. It is a shame that this joy, just a few days gone, has been utterly supplanted by my reaction to the behaviour of mankind on a grander scale.

A.D. 1914, August 4th

It has been ninety-nine years, almost to the day since I last wrote in this notebook. It took me several days to remember where I had hidden it. What do we find as I write? War once again, and on a scale even I have never seen before in all my many years. I yield! I wish to leave this world, and go, and let man destroy man as is his delight, and perhaps even his sole purpose. The world is full of darkness; machines now exist that fly and rumble over the ground to kill and destroy men in great numbers, and I fear the end of the whole world is nigh.

In the years since I last wrote, all I have discovered is that there seems to be another strong power towards Builth Wells or Rhayader that has the same 'depth' (I cannot find a better word) as the Darkgate in which I have now lived for so many years. If I believed there were any point, I might seek it out, but these days — especially these days — I see no point at all. Let the Yorebear escape as he will and be destroyed with the rest of mankind.

A.D. 1950, March 12th

For the first time in decades, perhaps even centuries, I feel alive. There is a sense that the Second World War is almost behind us and people may have learned the lessons at last! I dare to believe it will never happen again, and that there is hope! I have hope!

I think I will finally take a trip to Builth on the Thursday bus to look for the source of the Darkgate-like power that I have been sensing from that direction. I will take a Darkgate stone with me to help me search. I have recently been wondering if there might be *another* Darkgate! That might make things very, very much more interesting, and who knows, perhaps I'll find a way to use it to defeat the Yorebear at last! I can but hope.

A.D. 1950, March 16th

I have just returned from my trip to Builth. I did not find what I was looking for but there is definitely a strong Darkgate-like presence in that direction. Next stop, Rhayader. I'll take a trip on Monday; the paper says the weather should be nice.

A.D. 1972, May 9th

I have been asleep for years. I don't know whether to rejoice or worry — I haven't slept since 1618! Things are very different now. Women are wearing the most outrageous clothes: indecently short skirts, and even trousers, and tight tops that show their chests in detail. It's almost enough to attract my attention after all these years! And the music, such as it is, is a clashing drone to my ears. It is even pouring out of cars as they drive through the village. I find myself feeling misplaced and depressed. I have been alive for hundreds of years, and yet I have never felt like this before because, previously, I have lived through the changes and understood the affairs of the world going on around me. But now, after just twenty-two years, I feel like a foreigner from a far distant land, distinct from everyone around me, and more different than I have ever felt before. I am taking long walks in an attempt to keep my spirits up.

February 13th, 1989

It happened again. I have been asleep from 1976 until today. Once more things have changed and I can't keep up. After all I said, I find myself pining for the 1970s! In fact, I find myself wishing to return to a number of years from the past, starting with 1618.

I'm really quite concerned about these sleeps, I'm beginning to think the Darkgate is dying, or losing power; perhaps they are the same thing. It certainly seems weaker.

I still haven't been able to find the location of the other power source. I explored as far as Rhayader in 1975 but there was nothing there. The sense of power was stronger in that direction, however, so I might try Llangurig next.

December 23rd, 1998

This is bad. I'm really getting worried now. I was awake for only three days in 1989 before I fell asleep again, and I'm finding it hard to communicate with the Darkgate properly. I think it's taking back power from me to keep itself going. I'm seriously thinking about re-starting the Darkgate and putting the Pearls of Stone plan into action while I still can. If I fall asleep forever, or die (which are pretty much the same thing) will the Darkgate restart on its own? Will the Yorebear be released? I haven't got a clue.

I'm going to try to find the other Darkgate in Llangurig, or wherever it is, and I'll take this notebook with me in the hope that it will be useful to whoever is there, if anyone.

May 8th, 2005

The last seven years have been a blur. I've managed to fight with the Darkgate to keep myself awake but it's been like a half-dream the whole time. I've got to do something now. I'm making one last push to get the information in this book into the hands of someone who can help.

I'm in Llangurig at last, writing this while sat in a pub. Sadly there's no Darkgate here, but it's definitely close by. It's ironic that after all these centuries I find myself needing just a few more days, but not having the luxury.

I managed to change my appearance to make this trip, but I look a lot less human than I would like. There's a church here. I'm going to give this notebook to the rector. The publican says he's a new man from England, but seems honest and good and, so far, the village like him. A good man who can take on my work is what I need now.

I want to record that I have left sizeable stones, each about the size of a cannonball, in two places on my journey. I have deactivated them so that the Yorebear can't find them when he wakes up. One is in the churchyard in Rhayader; I will place the other in the churchyard here. It was not easy to carry them on the bus in my state! To activate them you need only touch them with a chipping from The Darkgate, or who knows a chipping from the other Darkgate, if it really exists. Good luck.

Once I've given my book to the rector, I'm going to try to make it back to Llandegley, and I think I will have to put my power back into the Darkgate in case it becomes unstable and detonates! Such an explosion would be large enough to remove continents. When Arthdu awakes, I expect to die. He may kill me himself, but I don't think he will have time. The power that remains in me will flood back into The Darkgate and I will be left aged 421 years old with no power to sustain me. In either case, I hope it's a quick death.

Good luck, and if it still means anything in this age,
God speed.
W.R.

Gundy finished reading and waited for Arthgwyn or Joanne to say something.

"Joanne," said Arthgwyn. "This is turning out to be one of the most heart-wrenching days I've had in centuries. That poor man! I know exactly how he feels; I've felt everything he wrote about, and he got quite close to Aberystwyth! If only I'd known!"

"There's something else," said Joanne. "We know what happened after he returned to Llandegley. It's in Pale's book."

"I take it from your tone that it's not pleasant?"

"Not exactly. Do you want to know?"

"I have found, over the years, that it is better to get these sorts of things over in one go. Tell me."

"Well, when Pale, Arthdu and the Horde awoke, which we now know was in 2005 — Pale's notes didn't record the date — they found Robertson standing outside the Darkgate. Probably the only reason they didn't kill him immediately for what he'd done to them was because they were so amazed to see him there. Robertson said he'd been waiting for them and that he expected to die, but that he believed the Yorebear himself could very well die soon because Robertson had left information with someone, telling them how to destroy him. Then, he couldn't say any more — he began to cough, he groaned and stumbled, and fell to the ground and died. Only a few seconds later, his body had almost completely decayed and a light came out from the Darkgate and touched the remnants and they disappeared. And that was that."

"Robertson *told* Arthdu that he could be dead soon?"

"That's what Pale wrote, yes."

"Oh dear. That does not sound wise. It's my guess that Arthdu would have realised he needed to put his plans into action sooner rather than later. Of course, just a few months after Robertson woke Arthdu, Teddy put him to sleep again, but for Arthdu that would only have reinforced the urgency of putting his plan into action, to gain complete control over the Darkgate and re-conquer the lands of Western England for Briton. But what can we do? What can we do, Joanne?"

Joanne glanced at Gundy, surprised to hear Arthgwyn sounding so fatalistic. Arthgwyn continued.

"We have nothing. Nothing! Robertson ruined it all by telling Arthdu that there is a plan to destroy him, and my dear Gwion died FOR NOTHING! My lovely man gone! And we've nothing to show for it! Nothing, noth…" and she drifted off into silence.

Joanne, tried to soldier on: "I don't know what we can do, but we've got to think of *something*, we can't just give up! There are people out there who need us to stay strong for them!"

"Ha! That sounds wonderful coming from you, Joanne! You're in the midst of running away!"

"Arthgwyn! Please! Stop it, I know you're upset — damaged

even — but, please, we can't fight each other!"

Arthgwyn was silent. The car trundled along, the was a faint hiss from the phone's speaker. A sigh from Arthgwyn.

"I lost the man who has meant more to me in all my years, and now I have to think of a way to kill my ex-lover, so I'm sorry for being angry. But you're right, I shouldn't be angry with you. We have to find a way to recover from this. *I* have to recover from this … Maybe we can make Robertson's "Pearls of Stone" plan work? Or maybe we simply don't have the time, but you're right we have to do what we can, even if it's not much."

"Well, if this Emily woman turns out to be an ally, that'll be one more person to help. I'm not sure she'll help if I tell her what she's getting herself into though."

"Then I'm not sure you should tell her."

"Can I really treat her like that? Is this her fight?"

"It's going to become her fight. She's going to be more and more under pressure for her stance on Live toys. She needs you to give her something to keep her out of the limelight, and The Dolls need her to help them get out of that gazebo."

"Hm," said Joanne, only partially convinced.

As Joanne and Arthgwyn, explored other ideas for gaining support or challenging Arthdu, Gundy rummaged through Rhiannon's bag in the back of the car. One by one, she pulled items out, held them in front of Bertie and played a game of 'hunt the sparkle' with him, but there was nothing of interest — he only saw sparkles on Gundy's Darkgate stone.

The unusual thing was that Rhiannon's bag contained very little: her phone, a hair brush, a mirror, some gum, a plastic packet of tissues, a mobile sat nav and a golden key. No make up; nothing to eat or drink; no sanitary products; no personal items such as pictures or nicknacks; no receipts from shops; somehow, it was slightly disturbing.

"What do you make of this Arthgwyn?" ask Gundy, and she

told her what she had found in Rhiannon's bag.

"That's a good question. I'm a little concerned to say, I think Rhiannon was more than just part of Arthdu's horde," began Arthgwyn, with tension in her voice. "*Maybe* she was a Yorebear."

"What? Oh my goodness! Really? We killed a Yorebear?!" said Joanne, the car weaving on the road for a moment.

"Well, no, I'm not sure. I don't understand how she *could* have been a Yorebear, nor how you could have killed her with a single Darkgate stone; I'm just saying it's one possibility — when I take a handbag outside, which is rare, my bag contains similar things: I have no need for food or drink, don't go shopping much, I don't need make up because — when it matters — I make the picocells change my appearance. Maybe she and I don't need the things other women need?" Arthgwyn paused. "The thing I'd like to know, is what the key is for." Gundy picked it up and examined it as they drove along. Arthgwyn continued. "We should look out for anything with a lock that Arthdu might like to keep from us; in the meantime, we need to find out what Simon and Teddy are doing, and organise a plan of attack with them."

"Agreed," said Joanne. With a jolt she remembered she'd promised to phone Simon. He and Teddy would be wondering what had happened to the rest of their family.

- CHAPTER 9 -

Ramgar and the War of Ess

Now that no one could eavesdrop her calls, Joanne rang Simon to tell him all that had happened, and to give him her new number. Before she could say any more, Simon blurted out that the three of them had just arrived in Llandegley and they hoped to find Ramgar, and he'd agreed it with the dolls, and … He waited for her objections, ready to provide a (short) list of reasons why it was a good idea. She paused, but agreed quietly. All she asked was that Simon and Teddy should find a way for them and Ramgar in stay touch, so they could act together, as a unit.

While Simon came to terms with his wife's pragmatic approach to the danger he was facing, Joanne reported on the recent events at home and in Llangurig, including the deaths of Gwion and Rhiannon, who's role she also had to establish, and summarised the contents of Robertson's book that had been so hard won but seemed to offer so little, and finally she explained why Gundy and she were still determined to travel to Hereford to meet Emily. At first, the roll-call of new dangers she and the boys had faced passed into Simon's mind as relatively neutral and dispassionate facts but, within seconds, a creeping, near-paralysis of what-might-have-been spread through him. As Joanne talked, he became distracted, repeatedly visualising dangers and attacks on his family: sometimes the scenarios ended well; sometimes they did not. He stopped her in mid-flow and explained what was bothering him.

She paused, uncertain, then half-heartedly tried to say that all would be well, and they would work together. She changed the conversation and mentioned Robertson's Pearls of Stone plan, but said they didn't have time to fully implement it today; it was already mid-afternoon. It needed more thought. Simon agreed, and that was it. They said their goodbyes and ended the call.

Still in a daze, Simon pocketed his phone and passed on Joanne's information to Ess and to Teddy, who nodded slowly while his fuzzy mind struggled to grasp it all. Simon's thoughts too, were in slow-motion. He studied the car's internal door release handle, and took it in his fingers. He pulled, felt the clunk of the door mechanism. A push on the door, parting with the rest of the car; the air flowing over its outer edge; the sounds as his foot pressed down on dry ground; Teddy inside the car, masked by the reflection of trees on his door window. He heard Nature, and felt Life, for a second.

Teddy called and waved to Simon to remind him to let him out. The request shattered Simon's daze; he pulled on Teddy's door handle, opened the door, un-did his seatbelt, and picked him up, lifting him around on his hip, as if he were a child, and set him on the ground. Then Simon knelt down to talk to Teddy, eye-to-eye.

"Teddy, you've done this sort of thing before. Do you think we're going to *kill* people?"

"Hmmm. I ffink der best way to survive is to try not to ... but der trying not to doesn't always work."

Simon stood up and, for a split second, pursed his lips with determination — then he slammed both car doors shut and they set off.

The time for contemplation was over; they were now in action.

::

They left the car up a bumpy, overgrown track, near the top of a partly wooded hill. To get as far as they had driven was jarring, slow and challenging for the car; it was not the kind of place dog walkers parked. It wasn't a perfect hiding place, but they had no time to find somewhere else. Simon minimised the risk by parking the car with the damaged side facing the densest part of the wood, the top edge of which was roughly half-way up the tallest of the several hills around Llandegley, on the other side of the valley from the Darkgate.

Simon and Teddy climbed the steep, wooded incline under cover of the trees and, as before, Ess travelled in the breast pocket of Simon's shirt. Teddy was almost beside himself with worry. The Darkgate was at most a mile away, and it called to him, gnawed at him, pulled him in the opposite direction from the one in which they were walking. He did his best to ignore it. As for Ess, he had the bearing of a man on his way to a funeral; probably his own.

After climbing for no more than five minutes, they left the top of the wood and started to look around for signs of Ramgar, hoping to see a gathering of sheep somewhere below them, or on a nearby hillside, ideally with a single brown 'sheep' in their midst. But they didn't really know what to expect. Maybe they should be looking for a group of Live toys instead. The only strategy they had was: (i) to climb to the very top of the hill and look around on all sides for some sort of unusual gathering, and (ii) for Teddy to ask local sheep if they knew anything about Ramgar. They were in the middle of doing (i), but (ii) didn't work because Simon scared the sheep too much. Teddy tried running off to talk to sheep on his own but they were not brave like the Flock sheep he'd met three years ago, they just froze when they saw him, let him run a little closer then bolted, leaving him shouting, "Come back! I want to talk to you!" Simon reminded him that shouting might not be a good idea if there were Hordesmen nearby.

All they could do was walk to the top of the hill, and if they didn't see any sign of Ramgar then they'd have to walk back down to the car and drive around looking for some sign, some clue, of where he was.

Then, when they were a hundred metres or so below the ridge, the sky lit up on the other side of the hill on which they stood. It was almost like lightning, but the clouds weren't dark enough and the light wasn't instant enough. This was definitely 'unusual'. Simon and Teddy looked at each other and, without a word, dashed to the top of the hill to look over the other side.

At the top, they kept low and peered down through the rustling grass and the browning bracken. Below, in a deep dip, surrounded by hills on all sides, was a collection of sheep and colourful spots; it was hard to estimate the number of sheep, perhaps fifty or sixty, and even harder to see what the spots were, but it was quite possible they were Live toys. For a moment they were unsure whether it really was Ramgar's camp or not, then a second explosion lit up a huge dome of translucent light that surrounded and protected the sheep and dots within.

"I think we've found Ramgar," said Simon dryly.

"I ffink so," agreed Teddy. Ess just looked forwards, expressionless.

As they studied the scene more carefully, they could see shadowy, dark-clothed figures dotted in twos and threes at locations all around the circumference of the dome. A small group of seven or eight figures were a couple of hundred metres below Simon and Teddy's position, with a larger gathering of ten or fifteen figures closer to the right hand side of the dome. On the left of the dome, a low hill covered in trees made it impossible to see if there were any of the Horde on that side; they decided to assume the worst. Finally, on the far side of the dome was a steep, shrub-covered, scrubby hill. Simon saw it and had an idea.

"Teddy, look over there: if we could get around there, without being seen, we wouldn't face much opposition; there's almost no one on that side, *and* there's that sort of wiggly copse of trees from top to bottom."

"But how can we penetrate the dome's defences?" asked Ess.

"I was hoping Teddy could help us with that one. Can you use your stone to make an opening in the dome's field?"

"I don't know, I could try…"

"The problem is, if you don't succeed soon after we break cover, The Hordesmen will see us because the dome is see-through, so we'd soon be under attack and, soon after that, dead, basically."

"Not if I make my own mini dome, actchully!" smiled Teddy.

"Good idea … but won't you have to lower your shield to do whatever you're going to do to get us through that big dome? Won't we be vulnerable?"

"Huh?" asked Teddy.

"Won't they be able to attack us?" explained Simon.

"Oh, yes," said Teddy, crestfallen. "Day will."

"Still, it's all we've got. Let's walk round there and see what it looks like from that side."

It took twenty minutes for them to wheel round, clockwise, while remaining unseen by The Hordesmen. They kept hidden below the ridge to the left, passed through the wood keeping well away from the dome and Hordesmen, round the back of the far ridge, keeping out of sight, then scrambled up and down into the green ribbon of trees they, crouching low and using the thick scrub and the wood for cover. Little stones dislodged, fell and bounced, making ticking sounds as they clacked onto other stones, bouncing again and again. The sound would be enough to attract someone's attention, so they had to drop down very slowly, metre by metre. At one point, they had to hide behind some rocks to avoid being seen by a Hordesman passing through the trees on patrol, but they remained undetected. It had taken ten or fifteen minutes to move from the top of the ridge to the last protected point near to the edge of the dome, but they hadn't been discovered. When they reached their target location near the edge of Ramgar's camp, not a single Hordesman was nearby. All they had to do now was rush for the dome and hope Teddy could break through.

While still hidden, Teddy lowered his stone's shield and concentrated on the dome. He felt what he wanted to do. He wanted to get in; he visualised the dome opening for them — then he told the stone he wanted it ... *now*. And they ran.

A beam of light shot out from Teddy's free paw towards the dome and met its surface. For a split second the whole dome flashed and thrashed with tendrils of translucent pink and red, then an immense white light burst outwards towards them, and ... blackness.

They woke up sometime later, confused and aching. Simon, in particular, felt awful. It was as if his body had been fried, and repeatedly hit with many small hammers. Ess just ached. Two sheep strode over to them.

"Maaah!" said the lead sheep to Teddy. "You're lucky to be alive, maaah!"

Teddy noticed his Darkgate stone had become blackened and porous, like volcanic rock.

"What happened?" asked Teddy.

"You attacked our mini Darkgate with a stone from the *same* Darkgate. Maaah! No one's supposed to do that," said the other sheep. "Your stone has run out of power now."

The first sheep continued. "Maaah! It's one thing for a crossbow flint to detonate on the outside of the protection field, but Ramgar says it's quite another to try to open a hole in our mini Darkgate's shield while still holding on to *your* stone! Maaah! That's not going to end well. I'm afraid our mini Darkgate automatically sent out a massive defensive pulse and stunned everyone in about a fifty metre distance of the edge of the dome. Maaah. It's weakened our mini Darkgate's power quite a lot," the sheep indicated with its nose towards the centre of the dome. "But, in a way, you did us a favour. We can't *make* it do that, but you did. It stunned you and almost all The Hordesmen. Maaah. There were two Hordesmen, right at the top of the ridge, who were unaffected but they ran off. We sent out a scout, a fast running tiger toy, and she saw them flee down the other side towards the Darkgate, presumably to call for reinforcements; the rest are just lying out there, stunned. Ramgar's been doing his best to revive you, of course. In the meantime, we've been able to gather up all the flints from their Darkgate crossbow bolts and add them to our pile; hopefully, that will make up for the power our mini Darkgate just used up. Still, overall, I think Ramgar will be pleased."

"Ramgar *is* pleased," said a dark, old voice. "How are you, Teddy?"

Teddy looked to his left and there was the familiar figure of a ram trotting through the milling sheep. And yet he looked older, even more wrinkled, and Teddy was concerned. It must have shown on his face.

"Yes, I'm looking a little older, aren't I?" Ramgar looked at Simon. "And who is this?"

"Dis is Simon, my owner and my ffrend, and in his pocket is Ess."

"Um, Teddy?" said Simon.

"Yes," said Teddy.

"I can't understand what anyone's saying."

"Can't you?" asked Teddy.

"Er, no. All I can hear is you and the sheep and the ram bleating to each other. Can Ramgar understand me?"

They turned their attention to Ramgar.

"I can indeed! Teddy, you'll need to translate for Simon: you and I can talk to each other because we have something in common; we have The Life inside us."

"The Life?"

"Yes, Teddy. The Life, as I call it, has kept me alive all these years. It was infused into me a very long time ago by a good man, and you have it too, to some extent; not as *much* as me, but more … *fitted* somehow — but that is not what we should be talking about. We need to talk about this," he said, trotting in a small circle, indicating the encampment of sheep and toys all around them.

"Now, are you three alright? As I think I heard Maapreen just say, I've been using a little of the power from the mini Darkgate to revive you early. Let's talk while they sleep." He tipped his head to the sleeping Hordesmen outside. "But first, I want to make sure you are all well."

On examination, Simon said he still felt full of adrenaline and pain, like he'd been bungee jumping and hit the water, but Teddy and Ess were now recovered. Ramgar tutted soothingly at Simon's aches and pains and touched him with his nose, triggering a quiet rush of power, and Simon felt a little better.

The pleasantries over, Ramgar explained what he was doing in Llandegley. He had returned from The Circle because someone needed to look after the sheep of The Way, who were loosing cohesion due to the frightening reports of killer sheep in England. His plans for reaching English sheep would have to wait because he'd experienced the weirdness in England for himself: there was a thin feeling of power in the air, almost like an electric drizzle, and it was making the sheep there act very strangely, and rather violently. He could sense it too but it had little effect on him. It affected his blacksheep servants though; all of them had left him, driven by something, enraged. So he thought it best to withdraw to Llandegley, to set up a base, and to try to help The Flocks nearby. He guessed the source of the problem was probably the Darkgate, and he wanted to be near, to see what he could do. On his journey, he had come across a number of Live toys, and he offered them his support and companionship. He explained that he did not know whether it would be safe in Llandegley or not, but many had stayed with him and walked with him, and the word spread that Ramgar was going to look after all the Live toys who needed help. It was not his intention but he realised that The Way was applicable to them too: a collection of scared individuals who needed a sense of belonging and togetherness in the face of a hostile world.

However, after his return, things had been difficult. There

were many sheep who didn't like the idea of Live toys following The Way. It was *their* Way; who were these interlopers? And Ramgar saw for himself that The Way had become organised, stiff, unyielding: he had a lot of work to do.

He had arrived in Llandegley by night and immediately took a Flock to the Darkgate. They had each picked up in their mouths all the stones and chippings that they could find that weather or some unknown process had split from the main Darkgate, the keener sheep even quietly dislodged some pieces with their hooves, and together they brought them back to their field. They piled them in the centre, Ramgar touched the construction with his nose and they had their own mini Darkgate.

Within the hour, an attack came from a single Hordesman, an assassin sent to kill Ramgar. When he fired his crossbow, the bolt hit the shield, exploded, stunning the attacker. They captured his crossbow, added its flints to their pile, and their Darkgate became stronger. Arthdu was livid that Ramgar was using parts of his own Darkgate against him and tried to control Ramgar's stones from afar, but for some reason he failed. Ramgar could feel what he was doing, but his tiny Darkgate was able to resist: it was nothing to do with Ramgar's conscious mind; whatever power he had just flowed from him, he couldn't explain it. It was done. Ramgar had a base, it was protected, and they were safe.

Ess spoke up.

"I know this sounds mercenary but, to defend the good you're doing here, why don't you make a pre-emptive strike on Arthdu and kill off as many Hordesmen as you can? You could easily weaken his forces and make him think twice about hurting you and your followers again. Sometimes, the end justifies the means you know."

"That," said Ramgar with a smile, "is not my Way; I do not believe violence helps. How can we defeat the enemy by becoming the enemy? I understand other people have other views on this, but for me this is not a path I can take. I would rather die than become an attacker myself."

Ess' face crumpled in disagreement. Ramgar continued.

"Nevertheless, I'm quite happy to defend myself and my
followers, like this," he said, indicating the shield. "Of course,
sometimes the blows of my attackers deflect off the shield and harm
them — and that saddens me — but I will not attack them myself."

Ess clearly did not agree, but kept quiet.

"Now," continued Ramgar. "Let's talk about why we're all
here. It's good to see you Teddy, but I take it you're not looking for
another lady teddy bear? In fact, I hear you have a partner now?"

"Yes I got a lovely lady bear now! And she's got me! She's
called Gundy."

"That is wonderful!" said Ramgar, genuinely touched.
"Hearing about love is refreshing, particularly now." And he sighed
happily. "It's out of love that I protect these sheep and Live toys,
and it drives me to promote The Way. And yet Arthdu, sees me as a
threat and wants to kill me! Well, I suppose I *am* a threat, although
not in the way he fears. When people see the deep peace of The Way,
after a life of fear and suffering, it challenges them, changes them.
We even have two Hordesmen in our camp now!"

"Are you mad?!" exclaimed Ess.

Ramgar considered. He pondered.

"No," he said calmly. "I don't believe I am. Although, it's good
to check occasionally," he added with a smile.

"Well. Okay. But aren't you concerned that one or both of
them might be, you know, a spy?"

"Not really. I've spoken with them both, listened to them very
carefully. I saw their pain and their desire to be calm after all these
years. I believe they are changed. I have those feelings myself. Of
course, there is a chance that I am wrong, but I don't think so in
this case. You should meet them."

Ess had previously dismissed The Way as waffle, but to stand
here and feel the air crackle as Ramgar spoke, and his poise and

steady, calm power ... it was not what he had expected. He looked around the camp, at the sheep, the toys, at Simon, and Teddy, at Ramgar, at Ramgar's eyes. For a moment he couldn't look away from those old eyes, until the pressure and darkness of Ess' past made him drop his gaze. He spoke quietly.

"Ramgar, I was going to come here, infiltrate Arthdu's camp, and do whatever I could to 'take him out', and most likely die in the process. I had a reason for dying, something to give my death meaning: to help avenge The Dolls." A cheeky smile crossed Ess' face. "But now I have a reason for *living* because I think we can make this work for you. I think we might actually have a chance of not being wiped out." He paused. "I need to think. Do you mind if I take a walk?"

"Not at all," said Ramgar. "May I ask: are you going to see The Hordesmen?"

"Oh, no," said Ess vaguely, his mind elsewhere. "I just want to think." Ramgar nodded, concerned, and watched Ess wander away.

Teddy's head leaned to one side, his mouth dropped open, and it was obvious he had a question brewing. He rolled it over in his mind for a moment.

"Ramgar, what happened to Maalaw and The Flock?"

"Ah. That. I'm sorry to say that was another of the reasons I realised I had to return here. As you know, Maalaw took over that Flock when Maaroon was killed. From what I've managed to piece together, she had been drugged and was pushed in front of a car, through a hole in a hedge that overlooked the road, leaving Maalaw in charge — but Maalaw was soon under the control of Arthdu or his agents. She was probably also drugged, and certainly had to tell her Flock things that were contrary to The Way: they had to learn to bite, to head-butt each other in preparation for fighting, and so on. One day she simply said 'no more'; the next day, she was dead. By the end of that day, a Hordesman had stolen the whole flock from their field and we never heard from them again; they probably ended up as killer sheep, or as meat."

"Oh my goodness!" blurted Teddy.

"Indeed," agreed Ramgar. "Soon after I heard that, I began the long walk back here. It's a good thing I did because I hear The Circle was destroyed by Hordesmen two days after I left."

::

One of the sheep stationed around the inner perimeter of Ramgar's dome bleated loudly for attention; Ramgar trotted over to see what the ewe wanted. Outside the dome, looking utterly terrified, were two Live toys trying to get to safety. For a few seconds, Ramgar lowered the shield, while they ran inside, and immediately raised it again. They were out of breath and had a hunted look, mostly because they had to avoid the two fleeing Hordesmen, and had run for their lives from the top of the ridge, through the sleeping soldiers of Arthdu: they'd realised they had a chance when they saw the Darkgate's pulse knock out everyone around the dome.

"They're coming! They're nearly here!" shouted a raggedy Live owl to Ramgar, with what little breath he had.

"Who's coming?" Ramgar asked.

"The men-things, on horses!" squeaked the owl's tiny teddy friend. "Loads of them!"

Ramgar nodded calmly. "Hm, I see. Well, there's no reason to worry. We're quite safe in here. Their crossbows can't do anything more than they've tried to do several times today, and yesterday, and the days before that!" The toys smiled a little and were welcomed by other Live toys, as Ramgar trotted off to talk to a sheep who needed his attention.

Simon and Teddy watched the activity around them, disconnected from it, now unsure what they were doing in this bizarre open place.

On the edge of the dome, Ess was still acting oddly. He was walking around the edge on his own, keeping himself mid-way between the perimeter guard sheep, talking to Live toys and looking thoughtfully out of the dome, his gaze zigzagging around the hill, up towards the ridge. As he stood by the edge of the dome, four or five toys walked up to him and stood side-by-side in a line without a word to each other.

"What are they *doing*?" asked Simon.

"I don't ffink I know..." said Teddy, his words drifting off as he continued to watch.

Less than a minute later it all became clear.

Another band of three Live toys arrived at the dome and Ramgar lowered the shield, and there was a cry.

"Now!"

A single word from Ess, which was the signal for him, and the Live toys with him, to rush out of the dome and into the scrub beyond. Ramgar shouted his objection; Simon bellowed, even Teddy called out for them to come back, but it was no good, Ramgar had to raise the shield again for the safety of all within, in case any of The Hordesmen were faking unconsciousness, and Ess was gone.

They asked around the dome for word of any who were missing, and concluded that Ess and five small teddies were gone, all taller than Ess, but none more than the height of a cat. A couple of teddies approached Ramgar to report that Ess had asked them what they thought about a direct attack on Arthdu. They had both replied they didn't believe in that sort of thing, but they hadn't thought anything of it since Ess had appeared to be merely gathering opinions. Obviously, he'd been doing far more than that.

As they were still trying to work out what Ess was doing, the first of the stunned Hordesmen began to stir. Within five minutes, another two were awake, and the three together methodically began to revive the others, all of them rubbing their sore heads and casting glances of pure hatred towards those inside the dome.

Simon was stomping up and down, frustrated, shouting and cursing and saying what idiots Ess and the teddies had been to leave, that it was dangerous, and that they would surely die for nothing. But Teddy wasn't so sure. To Teddy, it was simple: Ess was their friend; if he was gone then he was doing something to help them. Simon wanted to believe it, but how could a ten centimetre lump of plastic and five tiny teddies do anything? Even Teddy could see that Simon was worried for Ess' safety.

A sheep trotted up with more news. Five of the chippings from the mini Darkgate were missing. And it dawned on them what Ess was planning to do. And yet there had been no sign of an attack from them, even though they'd been outside the dome for several minutes.

Wherever they were, their safety became in greater doubt when reinforcement Hordesmen marched over the top of the hill and started their descent towards the dome. The full company of the original Hordesmen had now been revived, striding around, pointing at their colleagues marching down the hill, whispering to each other. The two groups of Arthdu's men met up and the original group were given replacement weapons, some taking crossbows, others preferring to brandish long, antique knives, which each carried strapped to their upper legs, but all of them were livid to have been stunned and humiliated. They separated into groups of three and four, and spread out left and right across the face of the hill down which the reinforcements had descended.

Without warning, a bolt of power shot out across the hillside from a group of three Hordesmen, slashed several hundred metres through the air, and disintegrated one of their companions. Immediately, the dead man's colleagues fired bolts in return, destroying all three of the first group in a fiery conflagration. Two more bolts of power flew from different locations, and in seconds Hordesmen across the hillside were firing at each other in a mass of roaring death.

"Cease fire!" bellowed a wise Hordesman. "Get down! They're making you fire at each other!" Most of The Hordesmen obeyed, with just a few stray shots in the next second or two. Ducking down as low as they could into the undergrowth, they looked around for signs of movement; they waited, scanned the hillside, hardly breathing, but saw nothing. The wise Hordesman called out again.

"Everyone fall back to my position, Now!" Still keeping low, The Hordesmen began to sprint, in twos and threes, towards his position, taking up a tight circular formation around him. They looked nervously around the hillside for any incoming flashes of power, but there were none. Within a couple of minutes, at least twenty Hordesmen had joined the circle, crossbows pointing outwards, visually searching the hill scrub for any sign of their attackers. A bird took off and a crossbow fired. It missed the bird but hit the ground nearby, detonated, and the bird was engulfed in the explosion that roared outwards and upwards. It fell to the ground, blackened and dead.

A few latecomers, who had run from almost the other side of the dome neared their compatriots, and the wise old Hordesman realised, with a look of horror, that he had made a mistake.

"It's a trap! Separate! NOW!" He yanked something from his cloak and shouted into it, "MASTER IT'S A TRA—" But it was too late: four blasts of light shot out from different locations in the undergrowth, trained on The Hordesmen's quivers. Three missed but one found its victim: a crossbow flint exploded, setting off the rest of the quiver's bolts, vastly enhancing the blast of heat and light, flashing out to consume the quivers of the other Hordesmen and, in an instant, a hot, bright-white blast scorched out across hundreds of metres of hillside scrub in all directions, annihilating everything in its instantly expanding circumference. It obliterated all the gathered Hordesmen, but it also destroyed those who had been walking to join them, and the shockwave hit Ramgar's shield.

The blast shook the dome and all its contents, to the very core of the mini Darkgate. A wave of heat passed through the inside of the dome but, as in Moccas, it was only highly uncomfortable, not lethal. Animals and Live toys screamed and bleated, but all were well, just very, very scared. Ess' plan had worked. Ramgar quickly trotted over to the mini Darkgate to check its status; the stones were still in one pile and essentially the proper colour. He bleated a grateful but sad, "Maaah".

Given the heat inside the dome, it seemed impossible that Ess or any of his helpers could have survived outside. Ramgar's face showed horror at what he had just witnessed, but he soon realised its implications.

"I think Ess may just have hastened our deaths," he said.

"Why do you say dat?" asked Teddy, panting with relief to be alive.

"Because they only thing that can reasonably happen next is for Arthdu to come here himself, full of anger at his lost Hordesmen, to kill us all."

Teddy gulped and translated for Simon.

They had to come to terms with a possible direct attack by Arthdu.

Simon looked around the dome for anything he could do to make himself useful, found nothing, and looked out of the dome in the vain hope of seeing movement and acting like a scout. Ramgar trotted up and down, deep in thought. Teddy looked at them both, concerned. Ramgar spoke.

"I'm sure Ess' reasons for committing suicide like that were something to do with proving his service to The Dolls with one last, grand gesture. He thought it would cleanse their memory of him, that it would earn their forgiveness. He might even be right. And yet his violence has probably killed us all, and he did this TO MAKE IT ALL BETTER FOR HIM WITH THE DOLLS?!" he boomed, with all the oratory power of a Victorian preacher. Sheep and toys looked at the ground; no one knew what to say. Teddy had never seen Ramgar raise his voice before; judging by the looks on the faces of the nearby sheep and toys, neither had they.

Teddy translated, and Simon replied.

"Ramgar, with respect, I don't agree. I think it was more than a selfish attempt to make amends. I think it was a misguided gift to us, using the only thing he knew: planning and strategy. What else could he do? He wasn't strong, but he was clever: I think he really believed this would help us, somehow. He'd *know* what would happen next. Maybe we're missing something? He admired you, Ramgar. He knew you couldn't do what he just did, or anything like it, so *he* did it instead." Simon too, found himself angry; angry at Ramgar, and not knowing why. Maybe he felt a pang of protection for the little figure who had just killed himself, but perhaps it was more because he saw something of himself in Ess.

Ramgar closed his eyes and took a moment. When he opened them again, he was more centred and calm.

"Perhaps you are right; perhaps not. However, I spoke in haste. I don't normally do that, but today is not a normal day. Whatever the reason for what Ess did, we need to protect ourselves against the oncoming attack."

::

About ten minutes later, a lone toy arrived at the dome and was allowed to enter. The toy, a dog with a large black nose, was brought to Ramgar and he saw the dog's fear; his need for peace and protection, and it revived the warmth and goodness under his aged, wooly exterior.

"Hello, my friend; it is good to see you made it safely. I apologise for what just happened, it was not our doing."

The dog quickly bowed to Ramgar and thanked him for his protection, before blurting out a warning.

"There are more men coming!" he said, nervously. "When I was up on the ridge, I could see them riding across the valley behind me … gaining on me … coming this way. They'll soon be here, if they keep riding at that pace!"

"It's okay. We're safe in here, for now," assured Ramgar, somewhat unconvincingly. "But may I ask: did you notice if one of the riders looked a fair bit larger than the others, in both height and girth?"

The dog thought, and nodded.

"Yes, I think so."

"Uh-oh," said Teddy.

Within a minute, fear had spread throughout the dome: Arthdu was coming. Sheep were bleating and running around, toys huddled together, and fear began to divide the two groups. Sheep questioned the toys' right to be in a Flock dome; the toys retorted that they'd been invited by Ramgar himself, so maybe the sheep were just a bit stupid, and they taunted them that at least toys didn't go around killing dogs and humans. Ramgar had to intervene.

"Listen to me EVERYONE!" he bellowed and bleated. "We are all in this together. We share this safety, and we share a common enemy. We need to look after each other — we are stronger when we stand *together*!"

"Maaah! Teddy started it all," shouted a sheep. "He messed up Maaroon's Flock!"

Ramgar was opening his mouth to retort, but a Live toy was faster.

"Rubbish!" he shouted. "It makes me wonder who's in control of all these sheep? Are they going to turn on us, like they do in England, eh?!"

Ramgar quickly responded to them.

"Both of you listen! Teddy put Arthdu to sleep for *three years*. He has saved sheep and toys alike from three years of Arthdu's oppression; we've had three years of peace because of Teddy, who is a Live toy and a friend of sheep. Teddy once told me, in tears, that he would die to protect a Flock, and I know from my heart that is *absolutely* true."

Ramgar paused and looked around, to test how well is words were working. There were no retaliatory comments.

"Now listen. It is my view that Arthdu has been using the

Darkgate to affect the sheep in Western England, in an attempt to induce fear and panic in the humans of that land, to make those people leave. If I'm right, he has a plan to invade and take over Western England for himself. I have no idea how he will do that, but he would not have begun to move if he didn't have that part of the plan in place too. When he attacks them, many will die: many sheep, many toys and many humans. All of them are just pawns in Arthdu's plans. So we will resist Arthdu, and we will do so together, because we all need each other; because we all need The Way, and because we are the best hope for those here in Llandegley, and our sisters and brothers in the West of England — and we will *win* because even the dimmest light can banish the darkness!"

A huge cheer went up, and although there wasn't an immediate embracing between sheep and toys, Ramgar's words had prevented any further in-fighting, for now.

A sheep ran up bleating uncontrollably. Ramgar, met her and touched her, nose-to-nose, to calm her. She settled.

"Crow says there's a human on a horse nearly at the top of the ridge, leading a force of Hordesmen — but he's not like any human Crow has seen before! I think, I think … Maaah! Maaah! Maaah!" and she lost control again. For a split-second, even Ramgar looked worried: there was only one being answering that description.

"Perhaps we will find out whether peace is stronger than war now," he said.

Teddy gulped.

Simon's confusion, due to the lack of translation, was resolved when Arthdu rode calmly over the brow of the hill, silhouetted by the darkening sky behind him.

- CHAPTER 10 -

Meeting Emily

The car's drone would almost have been soothing if they hadn't been on the way to meet a stranger in Hereford. Joanne had decided to take the Builth Wells route to Hereford, via Llanbedr, to avoid Llandegley: the idea of driving near Arthdu did not sit well with her. As they drove, Joanne and Gundy thought which, it turned out, was not a good thing — by the time they had crossed the border into England, they had convinced themselves that the meeting with Emily could well be a trap.

To make matters worse, as they passed over the border, things changed. They both felt a growing sizzle of power; in Joanne's case it was discerned as fear: her eyes wider; her breathing faster; in Gundy's case it felt more like adrenaline. Joanne looked around, hunted and distracted. Toys lay discarded and motionless on the ground outside houses, and the sight of them flushed her with fear. She imagined them creeping towards her, reaching out to her with dead eyes and fixed smiles, trying to touch her ... she screamed and accelerated the car to escape, feeling the panic rising. Puffing, she noticed Gundy out of the corner of her eye, gripped the steering wheel with terror, and braked hard ready to flee, but before the car had stopped, Gundy called to her:

"Joanne! Look at me. No, *look* at me — it's okay!"

With great difficulty, Joanne forced a look, and Gundy smiled and raised her paw. Joanne squeezed her eyes ready to die... but what she felt was a soothing glow, like a warm breeze flowing through her body, from front to back, and from that moment she had no further difficulty. Gundy couldn't explain how she knew what to do, and Joanne couldn't say what had changed her; all she knew was she was at peace for the first time that day.

After they resumed their journey, Gundy hid herself under Joanne's thin cardigan. If anyone saw her here, they were likely to accuse Joanne of being the worst ever mother for having a soft toy in the car. And if anyone should see that Gundy was a *Live* toy … it wasn't a good idea to think any further than that. Unfortunately, both Gundy and Joanne had already quietly thought well beyond that point to themselves.

The longer route had made them a quarter of an hour late for their cafe gathering, so hurried across the old bridge, along the streets of small shops and estate agents, across the cathedral grounds, and down the centuries-old lane that led to their meeting place.

Joanne had arranged a plan with Gundy: Gundy would wait outside with Oli, hidden under his blanket in the pushchair while Bertie held the door open, and Joanne would enter the cafe to find Emily to check all was well. If there was any trouble, Joanne would shout to Gundy, who would jump up out of the pushchair and use her Darkgate stone to fire through the cafe windows at the walls, causing confusion and allowing Joanne the chance to run out, grab the boys and escape. Joanne was frustrated at having to expose the boys to even this degree of danger — the idea had been for Gwion to look after the boys outside while Joanne dashed into the cafe — but she knew Gundy would do everything possible to protect them, and there was a new calm in her that she attributed to the influence of whatever Gundy had done to her in the car.

Joanne and Bertie opened the cafe door. A little bell tinkled above, and the chinks and tinks of spoons and crockery played louder in their ears; seconds later the warm aroma of coffee, tea and cakes triggered fleeting thoughts of food: Joanne moved Bertie next to the open door.

"Now Bertie, stay here and hold the door open. Can you do that?"

"Yes Mummy," smiled Bertie, already letting the door swing

back to the half-open position.

"No, you have to hold it fully open for mummy; if you can do that I'll give you *six* Jaffa cakes! ... Fully open, that's it."

He jammed his foot on the floor like a door stop. It was a little insecure but Bertie was very committed to the idea of eating Jaffa cakes, and he did a good enough job.

"Now, Bertie. Look around at all the people sitting down; can you see anyone with sparkles?" Bertie looked at each person in turn with a furrowed brow.

"No mummy," he replied.

"Good boy," she said with a smile and kissed him on the head. "Now, remember keep the door open and think of Jaffa cakes!"

Joanne scanned the cafe for the people she was hoping to meet, and scurried to the back, towards the only table with customers who approximately matched: a woman not much older than her, perhaps thirty-five to forty years old, and a younger woman somewhere between fifteen and twenty. But were they really mother and daughter? Certainly none of the other clientele matched the description: there were two older ladies engrossed in an important-looking conversation; a group of four young girls giggling and shrieking about something; a man and a woman in their fifties quietly drinking coffee, each reading, and a lone woman in her late seventies or early eighties looking wistfully out of the window. Joanne worked her way past chairs and people to the pair on the back table, glancing repeatedly over her shoulder to Bertie manning the door, smiling. She turned back to face the couple.

"Hi! I'm Joanne," she said, half-expecting them to look surprised and disconcerted.

"Hello! I recognised you from your video. Sorry we didn't say anything, just checking you out, actually. Lovely to meet you! I'm Emily and this is my daughter, Sophie. Yes, I know. I'm too young to have such a grown-up daughter, but I was young when I had her, you know. Spot of trouble. Wonderful man, quite blew my smokestack, but didn't last of course. She's the best daughter a mother could have though and … I believe I'm rabbiting."

"She does that," said Sophie, patting her mother on the arm with a smile and a trace of teenage embarrassment.

"Now then," continued Emily. "Where shall we go? Can't stay here of course. I suggest the lawn outside the cathedral. Open space. No one to overhear us, and yet lots of people around if any of us try anything naughty; there will be witnesses!" Emily's eyes twinkled in a fun and yet steely manner. It seemed nothing very much worried this woman.

Five minutes later, they had almost reached the Cathedral grounds. Emily had hardly stopped telling Bertie what a big, brave boy he'd been holding the door open for his mummy, while Sophie walked with him, holding his hand. Remembering Rhiannon's behaviour in flashbacks, Joanne kept an eye on Sophie, while pushing Oli and the still-hidden Gundy, and was trying to keep pace with Emily.

They stopped the pushchair in the middle of an empty expanse of grass near the cathedral's main entrance, and they all sat down. Baby Oli lay on the grass and kicked his feet and rolled around, while Bertie made daisy chains with Sophie in the late afternoon warmth. Only Gundy was unhappy, lying under the blanket in Oli's pushchair tapping her paws together, bored.

It was time for Emily and Joanne to talk.

"Emily," began Joanne. "You've been having a few difficulties recently, and so have we. We're hoping that we can help each other."

"Of course, that would be nice," agreed Emily. "And I'm beginning to believe that you're not about to arrest us or attack us … and hopefully you're becoming more certain that we're on the level too?"

"Yes, I think so. I'd got myself quite worried on the journey over here. But now's the time for us both to nail our colours to the mast. If you'll look into the pushchair, there's someone you need to meet."

"Exciting!" whispered Emily, clapping her hands together. She jumped up and she and Joanne looked into the pushchair. Joanne pulled back the covers to reveal Gundy, who was not looking very happy.

"Hello, I'm Gundy. I'm not normally this hot."

"Oh fantastic!" whispered Emily, gripping the pushchair's handle with glee. "Lovely to meet you, Gundy; sorry you're stuck in there. Marvellous idea though. Maybe we could get a pushchair for some of my 'boys' to travel around in ... Sophie, dear," said Emily with a cheeky smile. "Would you mind pushing a pushchair?"

"Mother!" said Sophie, wondering what people would think.

"So, what can we do for you, Joanne?" asked Emily, as if she was asking what Joanne would like from her shop. Emily sat down on the ground close to Joanne.

"First, there's a Live dog called Rufus. He's been hurt and needs someone to mend him. Can you help?"

"Oh gosh, poor thing. Absolutely I can help! I used to make my own line of soft toys for the shop, completely from scratch. Always carry a sewing kit in my handbag. Habit. So we should be able to sort him out in a few minutes. Where is he?"

"Well, that brings me to the second thing. Have you ever seen any Live dolls?"

"Dolls? Really? Wow!" said Emily, with obvious awe in her voice. "Live dolls are *rare*. I mean I've heard of them two or three times, but never seen any. And those I've heard about all seem to be in East Asia for some reason."

"Well, they're real, and they're near here, and they also need your help — but in a different way to Rufus: their human mother was killed."

"Killed! My goodness! Well, I'll have to make sure that doesn't happen to me! What do they need from me though?"

"They lived in a large house, which is to be sold, and they

need someone to buy the house and protect them."

"You want me to buy a *house*! Good grief! You don't want much do you!" laughed Emily. "How much is it worth?"

"According to the estate agent website, £950,000."

"Okay. Sounds like it might be quite a nice place. Could be an investment. Worth taking a look. I might need you to tell me more about the whole 'murder of their mother' thing before I can raise some enthusiasm about this though."

"Hm. Well, it's not totally clear what happened but, if you do buy the house, by the time the sale is complete it's very likely that either we'll all be dead or it will no longer be a problem."

"You know, Joanne, you're not selling this very well. Still, since I don't intend to die quite yet, and it sounds like a possible opportunity for me. If it looks good, do you think we could wangle it so I could stay there tonight? You said it's empty? Sophie and I can't really use our house outside Tewksbury at the moment — vigilantes you know — and we have a lot of toys, locked safely in a stock room, some Live, some not, so, later on, it might be a safe place for them. I was thinking about a hotel, or renting something, but this might be better. The money's not a problem as long as I like it and it looks like it will be an investment. Oh, and Sophie's now of an age when she'd like to start her own business — seventeen you know! How did she grow so big?! So I've been thinking about setting her up with a shop while I strike out and do other exciting things … perhaps like starting a refugee camp for Live toys!" Emily whispered the last few words in Joanne's ear. Joanne smiled.

"Have you got a phone, Emily?" asked Joanne.

"Yes. Do you want to make a call?"

"No. Not at all; in fact, I think they can track you from it when it's turned on. Could you turn it off?"

"Oh. Really? Oh, gosh. Yes, I suppose I'd better. But I was going to phone my solicitor. He's a good man, I've known him for years. Has his own Live toys, and has taken a few of mine off me in recent days, because of the Silly People."

"You could use one of the phone boxes over there," suggested Joanne.

Emily nodded and walked off to make the call. She hoped, somehow, to take possession of Mother's house today. When she returned she said that the solicitor had explained it would obviously be very hard to arrange in one afternoon, but he would make some discrete calls; perhaps they could arrange to rent the house while the purchase went through. Since there were no other people involved, and no mortgage required, he thought it might be possible. It was amazing what money could do. He had advised her she would need to do the whole thing as a trust, so her name wasn't involved, for now at least.

Despite, or perhaps because of, Emily's willingness to help, Joanne still found herself a little untrusting, even though she already enjoyed her company — it was just that failure to detect double dealing could be fatal, and that risk, however remote, was obviously not one to be dismissed lightly: it was hard to forget what had happened in Llangurig. However, she reminded herself that she'd seen a news article about Emily, that Emily and Sophie must have been through hard times as a result, and that she'd seen Emily's picture on Gwion's computer so she was surely the real thing. Moreover, Emily had had no reason whatsoever to trust Joanne, and yet had seemed to do so.

"Emily," began Joanne.

"Yes."

"Who's after you?"

"Ah, well, mostly vigilantes, but the police came around for a cup of tea yesterday."

"A cup of tea?"

"And a chat. Well, mostly a chat. They didn't touch their tea. A little bit rude really."

"What did they want to know?"

"It was strange. As far as I can see, I haven't broken any laws whatsoever, and yet they kept telling me I was endangering the public and I should stop helping toys unless I wanted to be arrested."

"Is it possible they are following you?"

"Well, it's *possible*. They are quite resourceful you know, the police," said Emily wryly.

"Indeed," agreed Joanne. "I've seen the news today and a lot of it is about Live toys so, if you're well-known for looking after such toys ..."

Emily nodded. "We need to do something that would throw them off the scent if they're following me." She brought her finger to her lips to think, and her brow furrowed.

Joanne spoke first. "Um, this is going to sound a bit cloak-and-dagger: can you disguise yourselves?"

"Ooh! Fun! Yes, I suppose that might work, if you could go and buy us some clothes and hats and things. *We* can't do it because they'd be following us and they'd see what we'd bought."

"Ah. Do you think they're watching us all right now?" asked Joanne, looking at the people sitting near them on the grass, those standing looking at the Cathedral, and people waiting on the street. "Because if they are watching you then I suppose they're watching *all* of us, and that would make it hard for us to buy things."

"True. Fiddlesticks ... Okay, where's your car?"

"In the little car park, just over the old bridge."

"Damn, and we're in a multi-story car park ... must be half a mile back there, so we can't just rush for a car either."

Sophie looked up from playing with Bertie. "I could go back to our car and drive it around a bit? That might make some of them follow me," she said with a smile.

"You've only just passed your test!"

"I need the practice then! Also they won't be looking for Joanne's car, so you should go with her," Sophie added, waiting for her mother's next move. Her mother smiled.

"You're my daughter alright!" she laughed. "Okay, but please be careful. Don't drive round and round in Hereford, just drive to Ledbury or something, it's easier driving. And go and stay with Lucy tonight."

"Okay!" grinned Sophie, victorious. But she had a thought. "Oh, you'll need to walk to the car with me, or they'll follow you and Joanne too; I suppose Joanne will need to pick you up once I've gone — and I'll have to make a pretend mummy in the seat next to me somehow … ah, yeah, I think I can manage that with the horse-mucking coat in the boot but … yes, stuffed with the emergency blanket. What do you think?"

"Excellent," said Joanne. "Sounds good. But I was thinking that the other thing we should do is take an indirect route to The Dolls. I'm pretty sure there's a back road; I'll have to look it up on a map. If we do that then we'll be able to see if someone's following us — we'll be taking a meandering route that no one else should take," she finished, pleased with her line of reasoning.

"And if there is someone following us," added Emily. "Can we do that taking-a-turn-really-quickly-to-lose-them thing? That would be cool!" Emily was enjoying this a bit too much for Joanne's taste.

A teenager walked by, holding her miniskirt down to stop the wind. It was enough for them to notice the cooling breeze that was now whispering across the cathedral green, and the darkening clouds.

"It's going to rain," stated Emily, looking up. "We should make a move."

::

They separated. Sophie and Emily walked back to their car. Emily retrieved the coat and blanket from the boot and made a rough dummy of herself out of view while Sophie 'checked the oil' with the car bonnet up so it was impossible for anyone to see what Emily was doing. All Emily had to do was sit the dummy in the seat, keep low and hide behind the car next to them while Sophie put the bonnet down, got in and drove away.

Ten minutes later Emily left her hiding place, walked out of the back of the car park where Joanne was waiting, and sat down in the passenger seat of Gwion's waiting car, next to Joanne. She turned to wave a greeting at the boys in the back and they all set off on their slightly-longer-than-usual journey to The Dolls.

Emily kept checking for cars following them. There was a red Renault immediately behind them, then a silver estate, and what seemed to be a dark green Volvo of some sort behind that, although it was hard for Emily to see. After a couple of miles of countryside, they turned right onto the Golden Valley road. The red car and the estate didn't follow, but the Volvo did. It kept its distance. It was enough to concern Emily.

The drive down the pleasant winding Golden Valley road was tense under under the threat of the chasing Volvo then, quite unexpectedly, it turned left in the village of Peterchurch and there was no one behind them at all.

Emily wasn't convinced. "We need to find somewhere to hide the car and wait for a few minutes, just to be sure." Joanne nodded and started to look for somewhere that would do. After a minute Emily shouted. "There!" and Joanne spun the wheel and skidded, only just under control, into a stoney car park surrounded on all sides by a Forestry Commission wood, with just the narrow, overgrown opening through which they had roared. Joanne hid the car behind a screen of trees and they waited. Thirty seconds later a black Peugeot estate shushed by with two men in the front seats. Another few seconds and a little old lady driving a small rounded car, then nothing for over twenty seconds. Joanne and Emily looked at each other.

"Those two men. Do you think they were following us?" asked Joanne.

"It's a possibility." Emily glanced sideways. She thought. "I suppose they'd turn round, and we'd see them pass us again. Shall we wait?"

"I'm not in a hurry, though Oli will need a feed soon."

Emily smiled kindly.

Two minutes later the black Peugeot, drove past them again, in the opposite direction, containing two concerned looking men.

"That *was* them! Well! Joanne! We *were* being followed! How super!"

Joanne smiled only slightly: "We should wait a few seconds, so they can't see us in their rear-view mirror."

"Quite right." Emily nodded, and they waited ... "There, that should be long enough."

Joanne edged the car over to the road, pulled out and accelerated away.

::

Fifteen minutes later, Joanne and Emily were struggling through the wood above the Dolls' house. Emily carried Oli in her arms while Joanne led Bertie through the trees hand-in-hand, carrying Gundy under her arm. They made slow progress.

"At least we've got Rhiannon's sat nav," said Joanne without thinking. Then she screwed up her eyes in stupidity.

"Who's Rhiannon," asked Emily.

Joanne swallowed.

"Rhiannon was ... um ... killed, earlier today. It was horrible."

Emily stopped walking and her mouth opened a crack.

"It was *my* fault," Gundy cried out from under Joanne's arm. "Rhiannon was threatening us, and was very likely going to kill us all. My job is to protect Bertie. He's my owner. They'd already killed The Dolls' mother. I had one chance," and Gundy burst in to tears. Joanne had never seen her cry like that before. She let go of Bertie's hand, set Gundy down, and reached out to stroke her head.

"No! Don't! I don't deserve it. I'm a murderer" Gundy called, a little too loud for comfort.

"Shh!" said Emily, partly to soothe and partly to stop Gundy from revealing their location. "I'm not saying it's right what you did … but … I'm having a hard time thinking what I would have done differently if someone was threatening Sophie."

"We're not saying it's right either," agreed Joanne. "We've talked about it and the alternative would have been to have let the children be hurt or killed."

"Well, look, we can talk about this later,"said Emily, her expression fully grim for the first time. "Let's just continue down to The Dolls."

There were no jolly smiles and no sense of camaraderie, just a feeling that they had a job to do. They trudged down the hill, through the trees, crunching over twigs, rustling through leaves, and pushing aside greenery that blocked their path. It seemed to Emily and Joanne to take a lot longer than the minutes that passed on Emily's Steiff watch.

"We're nearly there now," said Joanne at last. Emily nodded without smiling.

"Ooh, sparkles!" said Bertie happily, pointing towards some trees next to the perimeter fence around The Dolls' manor. Joanne's face flashed with terror.

"GET DOWN!" she shouted, grabbing Bertie to her and pulling Emily to the ground so that she lost her grip on Oli, who tumbled half on top of Joanne and half onto the ground. Something shot over their heads, and a moment later there was a huge explosion behind them, where the Hordesman's arrow stone had hit a tree fifty metres or so from their position. The force of the explosion, and a spray of forest fragments, blasted over the top of them; if they hadn't been on the ground already, the wooden shrapnel would have blasted into them, but instead they suffered no more than a few scratches and ringing ears.

Gundy leapt up, ran a few metres to the left and held her Darkgate stone like a compass again, and discharged three shots in the direction of their attacker, who was still roughly where Bertie had pointed. Although much weaker than the exploding Darkgate bolt, the first two blasts felled trees but the third thudded into the ground throwing up earth and sticks. The assailant screamed.

"Quickly, give me Arthgwyn's dart gun, Joanne!" demanded Gundy.

Joanne rummaged in her bag with shaky hands, pulled it out and threw it to Gundy, who caught it and padded off through the undergrowth towards the attacker. After a few seconds, she had disappeared into the bracken. There was shouting. The click of the sleep gun being fired twice. A blast from the Darkgate stone. They listened but only heard the sounds of the wood, and Bertie and Oli whimpering against their mother. Small twigs cracked, bracken rustled and Gundy appeared.

"He's asleep now. And I really mean asleep; he's not dead. A tree had fallen on him but he's okay. I blasted it so he'll be able to free himself when he wakes up tomorrow. I couldn't lift his crossbow though."

Joanne opened her arms to Gundy, who walked over and accepted the affection this time, then she held Gundy and the boys close to her. Emily walked over to them both, knelt down and put her arms around them all.

"Thank you, you amazing bear. I'm sorry. I'm sorry for not understanding what you're going through."

"It's still not right what I did though!" pleaded Gundy with big eyes.

"It's in the past. You're doing your best. That's all anyone can do." Emily breathed deeply. "I'd better earn my keep. Shall I grab his weapon?"

"If you don't mind," said Joanne. "But can you take Gundy with you, just in case?"

"Of course," said Emily putting out her arms and picking her up.

They rustled over to the still-smoking tree to locate the crossbow and quiver, next to the sleeping Hordesman. Putting Gundy down, Emily slipped the quiver over her left shoulder, and the crossbow's strap over her right, then picked Gundy up to carry her again.

"Bertie, are you alright sweet pea?" asked Joanne, hugging Oli to her, stroking his soft baby hair.

"Scary! Don't like it!" said Bertie.

"I know, I know. It was a bit scary, but you were a wonderful boy and you kept us all safe! You're a very good boy!" Bertie smiled between sniffs and hugs, and they and Oli made their way down to The Dolls' fence. Meeting up with Emily and Gundy when they got there. Carrying children and soft toys, the adults lifted their legs over the wire and descended into the garden.

::

At first, the Dolls' servants had been shocked to find several strangers in their garden, for the second time in one day. However, Gundy had visited the dolls before and was able to assure the servants that all was safe, and that the two big and two small humans were here for a reason. So, after a little to-ing and fro-ing, everyone was soon sitting in the gazebo taking tea and eating biscuits in the early evening air.

They each introduced themselves; Emily bubbled happily and admired The Dolls, who, in return soon realised that loving this woman might rather easy... Emily marvelled at The Dolls' beauty, their elegance, their darling little outfits and, more impressively, their cool-but-forceful ability to control the area in and around Bredwardine, with extensive influence beyond — and still to have time for tea.

As the last sips of tea were being drunk, Rufus chose the moment to limp out from under the seats where he had been resting. He hadn't wanted to dampen the mood, but now the conversation was in a lull …

"Hi. I'm Rufus, and you must be Emily?"

"That's right … Oh! Look at you! What happened?!"

"A garden fork."

"Ouch! You poor thing! Well I've got my sewing things; I think I have a job to do, yes? Do you mind?"

"Not at all," said Rufus, wincing slightly at the thought.

"Of course, come here; let's get this over with."

Emily stood up, then knelt down in front of the shaggy, damaged dog, gently slid her two palms underneath him, and scooped him up into her arms.

"Come here, my love. I'll make it all better now. Shh. You'll be fine."

The Dolls looked on, their eyes misting over with emotion, now truly hopeful that they had found someone who would look after them in the way they had always wanted.

"Emily," said Agnes.

"Yes," acknowledged Emily, while digging out her sewing kit from her handbag.

"This is a big thing to ask, and we've only just met you, so please feel free to refuse."

"Go on."

"Do you think, at some point, you might agree to try being our Mother?"

Emily put the sewing kit down on her lap and looked at Agnes with her head slightly on one side, heart filling with emotion. She would have paid any price to help them now. She agreed. Both Emily and The Dolls were overjoyed to have found each other, clapping, crying and exclaiming like Edwardian schoolgirls. Emily gently shook Agnes' tiny hand, and the deal was done.

::

As Emily carefully sewed Rufus back to health, Joanne realised there were two problems: First, since Emily would be staying with The Dolls, how could Joanne manage to usher Oli and Bertie and all their things back through the wood to the car on her own? What if there were another Hordesman, or if the one in the wood had woken up early? And second, how could Emily contact Sophie to let her know she was safe without revealing her new location? However if they phoned Sophie, even from the house phone, it was likely the police would be able to trace the position of Sophie's phone and, from that, back again to Emily's location.

Emily suggested Simon might be the solution to both problems, since he could come over to pick up Joanne and the boys, and he could phone Sophie from Llandegley and give her some sort of coded message.

Before they could do anything, however, Gundy felt something … Darkgate-y. She was just about to warn them when an arrow shot across the lawn, slammed into her stomach, and sent her flying backwards against the wall of the gazebo, smacking her head so badly that she lost consciousness immediately. Her paw fell open and the Darkgate stone dropped onto the floor. The arrow, tipped with its own stone rebounded from Gundy and clattered to the floorboards, having failed to penetrate Gundy's fur (due to its bluntness) or explode (due to her softness).

All eyes darted to the flowerbeds beyond the lawn, over which a Hordesman strode. He looked down at the flowers around him and ground one of the more delicate specimens into the dirt with his heel, then he looked up and sneered at them.

"So, it didn't … go … off," he said slowly. "Oh well. I'm a fantastic aim though, aren't I? Must have been a hundred feet!" he laughed, sticking his tongue out at the same time and waving a makeshift bow at them. "I *live* in a wood you know. I can make these things in my sleep. You *idiots*! And I always keep a few chippings spare in my pocket. Shame your dart gun didn't work very well on me eh? Not human see! Ha! At last I get some ACTION! Do you have any idea how long I've had to hang around your stupid house, you prissy little cows? Eh? *On my own*! I'll tell you: three YEARS!"

He walked slowly towards them, grinning with his black teeth. Emily eyed the crossbow and quiver she'd retrieved, lying on the grass, well out of reach. A fly buzzed around the Hordesman's face, intoxicated by his smell, and he watched it and stroked back his slick, obsidian hair, preening, then grabbed at the fly ripping it from the air and crushing it in his hand.

He looked up and they knew they were all going to die. Drawing his arm across his nose, he steadied himself and raised the bow at the gazebo: there was no escape; they were trapped in a shooting gallery. Joanne stood in front of the boys but knew she could not protect them.

"You should've killed me when you 'ad the chance up in the wood," he derided. "I'm goin' to enjoy this." He licked his lips and slowly, pointedly, aimed his bow, teasing them by gradually pulling the string more and more taught.

He focused fully on the gazebo. The grass rustled around him. He glanced down. Ten six-inch, steel blades rushed in and shone and were lifted above the lawn. Ten unseen creatures slashed in turn at the Hordesman's calves, spilling blood; severing, and maiming so that he screamed and stumbled and fell to his left and hit the ground reaching for his ankles. But ten blades kept hacking and stabbing and hacking. The Hordesman fought, and bled in a growing number of places, and tried to grasp his fallen bow with chopped fingers, and struggled, and bled and twitched. And then he stopped. The knives disappeared back into the grass and ten slight movements retreated and could not be seen.

Joanne felt queasy.

"What was that?!" she trembled.

"I think," said Agnes. "It will suffice to say, the servants recently found some tools in the tool shed, and felt we should be protected. But who can say for sure who did such a horrible, timely thing? It is impossible to see; someone really should cut the grass."

Many of The Dolls had hands to mouths, or hands flapping air at themselves, but none complained. Joanne looked over to Emily, to gauge her reaction. She was biting her lower lip, but nodding in agreement. Having faced death earlier, she was already beginning to be inured by the war in which they were all a part. Joanne said nothing.

- CHAPTER 11 -

The Hordesmen's Master

Judging by the steady charcoal and slate greys of the sky, it would rain soon, but first Teddy and Simon were going to be attacked by a Yorebear with the full power of an entire Darkgate at his disposal. Simon glanced at his watch, as if finding out that it was seven in the evening would be useful in some way.

In Simon's pocket, his phone vibrated. He pulled it out to see who was calling; it was Joanne. He pressed to accept the call, and put the phone to his ear.

"Hello?"

"Hello, it's me," she said, quietly. "We're stuck at The Dolls … and it's been a bit, well… How are *you* getting on? Any chance you could do us a little favour and pick us up?"

"Um, not really, no. I'm afraid Arthdu's just riding slowly down the hillside towards us."

There was silence at Joanne's end of the line.

"Oh my goodness."

"Yes," said Simon, his jaw tense at the sight of the Yorebear trotting ever closer. "Give the boys my love. Please. Hold them, and tell them I love them."

There was another silence. Simon continued.

"I'll be honest, I don't know what we can do, but if we can just stop him …"

"I know, I know. But every part of me wants you to run away right now and never to go back."

"I want to. I feel useless here. How can I help? I can't use a Darkgate stone, I'm the tallest creature around, so I'm probably going to be the first target, and earlier I tripped over a Live elephant and nearly broke my ankle, so I'm limping. The elephant wasn't too happy either."

"Can you ... *hobble* away?" Joanne asked. There was a pause; they both squeaked pathetically at the gallows humour.

"Seriously? No. Quite apart from the fact we're surrounded by Hordesmen; if Ramgar, or Teddy, or these sheep and toys need me, even for a moment, then that might be the moment that turns things around."

At the other end of the phone, Joanne made a sad little sound. She swallowed.

"I'll see you soon, okay? Hm? Soon. Okay?"

"Okay ... Love you."

"You too."

Simon ended the call and slipped the phone back into his pocket. For some reason he noticed he was hungry, yet he didn't want to eat a thing.

Arthdu wasn't in any particular rush. He was sizing them up, looking at each individual inside the dome. It was like he let his horse take a step per heartbeat, as it gradually edged lower through the heather and ferns.

Some distance down the slope, he pulled the reins to stop his horse. Arthdu looked around, nose in the air, almost sniffing. His Hordesmen stopped and turned to see what their master was doing. He could sense *something*. Scratching the bridge of his nose, his forehead furrowed and he looked around, lifting a now glowing hand out in front of him to search more keenly.

Whoever was hiding knew they were out of time; a blast of light shot out from the undergrowth, fifty or sixty metres to the right of Arthdu, perfectly on target. It slammed into him ... and did him no harm at all. He had his own defensive shield surrounding him.

The force of it did, however, knock him sideways off his horse and he fell onto the heather of the hill. Another shot, fired in haste, missed Arthdu but destroyed his horse, obliterating it in a whinny and a slash of yellow and white; another shot hit the ground nearby, but by now Arthdu was ready — he fired back, and the difference in force was immense: car-sized chunks of ground and vegetation were ripped out of the hill near the hidden attacker, in violent, roaring, blasts. The lone, remaining teddy fired again, almost hitting Arthdu's left shoulder, but now Arthdu had him — there was a rustle and Arthdu flicked his hand to position and fired again, ripping the hillside once more, then he and the remaining Hordesmen waited. All those in the dome held their breath, but there was no reply. Once more, Arthdu held his hand out, this time to feel for the teddy's stone. He indicated its position to the Hordesman standing nearest to the last blast impact, and watched him while he retrieved the stone, which was undamaged and as stable as when Ramgar had retrieved it. Arthdu lifted his hand into the air, ready, the Hordesman tossed the stone, and his master caught it, without the slightest change in expression. He slipped it into a pocket in his fur jerkin and turned to face Ramgar's dome.

"Nice try!" called Arthdu. "I wasn't expecting that from you, Ramgar; I thought you were weaker than that!"

"That wasn't my doing!" shouted Ramgar.

"Hah!" Arthdu boomed back. "There we are then. I didn't think so." He began to walk down the hill, just the sound of his feet brushing through the grass and undergrowth, and stopped a hundred metres or so above them.

"So. Are you all ready to die?" he asked calmly, looking around at those sheltered inside the dome.

No one answered; their fear wouldn't let them. Arthdu snarled in disgust and raised his hand: he breathed in deeply.

His entire body began to glow with the power of the Llandegley Darkgate. And he fired. White-red, hatred blasting out of his hand, shaking the entire dome, making an eardrum-splitting din that had toys, sheep, everyone screaming, bleating, certain that this was the end. It was just a matter of time; how could a handful of stones resist the power of a Darkgate …

The pathetic feeling of powerlessness that Teddy felt was almost as bad as the terror. He wished he could feel like he'd felt when he'd touched the Darkgate, full of anything-is-possible, full of power-and-potential. Suddenly, his stuffing filled with a spark of excitement: that was it! Paws over his ears, he ran towards the mini Darkgate in the centre of the dome. He reached it and immediately thrust his hand onto the pile of stones that was no more than half his height. Its contents rushed into him, the stones started to glow, and he could feel its pain. It wanted to fight back, it wanted to stop Arthdu, it wanted to stop him from controlling its bigger, related, stone parent. Teddy closed his eyes and felt through the air and ether for a connection to the main Llandegley Darkgate, he cocked his head to one side and searched for the link that Robertson had told them was to be found between the Pearls of Stone. The mini Darkgate helped him and he could see, in his mind's eye, white tendrils of tiny lights, flailing out of the mini Darkgate, first one way and then back again, like fingers trying to find a connection.

Teddy concentrated on trying to organise a flow of light from the mini Darkgate to the main Darkgate. He didn't know why, but he knew it was what he needed to do. He focussed, strained, pushed with his mind. And the lights began to swirl, in the darkness, slowly at first, then faster and faster. They gathered into a single, twisting stream, became coherent, and flowed away. He had sent a signal. A few seconds later a torrent of light returned and reached the light he controlled: Teddy could see the whole thing; the two Darkgates were now connected … and he could tell them what to do because, more than anything, they *wanted* him to be here with them, taking control. So he told the main Darkgate to stop sending strength to Arthdu. There was a thrashing, a difficulty, almost a pain, as if it didn't dare to cut off the power, but it obeyed and the huge flow that supplied Arthdu was vastly curtailed. The beam he was still firing at the dome, weakened and no longer made a noise because it was less powerful than the shield.

"No! NO! That is not allowed, it's *my* Darkgate, not yours!" shouted Arthdu.

Arthdu could see he had to fight, so he lowered his arm and closed his eyes to try to concentrate on his Darkgate and regain control, now raising both hands towards Teddy. But Teddy couldn't see; he was one with the joined Darkgate, feeling what it felt. He could simply feel the to and fro of his wishes and thoughts facing growing interference. The stones called out to Teddy for help, but it was no good. Teddy hadn't had hundreds of years of experience of connecting to a Darkgate. A mind-splitting, deep voice rose up inside his head, "I HAVE CONTROL!"

Through his dwindling link to the partially unified Darkgate, Teddy felt the blast leave Arthdu's hand. He tried to stop it, but it was in flight, loose and flashing through the air. He felt it slam into the dome, envelop it from side to side and turn it to a weak plasma which dissipated in seconds. The dome was gone; Teddy lost concentration, fell backwards onto his bottom, and his access to the mini Darkgate was no more. When he looked down, the stones were dark brown, almost black, peppered with tiny holes. They were not entirely exhausted, but they were useless against Arthdu's power.

The Horde roared in excitement and approval and started to fire at anything inside the dome's now non-existent perimeter: in seconds, Live toys and sheep were being slaughtered.

"Get down Simon!" shouted Teddy.

Simon was already ducking having been nearly hit twice in as many seconds and was floored by a nearby explosion.

"Stop!" shouted Ramgar in a massive voice, loud enough to be heard over the noise.

Arthdu complied and raised his hand to stop his forces. Silence fell.

"What do you want, freak?" said Arthdu.

Ramgar trotted towards him, unconcerned.

"If you want to kill me, then kill me," said Ramgar, smiling. "Leave these others alone, they are nothing to you."

"Unfortunately for you and for them, I do not agree," he said, raising his hand. He sniffed and fired directly at Ramgar at point blank range. But it didn't kill him. Somehow, Ramgar also had his own defence shield and he took the blast for several seconds; nevertheless, it was clear it was taking its toll on him. Grabbing a pawful of the worn out stones, Teddy did his best to make a forcefield with them, then he ran to join shields with Ramgar. It was still hopeless; it would only prolong things a few seconds at most, but Teddy couldn't just let Ramgar die.

"I'm going to kill you *both*! Perfect!" shouted Arthdu.

Teddy held the forcefield as long as he could but Arthdu was winning again, and the look of glee on his face showed he knew it. The blast was becoming painfully hot to Teddy's snout and Ramgar cried out in pain: finally the mini Darkgate stones were black and drained and full of holes.

"You're out of power, teddy bear," mocked Arthdu, as the protection faltered. "Now it's time to d—"

A thin bolt of power flashed across the scene and ripped clean through Arthdu and his defensive shield, knocking him backwards. He was in considerable pain and shocked to see a hole in the right of his chest. He clutched it, gasping and in panic, looking around wildly for his attacker. A superhumanly loud voice boomed from out of the dark wood on the small hill.

"It's me." There was a pause. "You know who I am, don't you?"

Arthdu struggled to gather enough breath to answer.

"Wh... What?!" he gasped out of disbelief. "Arthllwyd?!"

"NO! I'm CARREGllwyd," roared the voice, somehow able to hear him. "I'm not a bear; I'm a *man*!" he asserted.

"'Carreg' means stone, you know," retorted Arthdu, as best he could, sinking to the ground. "A cold, heartless stone. At least I loved your sister. Passionately," he spat.

"You never cared for her properly! You just wanted her for fun!" exclaimed Arthllwyd, rising just a little to Arthdu's taunt. And Arthllwyd fired again. A weak, fat, beam of heat and light that burned into Arthdu's stomach. He screamed and raised his arm to mark the launch of another retort but, just as his mouth formed the beginning of the first word, Arthllwyd fired again, a thinner beam, into Arthdu's chest, and he could no longer talk.

"What's the matter? Cat got your tongue? Can't get power from the Darkgate any more? Trying to work out why? Well, no matter. Know this: I have *let* you live this long. I could have killed you as soon as you stole my Darkgate, but I wasn't really in that frame of mind back then.

But, I've waited, and grown, and planned, and I realised what you could do for me — *have* done for me — and now how *wonderful* it is to watch your broken body like this at last." Arthdu's eyes raged with anger as Arthllwyd spoke from the trees. "I've used you to stir up trouble for me between England and Wales, not because I care about it like you do, but because it is useful for my greater strategy. But you are not allowed to finish off Teddy and his friends here because I need them, and because your usefulness is *over*." Fear replaced anger in Arthdu's eyes, but only for a moment.

Arthllwyd let loose a tight, powerful beam that surrounded Arthdu and shrivelled him to death in a microsecond. A moment later the beam changed, reversed, and he was drained to a husk; it was as if all the energy had been sucked out of him. The ash that remained fell onto the hillside.

"Woah! That was gooood!" thrilled Arthllwyd.

Even now, no one had seen his face.

The Horde were confused and scared; Teddy and the others, equally so for different reasons. Then the burning light returned: this time it was like a spray of water, back and forth, covering The Hordesmen. But it wasn't water, it was a fiery spray of superheated, white light, and they too burned and died like their master, their crossbow bolts exploding in chain reactions, ripping huge craters into the soil, while sheep and toys cowered.

For a moment there was silence. Complete, terrified silence.

"Nothing like a bit of a clean up!" continued Arthllwyd. "Much better, lovely! Now all I have to do is take back my Darkgate and remove its link to any Horde stragglers and … well, that's for me to know and you to guess. Anyway, I should introduce myself …"

By now, each and every being in Teddy's camp was absolutely terrified, utterly in contrast to Arthllwyd's deep, calm, now-playful voice. He strode out of the wood on foot, looking nothing like a Yorebear. He was tall and slim, with a sharply rugged face and shocking eyes like radioactive sapphires.

"Good day to you all! Or is it evening? It's that funny time of day when it's hard to tell isn't it? And the weather doesn't help," he said looking up at the gloomy, dark clouds.

As he walked, his curly, roasted coffee hair bobbed above his eyebrows at the front, and fell longer at the back, to his white, long-sleeved, open-necked shirt, tucked into perfectly fitted khaki chinos. Anyone would have believed he was in his thirties; in fact, he was 1,458.

"Hello, Teddy," he mouthed silently, pointing at the frightened bear, like he was a friend in the audience.

"So," he said, rising and falling almost musically. "We're just about done here, but before you go, there's someone I'd like you to meet. My daughter. Rhiannon."

Arthllwyd turned to look behind himself, as if introducing the next act, and there she was. Rhiannon, unharmed, professionally dressed and oozing smugness.

"Hello," she shouted over to Teddy. "You can tell your girlfriend that I'm fine. A nice little trick we've learned to do. Hurts a lot though, and dumps you naked in the most embarrassing places, but hey, I've found you can get out of anything if you say you're the victim of a practical joke, and ask if you can borrow some clothes. And don't worry, my father needs you so I have no intention of harming you. Just make sure your girlfriend doesn't come near me because I will kill her whatever my father says."

Arthllwyd looked at her with a playfully stern face and wagged his finger. Then he addressed them again.

"Right, go! Tell people what you have seen. Tell Gwyneth. This was the end of Cadarn, who became the bear-man, Arthdu, and the end of all the strategies and beliefs for which he stood. I have work to do, and the world will become a better place for it. You will help me when I am ready but, for now, you may go."

They stood, shell-shocked by what they'd heard, and it started to rain. A drop. A drop, a pause, a drop. Within a few seconds, the heavens opened and it began to drench sheep and toys and a lone human alike. Arthllwyd and Rhiannon drifted back into the wood, chatting quietly, a picocell shield over their heads to keep them dry. No one dared follow them, and the only signs that Arthdu and his Horde had ever existed were the black gashes punctuating the landscape. It was time to leave.

::

The first thing Simon did was call Joanne. He was alive; she was relieved. Simon promised to call Sophie to reassure her, but was told not to tell her what was happening in case her phone had been tapped. Then he would drive to The Dolls to pick up the family.

Joanne told Simon and Teddy not to worry about the Hordesmen at the Dolls manor house: Gundy would go out into the rain (wearing a poncho that the servants had thoughtfully fashioned for her out of an old plastic sack), to search the grounds and the surrounding land for Darkgate stones and any other Hordesmen, and Joanne would break into the house, go upstairs and ask Bertie to have a look out of the windows around the garden and over the road for sparkles ... but, if the dead Hordesman had been telling the truth about being alone, they should be safe. And, for the sake of the children, Gundy had disintegrated the Hordesman's slashed body.

All of this activity was probably unnecessary, since Arthllwyd had just implied that the remaining members of the Horde would not be alive for very much longer, but Joanne wanted to be sure.

If all was well, Teddy and Simon would simply drive up to the main entrance of the manor house to be reunited with their family, and they would talk with The Dolls, and they would go home.

::

It took forty minutes but Simon and Teddy arrived safely. They left the damaged car in the drive and walked carefully through the garden to the gazebo, still looking around for threats as they went, just in case.

As they came into view, Bertie ran to his daddy and they hugged, and Teddy ran to Gundy. Joanne hurried over and joined the family hug, with Oli, who was sleeping in her arms.

After a suitable lull, Agnes spoke.

"So, there's another Yorebear? I mean, I know Arthgwyn and Gwion called Arthdu the 'Third Yorebear', but I thought that was centuries out of date?!"

"There are only two now," said Simon grimly. He sighed. "I wish I knew what Arthllwyd wants from us…"

Teddy was more concerned about Gundy's safety; she rubbed her sore stomach while Teddy hugged her, and kissed her head at the back where it hurt, making her flinch. The thing that surprised him most was that she wasn't terrified about Rhiannon wanting to kill her. She just wrinkled her snout for a moment, and shrugged.

They phoned Arthgwyn and told her their news, and from back in the Aberystwyth Darkgate, she listened quietly to all that had just happened, beyond emotional breaking point. Nothing could express her feelings, so she didn't really have any now; she was numb. When she spoke she was worryingly calm.

"I suppose that's what dear Gwion must have meant when Gundy over-heard him say, 'That's not true'; I imagine Rhiannon had revealed who she was. It's almost unbelievable though. No one has heard *anything* from Arthllwyd in centuries, and I know Arthdu has been using the Llandegley Darkgate. It's odd: if Arthllwyd had been tapping the Llandegley Darkgate's power, Arthdu should have noticed ... strange that he didn't ... and Arthllwyd must have been drawing a *lot* of power, otherwise he couldn't be as strong as he is now. Maybe Arthdu wasn't as sensitive about these things as I am?"

"You can sense who's using the Darkgate in Llandegley?"

"Not who, no, but I can sense when it's being used, vaguely. That's how I knew when Arthdu was on the move again, and that's why Gwion suggested delivering a warning note to you."

She paused for a moment before continuing.

"You know ... all of you there, you're my only friends in this world now, so I think I should tell you everything. Arthdu — well 'Cadarn' really — was my first love, we were both seventeen, and Arthllwyd, or Carregllwyd as apparently he still wants to be known, is my older brother. From what you say, it seems, he can now change his appearance better than me! I know he used to look as bear-like as I do... Anyway, the three of us fell out with each other — learning to cope with what we had become affected us all badly, and we were at each other's throats like never before. We knew the damage we could do to each other, and separated. But there was something else drawing us apart, something I think Robertson felt too, to a lesser extent, when he was looking for the Darkgate here, and each of us was drawn to one of the three Darkgates ... Ah. Of course. Arthllwyd has been using the Saxon Darkgate. I'm not sure how he's managed to keep it secret but I bet that's it. That's where he got his power to survive all these years!"

But Gundy wanted clarification.

"Wait a minute; *three* Darkgates?"

"Yes, three. Didn't I ... oh. I remember now. I stopped Gwion from telling you. At the time, I didn't want to tell you more than necessary, I wasn't sure we could fully trust you, I'm sorry to say.

Yes, three. The Aberystwyth, Llandegley and Saxon Darkgates, but the Saxon gate is now in a town called Great Malvern. The Aberystwyth Darkgate is mine; Llandegley *was* Arthllwyd's but it was taken over by Arthdu for some reason, and Great Malvern gate was Arthdu's before it came under Saxon rule. He always hated them but, his power wasn't as well controlled back then; he couldn't defeat them *all*. Perhaps that's why he left..."

"I'm confused. Are you saying Teddy actually went to Arthllwyd's Darkgate, when he went to Llandegley?"

"Yes, that's right."

There was a pause. Arthgwyn continued in her somewhat disturbingly flat, calm voice.

"Well ... I'm going to need a lot of time to think about all this. I'd believed my brother had died five hundred years ago ... or faded to nothing. I'd missed him, grieved for falling out with him and never making amends, and couldn't bring myself to talk about him, because then I'd really have to admit he was gone. But now I find out he's not dead at all, he seems to have become a psychopathic murderer, who today killed my vicious ex-boyfriend, and I have a niece who killed my lover. Hmmm..." she drifted into silence. "I'd better go, it's been quite a day." They each mumbled goodbyes to her, wished her well, and Simon ended the call.

Then they sat there, listening to the sound of the rain on the gazebo roof.

- CHAPTER 12 -

The Lady on the Hill

Teddy travelled home in Gwion's car with Joanne and the boys, allowing Simon to deal with the heavy rain that was swirling in through the family car's windowless left side. But the rain was just the leading edge of a storm from Ireland and, an hour or so after they'd finally closed the front door on the day, it really pelted down. The wind and rain lashed at the stone walls and mossy slates of the house, and blew under gappy doors and through loose window frames. But they were warm and home at last.

Oli and Bertie were asleep by the time they reached the house and were carried to their beds; even Teddy and Gundy were exhausted. They plodded to their cupboard room and pulled their covers over themselves. Teddy fell asleep almost immediately but Gundy took a moment to reflect on the accidental killing of the Hordesman, and the relief of not having actually killed Rhiannon, before she too fell asleep hugging her beloved big partner, who was still muddy and scattered with bits of vegetation.

Joanne looked at Simon out of the corner of her eyes, and Simon looked back. Neither said a word.

"Would you really have left for your parents?" Simon asked.

"Of course, I had to protect the boys. Better than throwing myself at Arthdu without a thought for my family!"

And they argued, quietly so as not to wake the boys, alone, miles from anywhere, as the rain and wind swirled.

Later that night, a truce had been made and an awkward peace agreed — enough for them to get ready for bed. They sat up in silence, mulling over the things they'd seen that day, neither of them coping.

Simon sighed, as he remembered the explosion at Gaufron. His eyes opened wide with a spark of realisation. Reaching for his laptop, he did a search and found what he was looking for, pointing it out politely to Joanne:

Gas Explosion Likely Cause for Farm Destruction

A freak gas explosion is being blamed by police for destroying a farmhouse in Gaufron near Rhayader, mid-Wales. Although it is believed no one was hurt, the explosion killed several animals and reduced the farmhouse to rubble. Police say it is too early to be certain but suspect a build up of gas in the cellar was ignited by faulty wiring. 'It's lucky no one was killed. It was a huge explosion,' said PC Gareth Pemberton.

Reports of two other explosions, a few hundred metres along a track leading to the farm, were dismissed by PC Pemberton as 'nonsense' and the police say the case is now closed.

"The police are still acting strangely then," said Simon. "Do you think it's just the after-effects of Arthdu's work, or is Arthllwyd stopping the police from investigating?"

Joanne thought for a moment before answering in the kind of tone that suggests an argument isn't totally over. "It's hard to tell. I hope it's just the after-effects of the drugs Arthdu used on them. Will the police eventually look for the car?"

Simon didn't wait to find out. The next morning he phoned around, and a couple of days later, a friend of a friend had fixed the car, no questions asked — for a price — and Gwion's car was returned to Arthgwyn, who used it to drive up to Nant y Moch and the Elan Valley for long, windy, autumn walks under her cape, draped in the darkness of her wrecked life.

::

Each day Simon and Joanne awoke and wondered if today was the day the Dyfed-Powys police would question them due to the events of August 16th, 2008, or if Arthllwyd would burst into their lives, but weeks later no yorebear had appeared, nor had an officer knocked on the door of the cottage to ask about the events on the track leading up to a farm in Gaufron, or elsewhere. And no one was investigating Mother's death either. Emily and Sophie moved into Bredwardine Manor with ease — not only were the bank no longer trying to sell the property, Emily's purchase of the house had gone through remarkably easily. The most reasonable explanation — if an explanation were needed — was that Arthllwyd was somehow pulling strings for them ... but to what end? What use did he have for them? How could there be anything that he couldn't do himself?

The English panic about Live toys also ebbed. Newspapers, television and websites stopped reporting it, and even detailed web searches came up with little. Joanne noticed some people had deleted articles from their blogs, blogs that she knew had openly discussed Live toys in horrified prose. On the other hand, there were continued, occasional stories about sheep killing dogs and humans, which suggested Arthllwyd still had a plan for that part of Arthdu's strategy.

Whatever it was, it didn't involve suppressing the Dwarves. The Dolls reported that the Dwarves were again free to leave their *isclwylfa* and, when they had done so, had found the remains of several desiccated Hordesmen on the ground. They seemed to have died where they stood; the power that kept them alive removed so that they had aged to death in an instant. Arthgwyn suspected Arthllwyd had killed the Horde because he knew he could never trust them. The Hordesmen were gone for good.

::

Not surprisingly, the person worst affected by The Day was Arthgwyn. She was in mourning, and had slipped into a dark feeling of pointless, paralysing, aching weariness. Teddy and Gundy found they could connect with her Darkgate to soothe her — indeed the Darkgate seemed to delight in helping the two teddies — but it was never more than a temporary fix; Arthgwyn had lost too much.

Nevertheless, she would brighten for the sake of the boys when they visited. Despite her emotional state, Arthgwyn was true to her word — she did her best to remove the build-up of picocells from Bertie and Oli, then added a thin, skin of protective picocells to prevent further Darkgate influence. It seemed to work. Bertie could no longer see sparkles, nor cause power to leave his hands. Joanne felt a little sadness about the lost sparkles, but overall it was for the best. Arthgwyn mumbled that the family would need a check-up every few months, to make sure all was well, and they should look out for any signs of picocell activity in the boys.

As well as being broken by grief and loss, She was afraid: her brother, Arthllwyd, had never been like this before; his personality had been as much reshaped as his physical form. He was an unknown force, but clearly a deadly one. There were some moments when all she wanted to do was to meet up with him, to talk to him, to find out how he was after all these years; he was still her brother — but she had no idea how to go about it; and little energy to pursue the idea. Presumably, simply driving over to Llandegley and walking up to the Darkgate to find Arthllwyd would only get her killed. Or maybe he was in Great Malvern at the Saxon Darkgate? The uncertainty on this point only served to underline how little she knew about him.

But that led her to an even more disturbing discovery: she could no longer feel the presence of the Llandegley gate. After more than fourteen centuries, it was missing. Like a hole in her feelings. Gone. And it was another loss.

Arthgwyn said she was devising a plan, but she wouldn't talk about it yet. No one was sure whether it was a plan to meet her brother, or to destroy him. She just said she wanted to do some tests first, reading up on Gwion's research, and she shut herself in the Darkgate for weeks at a time. So, instead, Simon and Joanne and Teddy and Gundy, talked about what had happened. Over and over.

Rolling each detail around between themselves. Apart from the obvious questions about Arthllwyd, they realised there were two other questions for which they had no satisfactory answers.

First, exactly what happened years ago between Teddy being knocked out and him waking up riding on Naystraw the horse? They knew that Pale had knocked him out and poisoned him, but someone had found Teddy already tied to Naystraw, some distance from Llandegley, and that someone hadn't been Arthgwyn, and probably hadn't been Gwion either. There might be someone else out there who was involved in all this, someone who had pinned the note on the saddle and sent the dozy Naystraw on his way. Yet the note on Naystraw's saddle seemed to be in the same writing as the note Gwion had delivered through their door — how was that possible if they assumed Gwion had written it?

Second, why did the Hordesman go to Gaufron Farm when he did? In order to have arrived before Simon and Teddy, he would have left Llandegley at about the same time they were driving out of Aber' and, more mysteriously, *why* did he go there? Even Simon and Teddy had no idea they were going to visit until almost the last minute. But, if they assumed the Hordesman had been waiting there all the time, what had he been doing for three years? Was there some other explanation for his presence there?

::

As the weeks and months of uncertainty drifted by, they met up with Arthgwyn less and less frequently but, each time they did meet, she studied them carefully to check for picocell activity. To begin with Bertie and Oli showed no further signs of developing Darkgate traits; then, unexpectedly, Bertie's ability to see sparkles revived. It surprised them all. Later, it became clear that Oli could see them too, as he was fascinated by Gundy's stone. Arthgwyn investigated and worked out what had happened: it was the residual population of picocells unifying inside the boys. Those that had not been removed had realised they were weakened, so they had gradually migrated together to concentrate their abilities, but the worst the boys could do was send a small fizz through their hands, like a person touching a battery with their tongue, and they could see sparkles to some extent; that was it, and it got no worse, and Joanne was satisfied the Darkgate was no longer a threat to her family.

At about the same time, Mundy started to Wake Up. Simon thought it might be in response to the organised picocells in Oli, but Gundy believed Mundy was simply ready, now that Oli was hugging her and asking to take her everywhere with him. She was sluggish for weeks, but gradually learned to talk and walk, much as Oli was doing. Gundy joked that she and Teddy now had a baby, even though Mundy was taller than her; Teddy looked shocked that he might have become a father without realising it, and Gundy had to calm him down. He chuckled, and they hugged. And then, as happened many times every day, they remembered Arthllwyd had a plan for them.

::

Across the miles, a night-time hilltop edge was bathed in the sound of a woman crying out a ritual promise. She held a loose, dark grey garment to her cheek; vowing an oath of love, sealed by her tears.

The rite came to an end. She calmed herself, looked out over the moonlit view and placed the garment back into her shoulder bag, touching it one last time before covering it with the bag's flap — then with a flick of her head, she tossed her long, silver-lit hair behind her. Her face firmed into an unassailable resolve. As she took a full breath, she pulled her palms away from each other until they were a body's-width apart in front of her face. Power sparked between her hands; she closed her eyes and breathed out in peace, crackling fire between her separated palms and finger tips.

Mourning was over. Mair was ready.

Appendix - Welsh Pronunciation

English-only readers may find it hard to pronounce some of the Welsh words in this book. Although I've lived in Wales for over twenty years, you pretty much need to be Welsh to get the pronunciation perfectly, and even then things are pronounced differently in different parts of the country. So, this is just a rough guide to stop you murdering the language; if you want better results, ask a first-language Welsh-speaker.

Words in the book:

    Arthdu - ARRRTH-dee (with a rolled-R)
    Arthllwyd - ARRRTH-lloo-id (see the LL-sound below)
    Arthgwyn - ARRRTH-gwin
    Llandegley - llan-DARE-G-lee (see the LL-sound below)
    Llangurig - llan-G'EE-rig (see the LL-sound below)
    Gaufron - GYE-EE-vrown
    Peredur - peh-REH-deer
    Neuadd NAY-ath (a hard 'th' as in 'the') (means "hall")

General pronunciation:

    AU = "aye-ee" or "ee" or even "ah", depending on where you come from.
    DD = "th" as in "The"
    E = "air" or "e" as in "pen"
    EU = "aye"

F = v

LL = the sound made when you put your tongue to the roof of your mouth and

       blow quickly around the sides.

O = "aw" as in "caw"

R = "rrr" = a rolled 'r', a bit like a cat purring for 0.2 of a second.

U = "ee"

Note: 'll' and "dd" are letters in their own right in the Welsh alphabet, not two 'l's or two 'd's next to each other.

www.ingramcontent.com/pod-product-compliance
Lightning Source LLC
Chambersburg PA
CBHW070819120626
46556CB00002B/575